PRAISE FOR DIANE KELLY'S PAW ENFORCEMENT SERIES

"Kelly's writing is smart and laugh-out-loud funny."
—Kristan Higgins, *New York Times* bestselling author

"Humor, romance, and surprising LOL moments. What more can you ask for?"
—*Romance and Beyond*

"Fabulously fun and funny!"
—*Book Babe*

"An engaging read that I could not put down. I look forward to the next adventure of Megan and Brigit!"
—*SOS Aloha*

"Sparkling with surprises. Just like a tequila sunrise. You never know which way is up or out!"
—*Romance Junkies*

ABOVE THE
PAW

Diane Kelly

St. Martin's Paperbacks

This is a work of fiction. All of the characters, organizations, and events portrayed in this novel are either products of the author's imagination or are used fictitiously.

ABOVE THE PAW

Copyright © 2016 by Diane Kelly.

For information address St. Martin's Press, 175 Fifth Avenue, New York, NY 10010.

ISBN: 978-1-250-09484-1

Our books may be purchased in bulk for promotional, educational, or business use. Please contact your local bookseller or the Macmillan Corporate and Premium Sales Department at 1-800-221-7945, ext. 5442, or by e-mail at MacmillanSpecialMarkets@macmillan.com.

Printed in the United States of America

St. Martin's Paperbacks edition / December 2016

St. Martin's Paperbacks are published by St. Martin's Press, 175 Fifth Avenue, New York, NY 10010.

10 9 8 7 6 5 4 3 2 1

To Gene Edwards,
a larger-than-life character.
Rest in peace, good friend.

ACKNOWLEDGMENTS

As always, there are oodles of people to thank for making this book happen.

Thanks to my wonderful editor, Holly Ingraham, for your spot-on suggestions, for keeping me on a loose leash, and for letting my imagination roam.

Thanks to Sarah Melnyck, Paul Hochman, Allison Ziegler, and the rest of the team at St. Martin's who worked to get this book to readers.

Thanks to Danielle Fiorella and Jennifer Taylor for creating such fun book covers.

Thanks to my agent, Helen Breitwieser, for all of your work in furthering my writing career.

Thanks to Liz Bemis and the staff of Bemis Promotions for my great Web site and newsletters.

And finally, thanks to you fabulous readers who picked up this book. May you have a howling good time with Megan and Brigit!

ONE

BUSINESS, BUT NOT AS USUAL

The Dealer

"Things aren't looking too good for you, are they?"

God, how he'd love to wipe that smirk off the prick's face. Instead, the Dealer offered a shrug. "I'm not worried."

The prick snorted, clearly not buying it. "You should be."

The two locked stares for several moments. He was sick of demands, sick of threats, sick of people like the man sitting in front of him. Acid churned in his gut, threatening to eat its way through and dissolve him on the spot. But he'd be damned if he'd show any sign of weakness.

"Look," the guy said, the smirk softening a bit. "I need you, you need me. We help each other out. That's how this works."

That might be how it worked, but there were lines the Dealer had never crossed before. Lines he would *never* cross. There was too much at stake, too much he could lose. He looked the prick in the eye. "No deal."

TWO
THE PRICE OF FREEDOM

Fort Worth Police Officer Megan Luz

Hell couldn't be any hotter than Fort Worth, Texas, on the Fourth of July.

My polyester-blend police uniform stuck to my sweaty body as if I'd been shrink-wrapped. It didn't help that the darn thing was dark blue. The metal badge on my chest had heated in the sun, like a branding iron trying to sear my skin through the fabric. There wasn't a cloud in the sky, either. Relief would only come when the relentless sun fell below the horizon in another hour or two. I only hoped I'd last until then.

I glanced down at my furry, four-footed partner, Brigit. "How you holding up, girl?"

The large shepherd mix looked up at me, her tongue hanging out of her mouth as she panted. Her weary eyes said what her mouth couldn't. *This stinks.*

The two of us had been assigned to work the Independence Day celebration at the Panther City Pavilion. The full-day festival included pony rides, bounce houses, and face painting for the kids, as well as tubing on the adjacent Trinity River and live music for the adults. Of course the fireworks display scheduled for later tonight was for everyone.

To ensure the event was as family-friendly as possible, the chief had scheduled extra patrols to work the crowds, pulling officers in from other divisions throughout the city. Just as the police department had reported en masse to cover the various Independence Day events throughout the city, as well as to deal with the inevitable drunks the day would bring, so had the fire department beefed up its head count to deal with fires caused by errant Roman candles and accidents caused by the inevitable drunks.

Given my partner's olfactory capabilities, she and I had been assigned to work the entry gate. While I greeted attendees with a smile and a "How are you doing today, folks?", Brigit performed a sniff test on each of them, scenting for illegal drugs. Our mission was to prevent any such things from making their way into the venue.

While the heat was stifling, at least Brigit and I were in good company. Having appointed the subordinate members of his team to other duties, my boyfriend Seth worked the gate with us. He sported a pair of black boots, dark cargo pants, and a fitted T-shirt identifying him as a member of the Fort Worth Bomb Squad.

With broad, hard shoulders and powerful pecs, Seth was quite a sight to behold. Several women and a couple of teenaged girls in the vicinity were doing just that— beholding him. Yep, those hours spent perfecting his butterfly stroke in the city's swimming pools had certainly paid off. With his gorgeous green eyes, a strong jawline, and a sexy chin dimple that drew your eyes to his mouth, a girl could do much worse.

But what made him even more attractive was that he wasn't exactly model perfect. His ears were a little too big and his right cheek was tainted by a faint pink lemon-sized scar, a burn mark earned during his days with an army explosives ordnance disposal unit in Afghanistan. That scar wasn't the only one he'd earned in the army, and he'd gotten plenty before joining the military, too. But those scars were on the inside, invisible yet unhealed.

Seth worked now both as a firefighter and a member of the explosives unit for the city's fire department. So did his partner, a yellow lab named Blast who was sniffing the people coming through the gate for fireworks or explosives while Brigit sniffed them for drugs. They were a tag team in dog tags. *Sniff-sniff. Sniff-sniff.*

When a couple with a toddler in a stroller passed muster, I waved them in. "Enjoy yourselves."

The parents gave me a smile, while the kid pulled its fingers out of its mouth and reached for Brigit, giving her a friendly pat that resulted in a fur-coated hand. She held the hand up in front of her face, looking at it quizzically, too young to understand how her hand had suddenly sprouted hair.

Crouching down, I picked up the cooler I'd brought and poured more chilled water into Brigit's bowl. While I ran a hand over her neck, she furiously lapped up the liquid with a *slurp-slurp-slurp.* Blast shoved his face into the bowl next to hers to get at the water, too.

Seth held up a hand to stop the line of people streaming through the gate. "Give us just a second, folks."

Once the dogs had drunk their fill we resumed our duties.

Blast alerted on a group of five boys who appeared to be around twelve or thirteen, just old enough for their parents to send them to an event like this on their own.

Seth rewarded Blast's efforts with a "good boy" before turning to the bad boys. "You boys got fireworks on you?"

"Yeah," one said. He reached into his pocket and pulled out a handful of Black Cats, opening his palm to show them to Seth.

"Sorry, buddy," Seth said. "I'm going to have to take those."

Fireworks were illegal within the city limits and anyone caught with them faced a hefty fine. Of course the department tended to go easy on minors, merely confiscating their stashes and educating them on the law.

"Aw, man!" the kid complained. "I bought those with my lawn-mowing money."

"I feel you, kid," Seth said sympathetically. "But you gotta keep them outside the city limits. That's the law. They cause too many fires and injuries. We had one kid yesterday who blew half his finger off."

The boys exclaimed in unison, half disgusted, half intrigued by the carnage. I wasn't sure if Seth's story was true, but even if it wasn't, it *could* be.

"Tell your parents, okay?" Seth added. "They could be fined a lot of money if the fire department finds y'all with fireworks again."

"Okay," the kid muttered.

All of the boys emptied their pockets and Seth added

the take to the fireproof bin he'd brought to collect the contraband.

"Cool dogs," one of the boys said, eyeing Brigit and Blast, his resentment evaporating as fast as his adolescent sweat.

Seth reached into a pocket on his cargo pants and pulled out a trading card that featured a photo of Blast and some details about him. He held it out to the kid. "Would you like one of Blast's trading cards?"

The boy took the card. "Cool!"

The others clamored for cards. "I want one! I want one!"

Seth distributed cards among the boys. I, too, had a pocketful of cards made with Brigit's photo and details on them, including the fact that she'd been recruited from the city pound after impressing her first handler with her high energy and intelligence, two traits critical for a successful K-9. The card also noted that she'd graduated at the top of her training class. *Valedogtorian.* The boys left without their fireworks but at least they now had souvenirs to take home with them.

A few minutes later, a bosomy woman with hair the color of canned peaches approached. She was dressed in her trademark pink, all the way from her straw sun hat, down to her fitted knit dress, and ending at her wedge sandals. Trish LeGrande was a reporter for a TV station in Dallas. Though she'd worked her way up from PTA carnivals and charity bake sales to report on bigger stories, she still handled the occasional fluff piece. Her cameraman trailed along behind her, his equipment resting on his shoulder.

"Hello, Miss LeGrande," I said as she approached.

She stopped and tilted her head just so. "Have we met?"

"Several times," I said.

Though Trish and I had met when she'd reported on earlier cases I'd been involved in, she never seemed to remember me. It could be an honest mistake. After all, she surely met hundreds if not thousands of people when working her stories. Then again, she could just be a bitch.

She made no apology for failing to recognize me, which had me leaning toward *bitch*. Instead, she eyed Seth, running her eyes over his broad, well-muscled shoulders and firm pecs under the thinly veiled guise of reading his BOMB SQUAD T-shirt. She gushed in her breathy voice, "I'd love to get some footage of *you*."

I bet you would.

I stepped back to allow Trish and her cameraman to make stars of Seth and Blast. Who was I to stand in the way of their fifteen minutes of fame?

Trish scooted up next to Seth, draping a hand over his shoulder and smushing her boobs against his upper arm. *Yep, definitely a bitch.* Her cameraman stepped into place and gave a signal.

"Hello!" Trish purred at the lens. "I'm here at Panther Pavilion for the fabulous Fort Worth Fourth celebration! As you can see, we're in very good hands here. To ensure no illegal fireworks make their way into this family-friendly event, the bomb squad has its best two-footed and four-footed team members on duty." She bent down next to Blast. "Isn't that right, boy?" With that, she reached out and ruffled the dog's head. He looked up at her with gaga eyes and wagged his tail. *Damn him.*

Returning her attention to the camera, she stood. "Stay tuned for more footage throughout the day. Happy Fourth, everyone!"

She turned to Seth. "Thanks. You two will play great on screen."

"Anytime," he replied.

Damn him, too.

As soon as Trish and her cameraman were out of earshot, I stepped back into place next to Seth and mocked him in a cartoonish voice, *"Anytime."* I shook my head. "Pathetic."

Seth cut a look at me. "Jealous?"

I scoffed. "No."

He nudged me with his elbow. "Yes, you are."

I fingered the handle of my gun. "Don't make me shoot you."

A soft smile skittered over his mouth. "I like that you're jealous. It means you like me."

"I've let you see me naked. Of course I like you."

"How much?"

I scratched Brigit behind the ear. "Almost as much as I like my dog."

He dipped his head in acknowledgment. "I'll take it."

While Seth and I continued to welcome newcomers with smiles and verbal greetings, our dogs continued to stick out their noses and scent the air as the people slowly passed by. The crowd ebbed and flowed, at times arriving in small packs of one or two, other times congregating in large numbers at the gate. A half hour after Seth had confiscated the fireworks, a trio of twentyish Caucasian men approached, two with brown hair and one blond. All wore cargo shorts and T-shirts, but while the brown-haired boys wore tennis shoes the blond wore a pair of flip-flops. The blond elbowed the one to his right and pointed to a group of girls wearing skimpy bikini tops, short Daisy Duke shorts that barely covered their butts, and sandals. Yep, there was a lot of skin on display here today, much of it sunburned. One of the girls poured water from a bottle over her chest to cool herself off, providing the young men with some live soft-core porn.

Brigit plunked her butt down on the ground and raised her back leg to scratch her shoulder, the movement catching the blond's eye. The arm that had only recently been elbowing his friend now flew out reflexively to hold his friend back and the word "Cops!" sprang from his mouth. The three turned on their heels, hightailing it away from the entrance, the flip-flops living up to their name as they made their signature *flip-flop-flip-flop* sound. *Real subtle, huh?*

"We're up, Brigit." I unclipped her lead from her collar, gave her the order to stay by my side, and my partner and I headed out after them.

The one who'd spotted me cast a glance over his shoulder, his eyes widening in alarm when he saw me and Brigit in pursuit. Without a word to his friends, he took off running. *Flip-flop-flip-flop!* By the time the friends looked back, I was on them. "Stay right here!" I shouted, pointing to the ground as I sprinted past.

I continued after the blond. Given that he hadn't spent the last four hours being broiled by the sun, he had a distinct advantage. Still, I would've expected his footwear to slow him down. Those shoes were made to be an easy-on, easy-off option, not for running. *Flip-flop-flip-flop!*

Nonetheless, his fear fueled him, overcoming his poor choice in shoes.

"Stop!" I shouted after him.

He didn't stop. Instead he ran toward the Trinity River, cutting left and right around the people coming up the riverside trail. *Flip-flop-flip-flop!* As he darted around a stroller with a drooling toddler in it, his right shoe came off. His feet now gave off a *flip-flop* sound broken by a split-second pause as his bare foot hit the ground. *Flip-flop . . . flip-flop . . . flip-flop . . .*

"Stop or I'll deploy my dog!"

He made no move to slow down. *Flip-flop . . . flip-flop . . .* As he ran alongside the riverbank, he pulled something that looked like a small piece of trash from the pocket of his shorts and flung it as hard as he could out over the water.

"Last chance!" I hollered.

Still he ran on.

He couldn't say he hadn't been warned. I gave Brigit the order to take him down. She looked up at me as if to say *Really? You expect me to run all-out in this heat?* But she obeyed and took off after him. In seconds, she'd leaped onto his back and taken him down to the ground, the back of his tank top still gripped in her teeth.

I caught up with the two and issued the order for her to release him. She sat down and continued to pant, drool dropping from her lips and saturating the young man's back.

"On your knees," I ordered. "Hands behind your head."

Cursing, he pushed himself up from the dirt and attempted to eviscerate me with his gaze. Luckily for me, his eyes weren't laser beams. He put his hands behind his head, seeming to realize the jig was up.

I pushed the button on my shoulder-mounted radio to call for assistance. "Officer Luz requesting backup at the river just west of the entrance gate." I looked back to where I'd told the other two to wait, but they were gone. *Ugh.*

Yanking my cuffs from my belt, I secured them around the guy's wrists. *Click-click.* By this time, a crowd had gathered around and the current was carrying the item he'd tossed into the river downstream. I issued Brigit the order to watch the suspect and take him down again if he tried to flee.

I nudged the boy with my toe. "Try to run and she'll tear you apart."

He glanced at my dog, who sat rigid just three feet away, her brown eyes locked on him. *Nope, he's not going anywhere.*

Scurrying over to the bank, I crouched and reached for the baggie, stretching my arm as far as it would go. Just another inch . . . another inch . . . *oh, crap!* Physical laws kicked in and I fell forward into the muck. *Spluck.*

I stood, my knees muddy and the front of my uniform soaking wet, but at least I'd retrieved the baggie full of pills the kid had tried to ditch. I took off my sunglasses to better inspect the contents of the bag. Inside were three dozen or so pills and tablets in various shapes, sizes, and colors, a virtual candy store for someone looking to get high. Or dead.

Xanax, a drug designed to treat anxiety but sometimes mixed with other drugs in what some dubbed a "Xanax bomb."

Light green pills that said CIBA on one side, 3 on the other, what I recognized from my training as Ritalin.

White capsules that, if I had to hazard a guess, were what users would term Molly.

The quantity of pills told me that the kid wasn't a casual user. He was a dealer.

As I looked at the bag, a snarky male voice called, "Jesus, Luz! Did you fall in the river?"

I turned to find that my backup had arrived in the form of Derek "the Big Dick" Mackey, a cop who'd been my partner before Brigit. Derek was tall, broad, and as obnoxious as they come. He had rust-orange hair cut in a buzz cut, ruddy skin, and a close personal relationship with the chief. During the time when he was supposed to be training me, he'd taught me little other than how to be a crude, arrogant, and self-important ass. When he'd made one lewd comment too many, I'd somehow ended up with my Taser in my hand, delivering fifteen hundred volts to his genitalia. I claimed temporary insanity.

Fortunately, while his personal relationship with the chief usually worked only in Derek's favor, in that instance it worked in mine as well. Knowing I could paint a very colorful picture of just how offensive he'd been, Derek realized reporting me to Internal Affairs might end my law enforcement career but that his would take a hit as well. Instead, he'd taken the matter directly to the chief, who didn't want to see his golden boy in hot water and made me an offer I couldn't refuse—partner with Brigit or turn in my badge.

At first, the thought of being partnered with a K-9 sounded like a punishment, a burden. She wouldn't be able to help with paperwork or evidence, or question suspects. She wouldn't be able to engage in conversation during the dull moments on our shifts. Heck, she wouldn't even be able to open her own door! I'd be responsible for her while on duty and have to deal with her disgusting poop, not to mention the fact that proper bonding required that the dog live with its partner so she'd be mine 24/7, like a conjoined twin of another species.

Oh, how wrong I'd been.

Brigit proved to be incredibly smart and capable. While she couldn't open her door, she could sniff for drugs or disturbances, making searches much more efficient and productive. When a suspect led me on a foot chase and I ran out of steam, Brigit was there to pick up where I left off, continuing the pursuit until she caught the lawbreaker. She might not be able to engage in conversation, but she communicated quite well nonverbally and was a good listener when I needed to vent. I won't sugarcoat things. Having to feed and water her, and deal with all the fur and poop was no picnic. But she more than made up for it by providing me in return with free home security services and amiable companionship.

Brigit cast a glance at Derek. The dull look in her eyes, as well as the fact that her tail wasn't moving, told me she felt the same way about Derek as I did.

As Derek ripped a bite from the mustard-covered corn dog he was holding, I held up the plastic bag of pills and jerked my head to indicate the young man in cuffs. "He threw this in the river. I had to retrieve it."

"Let me see that," Derek said with his mouth full, treating me to a stomach-churning view of half-chewed animal innards, cornmeal, and mustard. As he snatched the bag from my hand, the sun glinted off his silver badge, burning a temporary white stripe across my field of vision. Derek examined the bag before swallowing his food, turning to the guy, and pointing an accusing half-eaten corn dog at him. "Bet you don't have a prescription for the Xanax and Ritalin, do ya?"

The scowl on the young man's face was his answer. *Nope. No Rx.* Looked like a judge would soon be issuing him a prescription for some jail time and probation.

A drop of mustard fell from the corn dog to Derek's shoe, leaving a bright yellow dot. He stuck his foot in Brigit's face. "Hey, dog. Clean that up."

Brigit gave Derek a look that said *My name isn't "dog" and, unless you want to share that corn dog, you can clean your own shoe, dumbass.*

When she turned her head away, he barked a laugh and wiped his shoe on the grass. Taking another bite of the corn dog, Derek manipulated the bag, more closely examining its varied contents. "What are these white pills? Is this Molly?" He looked to the young man for an answer.

The answer he received was, "I'm not telling you shit!"

Molly, short for "molecule," was the seemingly benign name for methylenedioxy-methamphetamine or MDMA, also otherwise known as ecstasy. The drug simultaneously boosted three brain chemicals—serotonin, dopamine, and norepinephrine. As I'd learned during training, the drug first surfaced as a club drug in the eighties and nineties, when it was known more commonly as XTC or X, but had had a recent resurgence in popularity, especially among the younger crowd and college students.

While the drug produced feelings of warmth, euphoria, exhilaration, affection, and unity, users paid the price for this high with nausea, chills, sweating, muscle cramps, involuntarily clenched teeth, and blurry vision. Users had succumbed to dehydration, seizures, and loss of consciousness. The drug caused restrictions in blood vessels, and could lead to heart attack or stroke. A stimulant, Molly increased the user's blood pressure and heart rate, which led to many becoming severely overheated, which in turn led to organ failure. Overdose cases with body temperatures of up to 107 degrees had been documented. And these were just the short-term problems with the drug. Depression and memory loss were more long-term complications. It was a big price to pay for a high that lasted only a few hours.

As with other unregulated street drugs, Molly suffered from a severe lack of quality control. While buyers might think they were getting pure MDMA, such was often not the case. The drug was often impure, cut with other drugs such as methylone, a related stimulant, with the end product varying wildly. Other times it was cut with flakka, a drug that was chemically related to bath salts, highly addictive, and had resulted in dozens of horrific deaths in south Florida, where a virtual epidemic was under way. Users could never be certain exactly what they were getting.

It seemed every time we turned around we heard reports of another Molly-related tragedy. While single-victim incidents were common, in one instance eleven students of Wesleyan University in Middletown,

Connecticut, had been hospitalized after taking the drug. And Molly wasn't just filling the news, it was filling the morgues, too. The problem with the drug came to a head after a string of deaths, including two at a New York City music festival, another at a concert in Boston, and yet another in Washington, D.C. Four deaths had been reported in Britain from the sale of a drug with a Superman logo. While the drug was purportedly Molly, it contained a lethal dose of another substance. Federal government reports indicated that over ten thousand people had ended up in emergency rooms for Molly-related health issues in a recent year. This kid wasn't offering his customers a good time. He was offering them the chance to unknowingly commit suicide. And while it might have been easy to write the victims off as stupid or reckless, many of those who'd succumbed had been otherwise good kids who'd simply made a poor decision. They didn't deserve to die.

Derek cut me a look of disgust and muttered, "You realize the street value of these pills is more than you and I earn in a week?"

I shrugged. "Nobody ever got rich being a cop." Not unless they were crooked. Those who joined the force did so for reasons other than the compensation. In my case, I'd joined to be an instrument of justice. Of course I hadn't realized when I'd signed up that justice was such an elusive concept. I stepped into place to pat the guy down. "Is there anything sharp in your pockets?"

"No," he snapped.

I patted him down, finding only a wallet in his pocket. According to the driver's license inside, the guy was twenty-one years old and named Graham. Appropriate name for a drug dealer, given that it was a homophone for gram. Still, he looked much more like the boy next door than the stereotypical drug dealer from the streets. Of course that was the problem these days. More and more everyday people had gotten into the drug game, and there was no stereotypical dealer anymore.

Per the license, Graham's last name was Hahn. Another card in his wallet indicated he was covered for health risks by his parents' Blue Cross Blue Shield insurance policy, while a third card showed he lacked only a single punch to earn a free haircut at Snippy's, a discount barbershop. A purple and white student ID pegged the kid as a student at Texas Christian University, or TCU, a local university that sat within the confines of my usual beat, the Western 1 Division. *Go Horned Frogs!*

I held out the wallet to Derek. "You'll take him in for me?"

While Brigit was great at taking suspects down, the fact that her special K-9 enclosure took up the entire backseat of my cruiser meant there was no room for transporting the suspects we apprehended. We had to turn them over to another officer. On the bright side, that meant we didn't have to deal with all of the paperwork that came with processing an arrestee and any evidence collected.

"A Molly dealer?" Derek snorted. "Hell, yeah, I'll take him in."

In 2012, Fort Worth police arrested seventeen students from TCU. The students, who included a number of football players, were charged with selling marijuana, ecstasy, cocaine, and prescription drugs. Since then, stopping the flow of drugs on campus and to the students had become a priority not only of Fort Worth PD, but of the university's police force, as well. With an enrollment of over ten thousand students who were constantly turning over, it wasn't an easy job keeping tabs on drug activity at the college. The arrest of this student would earn me and Brigit some gold stars. Of course I had no doubt that Derek would try to claim those gold stars for himself. The guy was nothing if not a narcissist.

While Derek polished off what remained of his corn dog, I read Hahn his rights. "You have the right to remain silent. Anything you say can and will be used against you in a court of law. You have the right to an attorney. If you cannot afford an attorney, one will be provided for you. Do you understand the rights I have just read to you?"

The kid snickered. *"No hablo inglés."*

I wasn't sure whether the kid was just being a turd in general, or whether the crack was intended to be more personally directed to me. While my first name was derived from my mother's Irish roots, my surname—Luz, which was on the name tag on my chest—came courtesy of my Mexican-American father. My lineage also boasted some Cherokee. Like my mixed-breed partner and most of the American population, I was a typical mutt, a little of this, a little of that, and none of it having much to do with who I really was.

I ignored the jibe, instead putting a hand on his arm to help him up. "On your feet."

He jerked out of my grasp, nearly falling to the side as he attempted to stand. No easy feat when you couldn't use your arms for balance. He should've let me help him. Oh, well. His problem, not mine.

Derek wiped his mouth with a napkin and looked

around for a trash can. Seeing none, he shoved the napkin into his pants pocket along with the baggie of drugs. As for the corn dog stick, he waved it in the air in front of Brigit. "Fetch, bitch!" he called to Brigit, hurling it toward the river.

Brigit made no move to retrieve the stick, instead tossing Derek a look that said *Bite me.*

As Derek hauled the suspect away, I walked toward the river to retrieve the wooden stick. Derek seemed to think being a cop meant he was above the law. Maybe I should've pressed the point by issuing him a citation for littering.

Brigit and I made our way back to rejoin Seth and Blast at the entry gate, where we continued to serve as a welcoming—or unwelcoming—committee, as circumstances dictated.

"Have a fun time."

"Enjoy yourselves."

"Sorry. No coolers allowed."

As we continued to work the gate, which sat near the law enforcement parking area, I saw Derek leave with both another corn dog and Graham Hahn. He returned without either an hour and a half later. Derek climbed out of his cruiser, shutting his door with far more force than necessary—*SLAM!*—and stormed toward me, looking as pissed off as I'd ever seen him.

"Everything all right?" I asked. "Corn dog give you heartburn?"

He ignored me, charging past as if I didn't exist. *Whatever.*

Seth cut his eyes to Derek's retreating back. "You ever get the urge to Taser that guy again?"

"All the time."

"I could arrange to turn a hose on him," Seth offered. "I can make it look like an accident."

"Thanks for the offer. Any more of Derek's BS and I just might take you up on it."

A few minutes later our shifts ended and other K-9 teams arrived to relieve us. Brigit and Blast exchanged butt sniffs and tail wags with the Belgian Malinois and black Lab that were taking over. The male officer with the Mal gave me a nod in greeting. "We'll take it from here. Go find some shade."

Shade? Heck, I'd rather see if the staff at one of the food trucks would let me sit in their freezer for a few minutes.

"Thanks." I raised a hand in good-bye as we headed off.

Seth did the same for his counterpart. "Later."

Beyond parched, we aimed straight for the concessions.

I spotted a sign up ahead with a yellow lemon on it. "A frozen lemonade would taste darn good about now."

"Let's do it."

Unfortunately, I wasn't the only one who'd had the thought. A dozen people stood in line at the booth. *Blurgh.* I hoped they'd spot me and Seth in line behind them and give us cuts. After all, we were public servants working to protect them while they enjoyed the day. But no. The only person who turned around was the woman in line right in front of me, and she gasped and backed away when she saw Brigit and Blast. Not a dog lover, evidently. So much for catching a break today.

Inch by inch, we made our way forward, finally

reaching the front of the line, where Seth placed our order. "Two frozen lemonades, please."

While he paid the woman at the counter, I grabbed a couple of spoons from the bin. We turned away from the booth, ripping off the lids and digging into the frozen concoction. The icy treat hit my taste buds and I cringed, both from the tart taste and the brain freeze. *Owww!*

Seth had a similar grimace on his face.

Once our instant migraines subsided, we set off again. Rather than fight the crowds and risk Brigit's and Blast's paws being stepped on, we stuck to the perimeter of the grounds, making our way along the fence until we reached the Trinity River at the northern border. Spotting a couple of ducks on the water, Blast went still, looking up at Seth for permission to give in to his instincts as a Labrador retriever and to round up the ducks.

Seth unclipped his leash. "Go for it, boy."

Blast leaped from the bank, belly flopping into the water, and took off swimming after the ducks he had no hope of ever catching.

Brigit dragged me closer to the riverbank, excitedly rearing up on two legs and barking up a storm. *Woof! Woof-woof woof!*

Might as well let the dog have some fun and cool off, right? I reached down and freed her from her lead. "Go on, Brig."

She dashed into the water, swimming after Blast. When the ducks took off faster than the dogs could ever hope to swim, they aborted their mission, instead swimming in circles around each other and playing chase.

Seth stepped to the edge of the water, bent down, and

scooped up a handful of river water, playfully sending it up in the air over my head, the resulting shower providing some welcome relief from the heat. Meandering through both the cities of Dallas and Fort Worth, the Trinity was far from the cleanest river around, but as far as I knew nobody had contracted cholera or dysentery from its waters.

I stepped to the edge of the river and raised my arms out to my sides for maximum exposure. "Splash me again," I begged, desperate to cool down.

"Okay," Seth replied. "Just remember you asked for it." He obliged, this time using both of his strong arms to scoop two generous handfuls of river water in my direction.

I turned my head skyward, closing my eyes. Instead of sprinkling down on me, the water hit me square in the chest. I lowered my arms and skewered Seth with my gaze. "Your aim was a little off."

A grin played about his lips. "No it wasn't."

A voice on my radio interrupted our conversation. "Officers requested to the stage. VIPs en route."

Darn. "Gotta go. Duty calls."

"Can you meet up to watch the fireworks?" Seth asked, cocking his head in question.

I raised my palms. While both police work and firefighter duties involved a significant amount of downtime, it was impossible to predict how a shift would go. A calm, quiet shift could turn on a dime, becoming a shit storm with no warning. I'd learned not to count my chickens. "I'll do my best."

I called out to Brigit, issuing the order for her to return to my side. She gave me a scornful look similar to the one she'd given Derek not long before, but nevertheless obeyed, climbing out of the river, her wet body looking scrawny compared to how fluffy she was dry. When she reached my side, I stuck a hand into my pocket and retrieved one of her favorite liver treats as a reward for her behavior. "Good girl."

I tossed a second treat to Blast, who remained in the water. He managed to snap it out of the air. "See you two later," I called as Brigit and I headed off.

THREE
SHAKE YOUR BOOTY

Sergeant Brigit

While taking a dip in the river had cooled Brigit down, it had also given her a serious case of flat fur. No self-respecting shepherd would go around looking like some pathetic short-haired breed. Of course there was only one remedy to that. *Shake.*

Brigit began her full-body shimmy, starting at her back end and working her way forward until she'd rid herself of most of the river water she'd soaked up. Her fur was once again proud and fluffy, as it should be. To her surprise, Megan had voiced no objection to being doused with the spray today.

Megan clipped her lead to her collar and Brigit walked by her partner's side. They passed a pony ride, where a half-dozen of the beasts were tethered to a metal wheel, taking toddlers and tykes in incessant circles. A small boy on a brown Shetland pony rocked in the saddle, kicked the pony in the ribs with his sneakers, and yelled, "Giddyup!" With its bridle tied to a metal pole and the weight of the other ponies acting as a counterbalance, the poor pony couldn't giddyup even if it wanted to.

Brigit's eyes met those of the pony. *I feel for you, buddy.* Perhaps their species should consider joining together, rising up, and overthrowing the humans. Then again, while Megan might technically be her boss, she was pretty much at Brigit's beck and call, feeding her, taking care of her poops, and reaching those hard-to-scratch areas, like the one at the base of her tail. *Hmm.* She'd have to give the idea more thought before fully committing to a coup.

As they approached a garbage can, Brigit spotted Derek standing in front of it. Derek was one of the few officers who never talked baby talk to her or gave her so much as a pat on the head. Brigit didn't like him at all, and she could tell Megan didn't like him, either. Her partner tended to stiffen when the guy came around and to hold Brigit closer, both of which the dog recognized as defensive postures.

For some reason, Derek was digging through the garbage can, tossing the contents onto the ground around the bin. Brigit's nose detected all of the tasty tidbits people had thrown away. Bits of barbecue. Nacho remnants. Pizza crust, her favorite. She'd love nothing more than to run over to the pile of food scraps and have a feast. But she knew Megan wouldn't be happy with her, even if she offered to share the smorgasbord. Sometimes there was just no pleasing people.

FOUR
NIP IT IN THE BUD

The Dealer

He cast a glance over his shoulder. She was gaining on him, virtually nipping at his heels. *Bitch*. But if she thought she'd ever get the best of him, she was sorely mistaken.

FIVE
STARS AND STRIPES

Megan

As Brigit and I approached the stage, I spotted Derek Mackey digging through a trash can, hurling food waste, dirty diapers, and other miscellaneous detritus to the ground. I wondered if whatever he was looking for was the reason he'd appeared so ticked off earlier.

"What're you doing?" I called as we drew near.

"None of your damn business!" he snapped, waving me away with his meaty hand.

He was acting like an ass, but I wasn't going to let his sour mood and disrespect get to me. *Why give the jerk what he wanted?* "Alrighty, then," I said cheerfully as my partner and I moved past. "Enjoy those scraps."

We continued on to the stage, where a band was setting up for a performance that was to begin in a few minutes. A lineup of politicians had gathered at the back of the platform. They ran the gamut from the city's mayor, to a member of the state House of Representatives, to a United States senator who was back from Washington, D.C., to spend the holiday with his family.

No doubt many in Congress went on break for the Fourth, returning to their home states to make appearances, assure their constituencies that they remembered from whence they came, and eat hot dogs and barbecue with their supporters.

Though not technically a politician, Police Chief Garelik had even turned out in uniform for the event, realizing it made an excellent PR opportunity for the department. With his broad, bulky build, silver hair, and chest adorned with medals, the chief looked both formidable and dignified. While the others took seats in an area at the back of the stage shaded by the broad tarp that hung over it, the chief stood at the front in clear view, letting those in attendance know that he and his officers were keeping an eagle eye on things.

When Chief Garelik spotted me and Brigit, he motioned for us to join him on the stage. As his golden boy's nemesis, I was far from the chief's favorite officer. But Brigit and I had played a major role in nabbing a number of violent criminals, and even he couldn't deny that the two of us were local heroes, our presence providing those in attendance something to rally around. The chief didn't like me but he did respect me, even if he disguised that respect in a wrap of snide comments and squinty-eyed sideways glances. I'd much prefer being respected to being liked, so all was good here.

As Brigit and I headed for the steps, my ears picked up comments from those in the crowd.

"Look! That's the K-9 team who took down that bomber!"

"Isn't that the two who caught that killer who was burglarizing houses?"

"Hey! It's the cops who captured the Berkeley Place Peeper!"

"Can I get a pic with you two?"

Given that the last statement was directed at me, I stopped and replied, "Sure." I stepped into place next to a thirtyish woman, instructed Brigit to sit at our feet, and smiled at the cell phone her companion had aimed our way. *Click!*

Far be it from me to gloat, but Brigit and I were minor celebrities around these parts. We did our job, and we did it with a dedication bordering on obsession.

"Thanks!"

"Anytime," I replied.

Brigit and I ascended the fold-out staircase on the side of the stage and took places next to the chief at the front. "Good afternoon, Chief."

He responded with a grunt. "Good? I've got sweat running down my ass crack, the sun in my eyes, and the mayor breathing down my neck. There's nothing good about this afternoon."

Every party needs a pooper. Looked like the chief had volunteered for the role today.

Any glory I'd expected from being featured on stage was short-lived. When the chief noticed Derek stepping away from the garbage can, he squeezed his shoulder mic. "Officer Mackey, report to the stage." In seconds, Derek was on the stage with us, standing on the other side of the chief, giving me his own squinty-eyed sideways glances. So much for my metaphorical moment in the sun.

On cue, a Boy Scout color guard presented the American and Texas flags, placing them in stands on the stage.

One of the boys stepped to the microphone. "Please join me in reciting the Pledge of Allegiance."

Derek, the chief, and I turned toward the flags, placed our right hands over our hearts, and murmured in unison with the crowd as they recited the pledge. Brigit took advantage of the opportunity to sniff the chief's shoe.

As the last line of the pledge was carried away on the breeze, five F-16s from the 301st Fighter Wing at the Naval Air Station Joint Reserve Base roared up in the sky and performed a low-altitude flyover, impressing the crowd with their precision turns and noisy engines. Brigit yelped—*Arp!*—and dropped to the floor of the stage, cowering in alarm.

"It's okay, girl." I knelt down next to her and ran a hand over her back. "It's just airplanes. They're loud but they won't hurt you." Why I felt the need to explain things to a dog that couldn't understand was beyond me. I think sometimes I forgot she was a dog rather than a person. At any rate, the soothing tone of my voice seemed to calm her and I could feel her stiff body relax under my touch.

I stood as one of the festival organizers stepped up to the mic. Dressed in red and white striped pants and a blue blouse emblazoned with white stars, the woman epitomized patriotism at its best—or worst, depending on your viewpoint. "Hello, everyone!" she cried. "Welcome to Fort Worth Fourth at Panther Pavilion!"

Lethargic from heat and humidity and hot dogs, the crowd offered only a smattering of applause. They'd come to the stage to hear the band, not a bunch of blowhards.

The woman didn't let the lukewarm welcome deter her from her mission. "We hope you all are having a wonderful time today. Don't forget to reapply your sunscreen! And be sure to stick around for tonight's fireworks followed by more live music. Now, it's my pleasure to introduce the mayor of Fort Worth, Mr. John Normangee!"

Another smattering of applause ensued, followed by the squall of a toddler whose snow cone had rolled out of its paper cup and fallen to the ground. *Tragic.*

While the kid's parents ushered him off to get a replacement, Mayor Normangee stepped up to the microphone and issued a greeting with the same practiced cheerfulness as the woman who'd introduced him. "Good afternoon to the fine folks of Fort Worth! So glad to see all of your faces here today. If you haven't tried the zip-line, be sure to give it a go! Lots of fun! Some exciting things are on the city council's agenda for the upcoming week. We'll be voting on the acquisition of land on Helmick Avenue for a new city park, contracts for infrastructure improvements, and rezoning requests for land along Bluebonnet Drive for a proposed multifamily development."

The lack of response from the audience indicated that they did not share the mayor's enthusiasm for city business.

The mayor gestured to the fortyish Latina woman standing behind him. "We're privileged to have our state representative here today to share a few words with us. Ladies and gentlemen, I give you Esperanza Espinoza!"

While the crowd's response to the mayor had been

lukewarm, the audience now threw their fists into the air and broke into chants of "Ess-ie! Ess-ie!"

Esperanza "Essie" Espinoza stepped forward, raising a hand to wave to the crowd. She was dressed casually in jeans and a T-shirt featuring a sequined American flag, her signature dark curls gathered in a bushy pony-tail at the nape of her neck. Before running for the Texas House of Representatives as an independent candidate six years ago, Essie had practiced labor law in Fort Worth, representing plaintiffs in wage disputes, discrim-ination cases, and other employment-related matters. The fact that she fought for the little guy, along with her sincere smile and approachability, had made her a popu-lar politician. She'd earned my vote. She'd gone on to gather fame and fans when she filibustered against a proposed bill that would have established a school voucher system.

"Happy Fourth of July, everyone!" She repeated the sentiment in Spanish. *"¡Feliz cuatro de julio a todos!"*

Her wishes earned her three times the applause as her predecessors, and one cry of *"ay yi yi!"* to which she responded with a laugh and *"Ay yi yi,* indeed. *¿Hace mucho calor hoy, no?* It's very hot today!"

Despite the fact that she'd merely stated the obvious in two languages, the crowd cheered her on. Esperanza lived up to her name, which meant "hope" in Spanish. She was a bright-eyed optimist, a woman of understated brilliance, a consensus builder who brought people to-gether rather than dividing them.

"I'm so glad to be home for the holidays so that I can spend the day with my husband and children." She blew kisses to her husband and three daughters, ranging in age from seven to thirteen, standing in the front row. She looked back up. "I'm also glad to spend the day with my constituents. I consider each and every one of you to be part of my extended family, and I'm proud to represent and work for all of you. I encourage you to contact me with any of your concerns. My office is only an e-mail or phone call away." She swiped her windswept bangs out of her eyes. "Senator Sutton will address you now and update us on what's going on in our nation's capital. Let's give him a nice welcome, shall we?" With that, she cast a look back at Senator Montgomery Sutton and motioned for him to step forward before applauding him and stepping aside.

Essie was definitely a class act. Though she'd tossed her hat in the ring for the U.S. Senator spot Monty Sutton now held, she'd made no snarky comments about her attempts to unseat him in the upcoming election in November. If only every politician could be so gracious and professional. Of course her restraint could also be due to the fact that Monty Sutton was a well-respected and well-liked politician, with impressive approval ratings. He'd held his office for four full terms so far. He, too, had earned my vote. At sixty-eight, he was older and more old-school than Essie in his appearance and demeanor, but he had an everyman quality about him, a grandfatherly sense of humor, and a record that proved him a thoughtful legislator. With his calm, reasonable demeanor and good people skills paired with his determination, he was a proven consensus builder and expert negotiator, able to bring the parties together to get things done. His integrity was beyond reproach, too. Unlike some of the more notorious members of national

governments, he'd never slept with an intern, sent a dick
pic to anyone, snorted cocaine off the breasts of a pros-
titute, or made implied references to blow jobs or the
size of another politician's gonads. He'd also never accepted campaign contributions from special interests,
as reflected in his slogan "Montgomery Sutton—The
Best Representation Money CAN'T Buy."

Senator Sutton stepped up to the microphone. He,
too, had set aside his business suits for more comfortable attire, though his navy pants, short-sleeved red polo
shirt, and loafers leaned more toward business casual.
The typical politician's American flag pin graced his
collar. His white hair gleamed in the sun and he dipped
his head to give a polite nod to the crowd.

Not to be outdone by Essie Espinoza's supporters,
Senator Sutton's small entourage near the stage raised
fists in the air and chanted. "Sut-ton! Sut-ton!"

When the chants subsided, Senator Sutton launched
into his speech, giving the crowd a quick update on the
latest news from Washington. "As y'all may have noticed, our middle class is shrinking, due in large part to
jobs moving overseas. To put Americans back to work,
I've proposed a bill known as the China–U.S. Partnership, or CUSP for short."

He went on to explain that the bill posed a challenge
to China's tradition of mercantilism under which it ex-
ported far more goods to other countries while enact-
ing protectionist measures, such as high tariffs, to limit
imports. Sutton was a longstanding member of the Senate's Foreign Relations Committee, as well as chair-
man of the Subcommittee on East Asia, the Pacific, and
International Cybersecurity Policy. Barbara Boxer and

former presidential candidate Marco Rubio served on the subcommittee with Sutton. Among other things, the subcommittee's duties included promoting U.S. trade and exports.

"I've done so much walking up and down the halls of the Senate Building in Washington to drum up support," he said, "I've just about worn out the soles of my shoes." When he lifted up one foot and wiggled it, the crowd chuckled. He waved a hand dismissively. "But that's enough shop talk. Y'all are here to have a good time and celebrate this glorious Independence Day."

His reference earned a few whoops and whistles.

"On this date in 1776," he said, shifting from current proposed legislation to a history lesson, "our forefathers dared to declare independence from England. We owe a lot to Benjamin Franklin, Samuel Adams, John Hancock, and those other rebellious upstarts." He paused for laughter, which the audience again provided. "Let's think about their words for a moment."

"Do we have to?" hollered a beer-bellied man, causing his buddies to erupt in laughter.

Senator Sutton, having dealt with hecklers for decades, was unfazed. "We sure do," he replied with a smile. He leaned closer to the mic and whispered. "Looks like we've got some rebellious upstarts here today, too."

Again the audience laughed.

When the senator spoke again, his words were slow and deliberate. "*We hold these truths to be self-evident, that all men are created equal, that they are endowed by their Creator with certain unalienable Rights, that among these are Life, Liberty and the pursuit of Happiness. That to secure these rights, Governments*

are instituted among Men, deriving their just powers
from the consent of the governed."

He paused a moment to let the words sink in. "What
does this mean?"

The beer-bellied man hollered again. "It means it's
time for another beer!"

At that point, Chief Garelik motioned for an officer
at the perimeter of the crowd to move in and let the
heckler know his jackassery wasn't appreciated.

"What this means," Sutton said, "is that every person is entitled to live, to be free, and to pursue those
things that will bring them joy, purpose, and satisfaction. Serving you all has brought me such joy, purpose,
and satisfaction. Of course it's brought me quite a few
headaches, too." His own chuckle echoed those of the
crowd. "It's my hope that each of you will find your
own particular source of joy, and that you will find it in
abundance. I wish I could do it for you, but as Benjamin Franklin noted, 'The Constitution only guaran-
tees the right to pursue happiness. You have to catch it
yourself.'"

"I caught happiness once!" the man in the crowd
yelled, undeterred by the cop standing next to him.
"Took two rounds of penicillin to clear it up!"

Sutton smiled. "You might want to find a different
source of happiness, son." His speech complete, he
raised a hand. "Enjoy the music, folks!"

As the politicians descended from the stage, the band
launched into a rock version of "America the Beautiful."

Brigit and I followed Derek and the chief down from
the stage. While the chief headed for the air-conditioned
trailer that served as FWPD's mobile command center,

Derek stalked off. Neither bade me and my partner good-bye.

I, on the other hand, took advantage of the opportunity to rub elbows with the senatorial candidates. Or at least I tried in Essie's case. As I walked toward her, an assistant with an earpiece swooped her away without so much as a glance in my direction. *Hmm.* Senator Sutton, on the other hand, put his hands on his knees and called out to Brigit. "Hey, there, girl!"

She tugged on the leash, knowing a "hey, girl" often came with a butt scratch.

I led my partner over and held out my hand, my pulse pounding. Given his tenure and success in Washington, D.C., Sutton was no stranger at the White House, often called in to offer advice and consultation. Standing here now, I was only one degree of separation from several U.S. presidents! "Hello, Senator Sutton. It's a p-pleasure to meet you."

He eyed my name badge. "You, too, Officer Luz. What a fine-looking K-9 you have here."

Brigit wagged her tail as he ran a hand over her head and neck.

"I couldn't ask for a better partner," I said.

He stood full upright. "You two enjoying yourselves today?"

Only if you call being on your feet for hours in the broiling sun enjoyable. "We sure are!" I lied.

He gave me a pat on the shoulder and a "you take care now" before stepping away to round up his wife.

I spent the rest of the day rotating duties with the other K-9 teams. Between drunken brawls, heatstroke, and lost children, first responders were kept busy all afternoon. Each time I passed the people floating in the river on inner tubes, I fought the urge to dive in. When the sun finally dipped below the horizon, it was all I could do not to send up a cheer. Of course the temperature was still in the nineties, but at least the sun was no longer scorching my skin and Brigit's fur.

As nine o'clock neared, I texted Seth. *Where are you?* *At the big truck* was his reply.

I strategically meandered my way over to the fire trucks and found Seth now decked out in his firefighter turnout gear and looking sexy as hell. The guy really made a yellow coat and helmet work for him.

While Brigit plopped down next to Blast on the dry grass, I leaned back against the truck next to Seth. Soon, the sounds of Sousa's songs blared from the speakers and the first firework streaked upward into the night sky, leaving a golden trail behind it. *POP!* Another followed behind, offering another *POP* followed by a crackling sizzle as sparks showered down. *POP! POP-POP-POP! POP-POP!*

Brigit emitted a nervous whine, her ears flattening back against her head. Though it was critical for a K-9 to be accustomed to gunfire and I'd been forced to subject her to gunshot noise during some of our training sessions, Brigit was smart enough to realize these sounds were different and potentially threatening. I stroked her back to reassure her. "It's okay, girl. Nothing to worry about."

Eventually, the bigger guns were brought out, treating us to one *KABOOM* after another, the sound waves reverberating off the truck behind me. I glanced over at

Seth only to find he'd closed his eyes. These *pops* and *kabooms* might be innocent enough, but Seth had heard many *pops* and *kabooms* in Afghanistan, *pops* and *kabooms* that meant his life, or those of other soldiers, could be in danger or, even worse, have just been cut short.

After looking around to make sure everyone's eyes were on the sky, I reached out and took Seth's hand in mine, giving it a gentle squeeze. Though he didn't open his eyes, he squeezed back.

Seth's radio and those of the firefighters around him came to life. "Grass fire reported near the portable toilets."

Seth opened his eyes. "Duty calls."

"More like *doody* calls," called one of the other men.

I roused Brigit and stepped away from the truck as the firefighters piled on to drive it across the field. They returned a few minutes later, just in time to see the grand finale as bursts of red, blue, yellow, green, and silver lit up the sky as if the heavens were raining glitter.

The headliner band immediately kicked in on the stage across the way, the diehards among the crowd heading in that direction to keep the night going while the older folks and families with small children began easing toward the exits. That was my cue to get back on patrol.

"I better go," I told Seth.

He slid me a sexy smile. "Meet you at your house for a shower later?"

I slid him a sexy smile right back. "I'll wash your back if you'll wash mine."

Brigit and I headed to the exit, stationing ourselves

next to the gate where we could keep a close eye out for drunks who might be planning to get behind the wheel. Officer Spalding, a beefy black cop, took up on the other side, giving me a chin lift in greeting. Spalding was a man of many muscles but few words.

As the beer-bellied heckler from earlier stumbled toward me, I held up a hand. "Hold on a second, buddy."

He stopped walking, but swayed in place as if slow dancing with himself.

I cocked my head. "You're looking a little tipsy, sir. How many have you had?"

"Not near enough!" he cackled.

One of his friends had the sense to shush him. "Be cool, man."

I turned to the friend. "How about you. How many have you had?"

"Only two," he said, "and one of those was at lunch-time."

The fact that he'd admitted to two told me he was likely being honest. It was the people who said "just one" that were usually lying. I pulled out my flashlight and shined it in his eyes. His pupils responded as they should, by retracting. He, too, responded like a sober person, by frowning and squinting into the light. "You driving your friend home?" I asked, hiking a thumb at beer-belly.

"Always do," he replied.

"All right, then." I swept my hand toward the exit. "Carry on." I could have issued beer-belly a citation for public intoxication, but he hadn't caused a fight, urinated on anything, or touched any women inappropriately. He'd caught some ten-proof happiness. I'd let him slide.

A few minutes later, Spalding performed essentially the same exchange with a group of young women, two of whom were teetering precariously on their wedge heels. "Who's driving?" he asked.

A young woman who looked annoyed, and thus sober, raised the keys in her hand and shook them. "That would be me. I drew the short straw and got designated driver."

"Be careful now, ladies." With that, he pointed to the gate, letting them know they were free to go.

The band continued to play and was into their sixth or seventh song when the flow wound down to a trickle. I could see a large group of people, mostly teens and people in their twenties, dancing in front of the stage, never mind the fact that the night was still warm enough to induce sweat when standing still. As I watched, the movement at the front of the crowd shifted, the dancers stepping back and growing still. Not ten seconds later, a call came across our radios. "EMTs and police needed at stage. Reports of an unconscious person on ground."

I looked over at Spalding.

"I've got things under control here," he said. In other words, he'd rather stay at the gate than work crowd control at the stage. I couldn't blame him. People loved tragedy, gaping and gawking when they should be getting the hell out of the way so the paramedics could tend to the victim.

"C'mon, Brig!" I took off at a run, my partner galloping alongside me.

We passed Derek, who appeared to be headed for the exit.

"They've called us to the stage!" I shouted.

He pointed at the watch on his wrist. "My shift is over."

Such dedication, huh?

By the time Brigit and I arrived at the stage, several other officers were already on hand, as were Trish Le-Grande and her cameraman. Officers shooed the crowd back from the collapsed girl so that paramedics could get to her. The EMT swarmed and hovered over her. One appeared to be checking her pulse, while another shined a light in her eyes. I couldn't see much of her at this point, other than thin legs with skin the warm brown of my own, tapering down to a pair of bejeweled sandals.

A girl and a boy, both of whom appeared to be around nineteen or twenty, stood at the front of the crowd, staring down at her. One of the boy's hands clutched his dark hair in a death grip while his eyes shined bright with fear. The girl openly sobbed, her hands cupped over her mouth, her auburn waves shaking as her shoulders heaved. *They must be friends of the victim.*

My suspicious were confirmed when a third EMT stepped over to the boy and girl to ask them questions. The two exchanged nervous glances before the girl said something to the EMT. He nodded and returned to the girl on the ground. As soon as the EMTs had the victim loaded into the ambulance, I'd make sure to get names and contact information from the two, just in case this wasn't a mere case of heatstroke.

Motion to my left caught my eye. Officer Hinojosa, a seasoned cop in his mid-thirties, stepped up next to me. "People have been dropping like flies today."

I cut a glance in his direction. "No kidding. Humans aren't meant to be out in this kind of heat."

When I turned back, the girl had been loaded onto a gurney and raised from the ground. One arm flopped lifelessly over the edge of the thin mattress. Her face was lax and innocent, like a sleeping child's. Her eyes were open, but barely, the slits big enough only to reflect the revolving lights of the ambulance. Still, though no life showed behind them, I felt as if the girl's eyes were imploring me to do something. But what could I do? She needed a doctor, not a cop.

As the paramedics slid her into the back of the ambulance and closed the doors, my gaze moved from the vehicle to the crowd. The girl who'd spoken to the paramedics was gone. So was the boy who'd been with her, the two of them disappearing like ghosts in the night air.

SIX
SIXTH SENSE

Brigit

She stood beside her partner in front of the stage. The band had stopped playing, the loud rock music replaced by the shrill scream of the siren coming from the ambulance. Sometimes Brigit's superior sense of hearing was a curse. She fought the urge to put her nose in the air and howl. Anything to drown out the earsplitting wail.

The lights atop the ambulance flashed, extra bright against the dark backdrop of night, burning her eyes. But those lights were nothing compared to the blinding flash when someone turned on the white spotlights on the front of the stage.

As Megan called again for the crowd to move back, Brigit's nose twitched instinctively, surveying the surroundings and detecting a number of smells. Sweat from the people who'd been dancing in front of the stage. Beer on the breath of those who'd gathered around, gaping at a young woman being loaded into the back of the ambulance. The stench of half-digested hot dog the girl had heaved all over herself before dropping to the grass.

Yep, there were all kinds of scents here.

But mostly what Brigit smelled was trouble.

SEVEN
THE COVER OF DARKNESS

The Dealer

The wail of the ambulance siren met his ears as his car pulled out of the parking lot. He turned to see the flashing lights, their reflection bouncing off the food booths and Porta Pottis.

Looked like he'd gotten out just in time.

He continued on, disappearing into the darkness.

EIGHT
CHAIN OF CUSTODY

Megan

Those of us who'd worked the Fourth of July celebration had been given the fifth off, and I'd intended to take full advantage of it by sleeping in until noon. Unfortunately, my partner had other plans. The sun had barely peeked over the horizon, the sky still hazy with an orangey-pink glow, when Brigit slid down from the bed and woofed softly to wake me. *Woof.*

"Please, Brigit," I moaned. "You went out at two A.M. Can't you hold it?" I pulled the sheet up over my head.

I'd nearly fallen back asleep when she woofed again, louder and more insistently. *Woof!*

I pulled the pillow over my head now, but it wasn't enough to drown her out.

Woof! Woof!

I tossed off the covers, sat up, and glared at her. "Next time you're napping I'm getting even."

I climbed out of bed and let her out the back door. Knowing she wouldn't be satisfied with just a potty break, I set about fixing her breakfast, spooning some wet food into a bowl for my partner to enjoy. As if the dog weren't pesky enough, my roommate's fluffy calico cat leaped up onto the counter and nudged my hand with her nose, feline code for *feed me now or I'll hork up a hairball in your closet.* Rolling my eyes, I retrieved a can of her wet food from the cabinet and set about filling her bowl, too. I pushed it to the back of the counter where she could eat in peace without Brigit trying to steal her meal.

After letting the dog back inside, I looked from one of the furry beasts to the other. "You're really the ones in charge, aren't you?"

They both cut me looks that said if I was just now figuring that out I was behind the curve.

" 'Mornin'." The five-feet-eleven-inch Amazon that was my roommate Frankie slunk into the room, her spiky blue hair sticking up in all directions. "What's for breakfast?"

"I gotta feed you now, too?"

She dropped into a seat at the table. "It would be nice."

I scoffed, but it was halfhearted and we both knew it. Frankie had taken me and Brigit in when I'd had no luck finding a house to rent that was both suitable and affordable. She'd taken a chance on us, having known us for only the fifteen minutes it had taken for me to nearly run her over in my squad car, discover she'd been dumped by her boyfriend, and return to the house to prevent her boyfriend from taking the television she'd helped pay for.

Luckily, things had worked out well for both of us. Brigit now had a nice yard to play and poop in, and I no longer had an upstairs neighbor with a prostate problem

who flushed his toilet all night long or a bastard land-
lord who refused to fix anything until the apartment
complex nearly burned down. Frankie gained a new
friend and a guard dog to keep her, her cat, and her valu-
ables safe. Of course the most valuable things she owned
were the TV I'd mentioned and the Luigino Atom Matrix
skates she used to play roller derby. Those skates cost
nearly five hundred dollars.

I fixed Frankie a bowl of Cocoa Puffs and made a
bowl of organic granola for myself.

Frankie had been working as a nighttime stocker in
a grocery store and still trying to figure out her life plan
when Seth suggested she might enjoy the physical challenges of being a firefighter. It was as if a lightbulb had
gone off in her head. She'd immediately applied for a
position and was currently working her way through the
required training, which took several weeks.

"What's up in training today?" I asked her.

"More physical testing," she said. "They're also making us climb an aerial ladder today. Gotta make sure
we're not afraid of heights."

"You'll do great. You're not afraid of anything."

"That's not true." She smirked. "I'm afraid the Fort
Worth Whoop Ass might lose this weekend's bout
against the Sherman She-Devils."

As we ate, my cell phone pinged with an incoming
text. It was from Seth. *Up yet? Dog park?*

I texted him back. *We'll be ready in half an hour.* It
was crazy early, sure, but if we didn't get the dogs to
the park by eight o'clock, it would be too hot for them
to run around and play.

I finished my cereal and rinsed the bowl in the sink,

leaving Frankie at the table with Zoe on her lap. I showered, washing my own back this time around, and dressed in shorts, a tank top, and sneakers. Seth came to the door as I was rounding up my dog park bag, which held a cooler of cold water, a plastic bowl, and an assortment of throw toys including a Frisbee, a tennis ball, and squeaky squirrel. No need for me to call Brigit. She'd heard Seth's car pull up and was already at the front door, sniffing at the bottom and wagging her tail as if to say *Our dates are here!*

As we stepped onto the porch, Brigit and Blast greeted each other with a playful tussle that ended up with Blast on his back and Brigit hovering over him, chewing affectionately on his neck. Seth and I did essentially the same, though our tussle culminated in a kiss. Much less slobber.

Seth rested his forehead on mine, his green eyes looking into mine. "How about another shower before we go?"

"I've had two in the last six hours. I'm plenty clean."

A grin tugged at his lips. "I could get you dirty."

I pushed him back. "Behave yourself."

He raised his palms in surrender. "Can't blame a guy for trying."

He took the bag from me and stashed it in the trunk while I loaded the dogs into the back of his seventies-era Nova. The muscle car sported blue paint with bright orange flames down the side and license plates that read KABOOM, apropos for a member of the city's bomb squad.

Once the dogs were situated, we humans slid into the front, sitting side by side on the bench seat. My skin stuck to the duct-taped vinyl, but it was a small price to pay to get to sit thigh to thigh with Seth.

Seth pulled into the dog park, taking a spot near the chain-link fence that enclosed the area. As Blast and Brigit descended from the backseat, an adorable rust and white papillon rushed the fence, barking up a storm.

"Hello, Lady!" I called to the dog.

Lady Fenton was one of Brigit's dog park pals and seven pounds of pure attitude. I think that's why Brigit liked the fluffy little dog so much. A Rottweiler or mastiff had sheer size on their side, and all they had to do to look tough was stand up. But for a tiny little thing like Lady to show no fear among dogs ten or more times her size was truly courageous.

I raised a hand to her owner, who offered a friendly smile.

We let Brigit and Blast in through the double gates, and they joined with Lady, trotting off to greet their buddies and make the acquaintance of the dogs they hadn't met before.

Seth and I found a spot to stand in the shade of a live oak. There, we did the same things the dogs had done— greeted the people we recognized and introduced ourselves to those we didn't. We made small talk, the conversation starting with the weather and someone asking the inevitable question, "Hot enough for ya?'"

We all agreed that, indeed, it was hot enough for each of us. A man named Pete who owned a boxer said, "Hell, it's hot enough for Satan himself!"

A sixtyish man with short and wiry gray hair not unlike that of his schnauzer took a sip from his water bottle and eyed Seth. "That reporter from Dallas with the big bazoombas said some girl nearly died last night at Panther Pavilion. You know anything about that?"

"Little bit," he said.

"What happened?" he asked. "Was it heatstroke?"

"Sorry," he replied, "but medical information is confidential. I'm not allowed to talk about that kind of thing."

The man scowled, insulted.

Brigit loped up, stuck her snout into the bag at my feet, and pulled out the Frisbee. Blast grabbed the other side and the two engaged in a brief tug-of-war until Seth managed to wrangle it away from both of them. He pulled his arm back and sent it sailing across the park. "Go get it!"

He didn't have to tell them twice. They were off in an instant, kicking up dirt and grass in their determined quest to be the one who snatched the disc out of the air.

Brigit won, circling back and dropping the disc at my feet. I tossed it this time, though my throw didn't have nearly the reach of Seth's.

A few minutes later, the dogs flopped down at our feet, tuckered out from the activity and the heat. We offered them some cold water, which they drank with gusto. *Slurp-slurp-slurp!*

After bidding the group good-bye, Seth and I led the dogs back to the car.

"So," I said, once we were seated inside, "what happened to the girl?"

"You heard me. That's private information."

I snorted. "Right." He might not be permitted to share private medical information with the general public, but

I was a fellow first responder, not to mention his girl-friend.

He cut a look my way and spoke in a whisper, as if that somehow negated his breach of confidentiality. "She's still in the hospital. Bad reaction to Molly."

"Molly?" *Dammit!* She—or someone who'd sold her the drug—had sneaked it past the K-9 units. I knew we couldn't be everywhere, and that people possessing drugs would take pains to avoid the K-9 teams, but it still rankled. "Is she going to be okay?"

"Who knows," he said on a sigh. "Last I heard it wasn't looking good."

I closed my eyes for a moment. No doubt the girl's parents were going through hell right now. The kids who took these drugs didn't seem to realize the risk they were taking, the danger they were putting themselves in, that they were essentially practicing medicine on themselves without the benefit of a medical school education and a regulated pharmaceutical company producing the drug. They might as well be playing Russian roulette.

We returned to my house and spent a lazy day on the couch watching movies, sometimes using our dogs for pillows, other times being used as pillows by our dogs. Though my eyes were glued to the screen, my mind was in that hospital room with the young girl I'd seen being loaded into the ambulance. *Would she survive? If she did, would she have permanent brain or organ damage?*

The same questions still ran through my mind when I arrived at work shortly before eight Thursday morning. I stepped up to the front desk to consult with Melinda, a fortyish blue-eyed, bushy-haired blonde who served as the W1 Division's office manager/administrative guru/ receptionist. Melinda was the cog around which the entire division circled, the scheduler, the keeper of information, the guardian of the key to the supply closet. In other words, the rest of us might carry guns and night sticks, but she wielded the real power.

"Good morning, Melinda," I greeted her. "Can you print me out a copy of the arrest report on Graham Hahn?"

"I could," she replied. "But what's the point?"

"What do you mean?"

"I was here when Officer Mackey brought the kid in. We had to let him go. Somewhere between Panther Pavilion and the station Derek lost the evidence."

My mind took a second to process that piece of information before my mouth cried, "He *what*?!?"

"You heard me," the no-nonsense Melinda replied. "The drugs were gone. Hahn was released. End of story."

"But Hahn had thousands of dollars' worth of pills!" I cried, as if that could somehow make the evidence materialize. "He wasn't just using the drugs. He was selling them!"

"Yet they're still gone," Melinda said. "Now can I get back to my other work or is there something else I can help you with?"

"No," I told her, fuming so hard it was a wonder flames weren't shooting out of my nostrils. "That's all I need. Thanks for the information."

She angled her head to indicate the hallway to my left and spoke under her breath. "Derek's in the men's room if you want to give him some hell."

"Oh, you know I do!"

I stormed down the hall and positioned myself across from the men's room door with my back to the wall, Brigit sitting at my feet. When the door swung open a moment later and Derek stepped out, I was on him in a heartbeat, my face only inches from his. "You lost evidence and botched my arrest? How could you!"

He frowned, but was otherwise nonchalant. "The drugs either fell out of my pocket or I accidentally threw them away with some other trash. As they say, shit happens."

Shit happens? That's his response? While Derek worked as a training officer on occasion, he'd been flying solo for the past few weeks. Too bad. If he'd had a partner or trainee with him, maybe he or she would've kept a closer eye on the drugs and prevented them from being misplaced.

"So that's a 'yes,' then?" I demanded. "You admit you screwed up?"

The Big Dick stiffened and glared down at me. "You best step back, Megan."

"Don't tell me to step back!" I snapped. "There's a girl in the hospital clinging to life, Derek! She was at Panther Pavilion and had a bad reaction to Molly. There's a chance she bought it from Hahn. And now he's gotten off scot-free!"

He waved a dismissive hand. "That boy isn't the only one dealing Molly in Fort Worth. Hell, he probably wasn't the only one selling Molly at the pavilion. Besides, if anyone's to blame, it's you and little miss sniffy." He gestured to Brigit. "You two were supposed to catch anyone trying to bring drugs into the event and that little pecker-head snuck right past you at the gate. Now get off my ass and get out of my way."

I got off his ass, but I didn't get out of his way. Nonetheless, he circled around me and stalked down the hall and out of the building to begin his shift.

"Bastard," I muttered after him.

The guy was infuriating, mostly because he kind of had a point. It was the job of the K-9 teams to find drugs. Even if the Big Dick hadn't lost the evidence and Graham Hahn was sitting in jail right now, the girl would still be in the hospital, hooked up to God knows what machines.

Just after Derek went out the door, Detective Audrey Jackson entered through them. Detective Jackson was in her early forties, with dark skin and hair she wore in short, perky braids. She'd taken me under her wing and allowed me to assist in an unofficial capacity in a couple of her investigations. She knew I hoped to make detective one day, and she'd become a wonderful mentor for me.

She raised a brow. "Why do you look like you want to hit something?"

Apparently my Irish temper was showing itself. "Because I found out Derek lost critical evidence in one of my arrests."

"The Hahn case?"

"Yep," I growled.

"About that," she said quietly, angling her head to indicate her office down the hall. "Let's talk."

I followed her down the hall, Brigit's nails *click-click-clicking* on the tile floor as we went. Jackson held the door open for me and my partner, closing it once we were inside. I took a seat in one of the chairs facing her desk while she dropped into the rolling chair behind it.

She eyed me intently. "You think Derek really lost those drugs?"

I wasn't quite sure what she was getting at, but her question gave me an uneasy feeling. "As opposed to what?"

She lifted one shoulder and let it drop. "As opposed to keeping the drugs himself, or maybe selling them."

No beating around the bush. That was one of the many things I respected about the detective. She didn't waste anyone's time, especially her own.

I felt my eyes widen of their own accord. "You think Derek stole the drugs?"

She gave me a patient smile. "I'm asking *you* that question, Megan. You recently spent months as his partner. Aside from the chief, you probably know him better than anyone on this force."

What she was really asking was whether I thought Derek could be a crooked cop. My mind tossed the thought around, tried it on for size. Derek Mackey was a jackass, no doubt about that. He was rude to both his coworkers and suspects. He didn't use enough deodorant and was in constant need of a breath mint. He liked to bang his dick and had been rougher than necessary with some of the people he'd arrested. His reports looked like they'd been written by a second-grader. His grammar was deplorable, his vocabulary limited, and he'd never mastered the rules of punctuation. He— *Wait. Where am I going with this?* Oh, yeah. Derek was a very big, very pointy thorn in my side, not to mention an absolute asshole. But a crooked cop? I shook my head.

"No. No, I don't think he stole the drugs. I think he's a sloppy cop, not a bad one."

She dipped her head in acknowledgment. "All right, then. I know I can count on you to give me an honest opinion."

"Thank you, Detective."

She gave me another patient smile. "Just because I'm sure you're being honest doesn't mean I'm sure you're right. Opinion and fact are two different things."

I crossed my arms over my chest. "Way to burst my bubble."

"I'm only being honest, too. I know that's what you want."

She had me there.

She leaned forward, picked up the stapler from her desk, and brandished it. "Between you, me, and the stapler here," she said in a quiet voice, "this isn't the first time Mackey has lost evidence."

Uh-oh. A warning tingle began to make its way up my spine. Unfortunately, more than a few members of law enforcement had been caught pilfering drug evidence to feed their own addictions. Still, Derek and I had been partners for months. I'd gotten to know the guy well. *Too well,* really. Derek had been known to have a few too many beers now and then when out with the boys, but nothing he'd ever said or done had hinted at any sort of illegal drug use. On the other hand, people could hide their addictions well, especially when the consequences of others finding out would be great. "The other lost evidence," I said, "was it drugs, too?"

"No," she said, "it was cash. Two grand, to be exact. It was years ago, when he was new on the job. He and his training partner busted a guy for selling stolen merchandise out of his apartment. Derek claims he left the cash behind on the kitchen counter, but it wasn't there when they went back."

"Was it possible someone else had a key to the apartment? Maybe the fence's friend or girlfriend or family member went in and took the money."

"It's possible," she said, "which is why Derek was given only a stern lecture and was allowed to keep his job. Every cop makes mistakes on occasion, and there was enough stolen property seized to convict the guy three times over."

Unlike the current case, where the loss of evidence ended any chance of prosecution, the misplaced cash hadn't prevented the lawbreakers from being prosecuted. Good thing.

"His stats are down, too," Jackson said. "Over the last month, he's issued fewer citations and made the least number of arrests of any officer in W1."

"That doesn't necessarily mean he's crooked," I said. "It probably just means he's lazy."

Derek didn't like the day-to-day grunt work that came with being a cop. I knew that for a fact because, when we'd been partners, he'd made me handle all of the boring, routine stuff. Rather, he lived for the large newsmaking busts, the ones that posed the potential for both violence and heroism. He liked to go toe-to-toe with criminals, to bust heads. Issuing a speeding ticket to a soccer mom who was running late picking her kids up from practice was something he considered beneath him. I told Jackson as much. Not that any of this excused his behavior. But it did explain it.

"What you say may be true," she agreed, "but he's got to do his job, whether he thinks these things are beneath him or not. He might be Chief Garelik's golden boy, but numbers don't lie. If Mackey's stats don't improve, he's going to have to answer for them. Captain Leone's ready to go head-to-head with the chief if necessary."

"Is Derek aware of this?" I asked.

"Oh, hell, yeah," she said. "The captain called him in and they had a come-to-Jesus meeting."

With any luck, Derek would see the light and change his ways, stop leaving the routine police work to the rest of us.

"Getting back to the matter at hand," Jackson continued, "once I check my voice and e-mails, I'm off to the hospital. Gonna see what I can get out of Miranda Hernandez. She's the girl who collapsed at Panther Pavilion. Hopefully she'll tell me who she bought the Molly from so we can get a bust out of this."

"I was there when the ambulance t-took her away," I said. "I saw the EMTs speak with a tall, skinny guy with dark hair and a girl with wavy red hair. They looked pretty freaked out. The girl was crying. I'd planned to check in with them, but they left before I had a chance."

She offered a harrumph that said when people don't stick around a crime scene, there's usually a reason. "You think you could identify them?"

"I don't know," I said. "I only got a quick look and the lighting wasn't good."

"I'll see if the EMTs got their names," she said. "You best get out on the road now. This city needs you and your partner on the job."

I stood and led Brigit to the door. "Have a good day, Detective!" I called back over my shoulder.

Officer Hinojosa drifted past in the hall, good-naturedly muttering, "Suck-up."

I blew him a raspberry. *Pffft*.

NINE
GETTING OUR LICKS IN

Brigit

Brigit wasn't sure why her partner stuck out her tongue and made that odd sound. What did *pffft* mean, anyway? Humans could be so odd. If a dog stuck out its tongue, it meant business. Something was getting licked.

TEN
LET'S MAKE A DEAL

The Dealer

"A half million up front," the guy said. "Another five hundred large when you deliver."

The Dealer couldn't believe he was even considering the offer. He'd never taken this kind of money before, and there was no guarantee he could deliver everything the guy was asking for. Taking the money would go against everything he—and the piece of metal on his chest—stood for. Maybe he should just stand up and walk away, leave all of this behind him.

He took a long sip of his whiskey, savoring the burn on his tongue as he bought himself another moment to mull things over, to consider all the pros and cons . . .

"Hello?" the guy snapped impatiently. "We got a deal or not?"

He sent the guy a cold stare. "What if I don't deliver?"

The guy smirked. "You mean what if you *can't*?"

Fucker. This exchange had begun to feel more like a castration than a conversation.

The guy tossed back the bourbon in his glass. "If you can't deliver, but we can tell you've tried?" He belched a nasty chuckle. "You can keep the down payment. Consider it the equivalent of a pity fuck."

ELEVEN
PARTY POOPERS

Megan

Friday night, Seth was on duty at the firehouse and Frankie's boyfriend Zach had planned to play poker with friends. So Frankie and I did the only thing two self-respecting young women would do on a weekend when they were man-free. We rounded up as many of our single friends as we could find and headed to a bar for—

"Girls' night!" we cried in unison, clinking our glasses. Some contained wine. Some were rimmed in salt and contained a frozen margarita. Tonight, I'd opted for a blue Hawaiian. It was the closest I'd get to a beautiful beach here in north Texas.

The faces at the table ranged wildly. Across from me sat my fresh-faced coworker Summer, who had lively blond curls and a sunny disposition that matched her name perfectly. On either side of Summer sat a couple of Frankie's roller derby teammates from the Whoop Ass. Raven had jet-black hair that fell past the half-dozen piercings in her ears to her shoulders, ending in a blunt edge. Mia was a femininely fierce Asian in a dainty pink lace dress and combat boots. The gem hanging from the silver chain around her neck looked frighteningly like a human tooth. I decided it was best not to ask. But despite the differences in our appearances, we had one thing in common. We were all women who didn't back down from challenges.

The waiter arrived with a heaping platter of nachos, another heaping platter of curly fries, and another piled with fried pickles, the trifecta of gluttony, a gastrological challenge. "Here you go, ladies."

We pushed our glasses and silverware aside to make room for the feast. After plunking the food down in front of us, he gave us a smile and said, "Enjoy!"

Raven watched him go. "Nice ass on that one."

While part of me was tempted to chastise her for objectifying the guy, for treating him as nothing more than a piece of meat, one glance at his retreating form told me she hadn't been wrong. I'd save the lecture for another time.

Summer dipped a fried pickle in ketchup and held it up in front of her. "I'm pushing thirty. I wonder how much longer I'll be able to eat like this without consequences?"

She had a point. While we'd had to pass multiple physical tests in order to successfully graduate from the police academy, our jobs as beat cops required surprisingly little movement. We spent most of the day sitting on our butts in our cruisers, driving around. Given that I was paired with a K-9 who took several potty breaks a day and liked to explore a little, I got more exercise than most officers. I also watched what I ate and jogged on occasion to keep in decent shape. Still, I was no Jillian Michaels.

"Play derby," Frankie suggested to Summer. "Rollerskating burns over three hundred calories an hour."

"No kidding?" Summer said. "Maybe I should trade in my squad car for a pair of skates."

"Or a hoverboard," Mia suggested. "It wouldn't be much exercise, but it would be fun to ride."

"Yeah, and if the hoverboard catches fire," Frankie replied, fishing a curly fry from the pile, "I'll come put it out."

Our conversation meandered from there to modes of transportation that, as kids, we'd thought would be everyday by now. Jet packs. Flying cars. Solar-powered trains.

I twirled my glass between my fingers. "Speaking of the future, has anyone decided who they're going to vote for in the Senate race?"

Raven stopped with her wineglass halfway to her lips. "There's an election this year?"

"Haven't you seen the signs?" I asked. "They're everywhere. Heck, there's even one behind the bar." I pointed to the back of the bar where one of Essie Espinoza's signs leaned back against the mirror, supported on one side by a bottle of Tito's Vodka, on the other by a Shiner Bock longneck. The sign featured a silhouette of Essie looking upward, her bushy hair softening her face, along with the slogan ESPERANZA ESPINOZA—OUR HOPE FOR THE FUTURE.

Mia shrugged. "I never vote. I don't think it really matters. All of the candidates are pretty much the same."

Voter apathy. Not unusual, though a person like me

who worked for the government found it frustrating at times how little people seemed to care. At least in this particular contest it might not make that much difference. Both Senator Sutton and Essie Espinoza had good ideas and reputations. Voters really couldn't go wrong either way.

During round two of drinks, our topic ventured back to men, with everyone contributing their dating woes, including Mia's boyfriend with the mommy issues to Summer's last Internet date that ended with the guy's offer to suck her toes.

I choked on my drink. "Ew!"

Raven snorted. "That's nothing. I once had a guy offer to—"

I poked my index fingers into my ears and recited, "La-la-la!"

Though Raven's lips continued to move, I had no idea what she said, and for that I will remain eternally grateful. Whatever the guy had proposed to do to her sent everyone but me into a giggle fit.

I turned to Frankie. "I never did ask. How'd the aerial ladder training go?"

She cringed. "Honestly? Climbing to the top of a high ladder with over forty pounds of gear on wasn't easy. I felt like my air tank was going to pull me backward. But nothing like the fear of plummeting to your death to motivate a woman to hold on tight and move fast."

"Good for you," I said, raising my glass again in salute. I could relate to her ordeal. During my K-9 training, we officers had to don bite suits and experience a dog attack. I'd wet myself. Fortunately, it had been a hot day and the suit already reeked of sweat, so nobody noticed. Well, nobody other than Brigit, that is. She'd twitched her nostrils near my crotch and given me a look of disappointment.

By midnight and round three, we'd switched to non-alcoholic drinks such as soda or tea and devolved into a debate over the relative merits of shaving versus waxing, and liquid eyeliner versus pencil.

Summer stirred the remnants of melted margarita in her glass. "Liquid eyeliner takes too long to dry and I always end up smearing it."

Frankie disagreed. "But pencil wears off too easy."

Summer shrugged. "Then you reapply."

While my spare time was generally spent in much more intellectual pursuits such as reading, watching the Discovery or History channels, or checking out the exhibits at a local museum, I had to admit the inane conversation was relaxing and entertaining, even if pointless. It felt good to kick back, to forget for a few moments about Miranda Hernandez lying in a hospital bed with machines doing the jobs her organs used to do. To forget about my failure to keep drugs out of the hands of young men and women who were barely more than children. To forget about my former partner whose slipshod approach to policing had led to a drug dealer being put back out on the streets.

It also felt good to be part of a group, fully accepted for who I was. Such had not always been the case. When I'd been a young girl, my uncontrollable stutter led to stares, teasing, and pity, making me horribly self-conscious. I'd retreated away from other children and into books, discovering a love of mysteries, putting together the clues and trying to figure out whodunit before the final reveal. As a twirler for the high school band, I'd been accepted as part of the crowd, but I'd remained the quiet girl on the fringes. Same for college. I'd hung with some girls from my dorm, but I was always on the edge of the group, barely there. It wasn't until I'd had success on the force that I'd really begun to find my place in the world and to realize my stutter didn't define me. I'd become more confident, more comfortable, more *me*.

My phone jiggled with an incoming text. I'd expected it to be Seth checking in on how our girls' night out was going, but the readout indicated it was Detective Jackson. *Any chance you can meet me at station? I'd like your input.*

I texted her back immediately. *On my way.* I had no idea why she was summoning me, but my guess would be it had something to do with the girl who'd passed out at the Fourth of July event. A queasy feeling invaded me at the thought that she might have taken a turn for the worse. I looked up at the group at the table. "Duty calls. I've got to head in to work."

Frankie nodded. "One of the others can take me home."

I bade everyone good-bye and headed out to my metallic-blue Smart Car. Two guys on their way in cast looks at my bare legs. I was equally offended and flattered, a conflicted feminist. I swung by my house and picked up Brigit. Habit, I guess. It's not that I thought she'd be able to add to the conversation. But it just seemed right to have her along with me when I was performing police work.

On the drive over, I slowed as I passed a seedy apartment complex. I knew from experience that the road here had a number of deep potholes the city had yet to fill. While the holes posed no problem for my squad car, my tiny Smart Car was another story. Hit one too fast and I could end up windshield-down on the asphalt.

A black-and-white cruiser in the parking lot of the complex caught my eye. Derek sat behind the wheel, looking up at Flynn Blythe, a tall, skinny ex-con with a short gray braid at the back of his neck. Blythe was a sorry statistic, a repeat offender. He'd been in an out of prison a half-dozen times during his sixty-five years on this earth, the length of his braid in his collection of profile mug shots depicting how long it had been since his last release. While his first arrest had been for selling LSD in the early seventies, most recently Blythe had spent a decade in the prison in Huntsville for illegally possessing a firearm and for selling crack, a drug that was considered yesterday's news by the time he was released. Blythe was on parole, but didn't enjoy having what he called a "babysitter," and gave his poor parole officer a hell of a time, though always stopping just short of a violation that would land his bony butt back in the slammer. We officers checked in on Blythe on occasion, to make sure he was keeping his nose clean. Looked like it was Derek's turn tonight.

I weaved my way through the obstacle course of potholes and continued on my way. Ten minutes later, I pulled into the W1 station, parked, and the two of us went inside.

Detective Jackson's office door was cracked only an inch or two. I knocked lightly. *Rap-rap-rap.*

"Come in!" she called.

I opened the door and Brigit and I stepped inside.

She smiled down at my partner. "Hey, Sergeant."

Brigit wagged her tail in greeting.

Jackson motioned at the door. "Shut it all the way."

I pushed the door closed behind me and turned to find her looking me up and down. She'd seen me in civilian clothes before, but they'd always been fairly business-like and conservative. She'd never seen me in a denim miniskirt, wedges, and an off-the-shoulder blouse. My heavy makeup, dangly earrings, and trio of noisy bangle bracelets seemed to throw her, too.

She tilted her head. "You look . . ."

What was she going to say? That I looked like a bimbo? I only hoped she hadn't lost respect for me, that her image of me as a smart, discerning woman hadn't changed.

". . . different," she finished.

"Different?" I repeated.

She raised a shoulder. "I didn't mean anything by it. It's just that you look nothing like an off-duty cop."

I wasn't sure if that was a good thing or a bad thing. "I was out having drinks with friends."

A soft smile flickered across her lips. "Girls' night out, huh? I remember those days. Sorry I had to interrupt it."

She gestured for me to take a seat. I perched on the edge while Brigit snuffled around the room, checking things out.

The detective twiddled her pen in her fingers. "We've got three more kids in the hospital. Two are TCU students. The third was an old high school friend visiting from out of town for the weekend. All had a bad reaction to Molly when they were dancing at a nightclub near the university tonight."

"Oh, no! That's awful news."

"Tell me about it. This has got to stop. The media is riding Chief Garelik's ass, he's riding Captain Leone's, and the captain's riding mine in return. I'm going to see what information I can get from these kids tomorrow, but if they don't cough up some names we'll need to send someone in undercover at the university. Clearly there's a link there. Someone who's dealing or has a connection to a major supplier."

"Sure seems that w-way."

"You've worked with the rookies doing your K-9 demonstrations. Who would you recommend? It's got to be someone who can pass for a college kid, but who's also smart enough to pull this off. Someone who can think on their feet and improvise."

A lineup of the most recent police academy graduates popped into my head and I mentally scanned the faces in the image.

There was the blond country boy with the thick east Texas accent. He had a youthful look about him. Problem was, he lacked the confidence that would come with experience, and, for lack of a better term, came off as a bit of a hick. Many of the students who attended TCU, which was a pricey private school, came from well-heeled families in the state's larger cities. He'd stick out like a sore thumb.

A young black female recruit could fit the bill. She was smart and insightful and kept calm under pressure. Unfortunately, though, I recalled she'd mentioned her mother's ongoing battle with cancer. Going undercover limited an officer's ability to interact with the people from their real lives. She was unlikely to be interested in the gig.

My mind's eye skimmed to the end of the row. Each recruit had a reason for me to reject them. One had spilled the beans about the surprise birthday cake for the captain and obviously couldn't keep a secret. Another lacked the tact needed to make friends at the college. The final one was a nerd who'd memorized every city ordinance and the entire Texas Penal Code. He'd never fit in with the college party crowd.

"What about me?" I asked.

Truth be told, the thought of posing as a student didn't excite me much. I'd been there, done that, got the T-shirt. While I'd had some fun times at college, made some good memories, I'd moved on from that phase of life and had no interest in going back. There'd been so much drama, so much time and energy focused on getting laid, and so much puke from kids who couldn't hold their liquor. I'd held more than one girl's hair back as she'd emptied her stomach into the community toilet. I enjoyed being an adult. Still, I'd taken this job as a cop with the hope and plan of eventually making detective. I'd reach that goal sooner if I played nice, worked hard, and brought down as many bad guys as possible, even if it meant going back to school and holding more hair back out of more puke. Besides, I'd never done undercover work and would love to get some experience.

"You?" Jackson snorted. "You're kidding me, right?"

I wasn't kidding her, but was I kidding myself? *Could*

I do this? Pretend to be someone I'm not to take down a drug dealer? . . . Of course I could!

"I haven't been out of college long," I reminded her. "I know the drill. And you know there's no officer more dedicated than me." It wasn't bragging. It was the truth. My job wasn't just a paycheck to me. It was a virtual obsession.

"You are dedicated. I can't deny that." Jackson unabashedly looked me up and down. "Honestly? I wouldn't have thought you'd fit the bill at all. But seeing you like that—" She gestured to my outfit. "I don't think it's such a stretch for you to pass as a college kid." She looked at my face and squinted, still assessing me. "How old are you anyway?"

"Twenty-five."

She put her hands palms down on her desk and sat up. "Well, you're nineteen again now, Officer Luz. I'll get you a driver's license and student ID with an alias. I'll also contact the university, see if they can get you Miranda Hernandez's bed in the dorm."

My heart slithered down to my ankles. When I spoke, my voice squeaked. "Miranda died?"

"No," the detective said, "she's still hanging on. But given her tenuous condition her parents withdrew her from school for the second summer session. No sense paying all that tuition, room, and board if she can't go to class."

I exhaled in relief and my heart hopped back into place. "Could you lead with that, next time?"

"Oops." The detective cracked a mirthless smile. "It'll be a few days before the doctors can accurately assess the full extent of her organ damage. But she looked pretty bad to me."

I could only imagine how traumatic all of this must be not only for Miranda, but also for her parents. *Would her organs recover from the hyperthermia? Would she need a transplant?* Only time would tell. "Did she tell you anything?"

Jackson's smile performed a 180, becoming a frown. "Not in words. She was too sedated for conversation. But her parents gave me some information and I read between the lines. Miranda's only seventeen, an incoming freshman who decided to start in the summer session. Judging from how overbearing her parents are, I'm guessing she was eager to get away from home as soon as possible. That might be why she tried the Molly. To spread her wings a little, experiment. I get the feeling she didn't have much freedom growing up and that her parents kept her on a short leash."

Brigit's ears perked and she raised her head at the word "leash."

Jackson stroked my partner's back. "Sorry, girl. Bad word choice." She looked back up at me. "Miranda's parents have no idea where she might have obtained the drugs. They know she'd made some new friends this summer, but she didn't give them a lot of details."

"What about the two who were with Miranda on the Fourth of July? The red-haired girl and the boy?" I asked. "Did you get in touch with the EMTs? Find out if they knew the kids' names?"

"I spoke with the paramedics," she replied, "but unfortunately they were in such a rush to get Miranda to the hospital that they only had time to ask them a few quick questions about their patient. What she'd taken, whether she'd had anything to drink, any allergies they knew of. That kind of thing."

Darn.

"I've been in touch with the university's police department," the detective continued. "They told me that both of tonight's victims who attended TCU lived in the same dorm as Hernandez. It could just be coincidence, but my gut and experience tells me there's a connection. Someone in that dorm is either selling the drugs to the other residents or hooking them up with a dealer."

"What about Graham Hahn?" I asked. "Did he live in the same dorm?"

"Nope. The address on file with the college indicated he lived in an off-campus apartment. They said he's no longer a student there. He flunked out spring semester."

Why was I not surprised? "Does there seem to be any other connection between Hahn and the victims?"

"None that I can find." The detective turned her computer screen to face me. "This is one of tonight's victims."

She'd pulled up a Facebook page for a girl named Ashleigh White. Ashleigh's profile picture showed a smiling girl with straight brown hair, a bright smile, and hazel eyes. She wore a purple TCU tee and ball cap. Her right hand was raised in the horned frog sign, her index and middle fingers crooked, the other fingers and thumb folded inward. She might lack the sense to stay away from drugs, but no one could say she lacked school spirit. Her friends list appeared below.

The detective scrolled downward. "I've been down this entire list and didn't see Graham Hahn on it. He's not on the lists for the other two victims, either. Besides, all of the kids tonight are only nineteen, lowerclassmen who just completed their freshman year. Graham was twenty-one. He was in his junior year."

In other words, it was less likely they'd crossed paths than if all of them had been the same age and in the same class.

She reached over, pulled a stack of papers from her printer's output tray, and held them out to me. I took the pages from her. They were printouts of the Facebook friends from Ashleigh White's page, as well as the pages for Miranda Hernandez and a boy named Colby Tibbs. He must have been tonight's male victim.

"Look those over," she said. "Take some time tomorrow to figure out which of their friends attend the university and familiarize yourself with the names so you'll know who to cozy up to at the school."

Could I really do this? Pretend to be a college student and infiltrate the party crowd on campus to track down drug dealers? Though I'd volunteered and been so certain a moment ago, now I wasn't entirely sure. But if Jackson thought I could, I should have that same confidence in myself.

"What about Brigit?" I asked. The thought of being separated from my partner for an indefinite length of time tied my insides in knots. Who would take care of her? Would she be assigned to a new, temporary handler while I was undercover? If so, would that officer take good care of her? Buy the expensive treats she liked? Trim her toenails? Rub her belly? Let her sleep in his or her bed? Give her a kiss on the snout and call her *sweetie-poopie Briggie Boo*?

Jackson mulled the situation over for a moment. "Take her with you."

"Won't she raise suspicions?" Brigit wasn't exactly a tiny Chihuahua like Elle Woods carried in her purse to law school in *Legally Blonde*.

"Ever heard of hiding in plain sight? Being so out and open will throw people off. Besides, it seems like everyone's got a service dog of some sort or another these days."

An overstatement, sure, but it was also true that the capabilities of canines had only begun to be tapped. Not only were they useful in many aspects of law enforcement, but they could detect bed bugs, cancers, even wildlife scat to help conservationists track animals less intrusively. Dogs helped those with mobility issues turn on lights, retrieve items, and even push buttons on elevators and at crosswalks. Service dogs assisted people who suffered from cerebral palsy, muscular dystrophy, Down syndrome, and autism. Dogs were now being used in physical rehabilitation, engaging in throwing games with patients. They were also used in psychiatric treatment programs and as emotional support animals. Dogs had been trained to help the hearing impaired by notifying their humans with a nudge when their name was called, or a doorbell, alarm clock, or smoke alarm went off. Companion dogs helped wounded veterans regain their independence and deal with PTSD. Dogs were even being used in courtrooms to calm nervous witnesses, such as abused children.

"Epilepsy," I said, thinking aloud. "I could tell people I have epilepsy and that Brigit is trained to give me an alert of oncoming seizures."

"Works for me," Jackson said. "She'll be a help. She'll be able to sniff out any drugs that might be in the dorm."

I realized then that, even if any TCU students had seen me and Brigit at Panther Pavilion or had seen our pictures in news reports regarding our recent arrests of a notorious peeping Tom and a violent escaped convict, they'd likely have trouble identifying us. I'd had my hair pulled back into the usual tight bun in the photos and when I'd been on duty. Plus, I'd been wearing little makeup and had sunglasses on for most of the day on the Fourth. And as much as I thought Brigit was a one-in-a-million dog, the truth of the matter was that she looked pretty much like every other shepherd out there. Her capabilities, not her appearance, was what distinguished her from other dogs.

Jackson stifled a yawn. "I want to move on this ASAP. The second summer session starts Monday so the timing is good. Spend tomorrow packing up and getting your things in order. Swing by here first thing Monday morning to get your new identity."

I couldn't wait to see who I would become.

"Any chance that missing evidence has shown up?" I asked.

"The drugs?" she asked.

I nodded.

"No. Why?"

Why? Because seeing Derek at Flynn Blythe's apartment had made my insides feel prickly. Had Derek simply been checking in on Blythe, or could he have been selling Blythe the drugs we'd taken from Graham Hahn? Would Derek not only risk his job and his standing as the chief's golden boy, but also disgrace the badge by stealing and selling drug evidence? While I didn't quite believe it, didn't quite *want* to believe it, I knew I had to share the information about Derek's visit to Blythe's place with Detective Jackson.

"I saw Officer Mackey on my drive over," I told her. "He was talking to Flynn Blythe in the parking lot of his apartment."

"You see anything change hands?"

"No." That was a good sign, wasn't it? I said a silent prayer that Derck was innocent. I mean, I hated thc guy and all, but despite his shortcomings he was an asset to the force. When an officer was needed to go into a dangerous situation, Derek was the first to raise his hand. Besides, any scandal would make the entire FWPD look bad and reflect on all of us officers. With the media blitz regarding officer-involved shootings of unarmed civilians, police had taken enough hits lately. We didn't need any more.

Detective Jackson was quiet a moment. "This information about Mackey, his visit to Flynn Blythe. Keep that between you and me, all right?"

I swallowed to force down the lump in my throat. "Yes, ma'am."

Seth had the day off on Saturday, and we spent it together, preparing me and Brigit for our upcoming role as a college coed and her service dog.

As we ate a quick and easy brunch of toast and jelly at my kitchen table, I looked up service dog vests online, turning my laptop to face Brigit when I had a screen of options pulled up. "Which color do you like, Brig?"

Seth washed his bite down with a swig of coffee. "Dogs are color-blind. It's not going to matter to her."

He had a point. And it's not like she could tell me her preference anyway. Still, asking had seemed like the polite thing to do. Sometimes I almost forgot that my partner wasn't human.

"What do you think, then?" I asked Seth, turning the screen his way now.

His gaze slid across the screen. "The pink one," he said. "She'll look less tough in it."

"Good point." I entered an order for an extra-large vest, adding a new nylon chew bone and three canisters of her favorite treats to the cyber shopping cart. I paid extra, exorbitant fees for overnight shipping and Sunday delivery, but they couldn't be avoided. Besides, the department would reimburse me, at least for the vest.

We finished our meal, left the dogs lounging on the living room sofa, and headed out for more shopping. We aimed for the local Walmart, where I purchased a couple of purple and white T-shirts with the TCU logo and horned frog mascot. Given that I'd long since gotten rid of the worn-out bedspread and sheets that had graced my dormitory bed back in my real college days, I headed for the bedding department next. I looked over the options in twin size, and selected one in a lime-green, lemon-yellow, and hot-pink striped print, adding a trio of cute decorative pillows to the mix. A desk lamp with pink beading on the shade seemed like the perfect complement, so I put that in the cart, too. In the office supply aisle, I grabbed a couple of spiral notebooks and a package of gel pens with ink in various colors.

As we rolled past the women's lingerie department,

Seth reached out, grabbed a package of plain white briefs that went clear up to the waist, and tossed them into the buggy.

I stopped and looked down into the cart. "What are those hideous things for?"

He scowled. "I don't want those college boys getting any ideas."

"They're not going to be seeing my underwear."

"They might sneak a peek at your laundry, maybe try to catch a glimpse of you getting dressed while your roommate's heading in or out the door."

I doubted any boy would go to so much trouble given that there was no end of pretty women strutting around nude all over the Internet. Besides, while I could hold my own, I wasn't exactly a sexy bombshell like Sofía Vergara.

"While we're at it," he added, "let's get a teddy bear for your bed. Nothing turns a guy off like a stuffed animal staring at him while he's trying to make a move." He lifted his head and glanced around for the toy department.

"I'm not planning to invite any boys back to my room." I rolled my eyes. "Besides, there's an attractive girl everywhere you look on the TCU campus. Nobody's g-going to be making moves on me."

He looked down at me, a brow raised. "Wanna bet? I remember what it was like to be in my early twenties. If I'd seen a girl like you back then, with your long black hair and those big brown eyes and nice legs, I'd have made a fool of myself trying to get your attention."

So help me, I warmed at the flattery. "All right. If it will make you happy."

I humored him by keeping the granny panties and letting him buy me the biggest stuffed teddy bear the store offered. I also bought glittery nail polish and a slew of makeup in shades far more vibrant than my usual choices, as well as some gaudy, colorful jewelry and a movie poster featuring Chris Hemsworth as Thor, his eyes narrowed in an intent look that could be interpreted as either rage or seduction. I chose to assume the latter, as well as the fact that the look was intended solely for me.

As we carried the purchases out to my car, Seth inquired about my major. "What are you going to study?"

"I'm not sure." Detective Jackson had left that decision up to me, and I hadn't made up my mind yet. Part of me thought I should take classes in criminal justice. That had been my major at Sam Houston State and I could easily ace the courses without having to study. But another part of me saw this undercover gig as an opportunity to expand my knowledge base, to try something new and different.

"Take physics," Seth said, putting the last of the bags in his trunk and slamming it shut. "All the guys in your classes will be nerds."

"Hey." I crossed my arms over my chest in indignation. "Smart is the new sexy."

A grin played about his lips as he reached out to play with a tendril of my hair. "Tell me about it."

TWELVE

GOOD THINGS COME IN SMALL PACKAGES

Brigit

BARK-BARK-BARK-BARK-BARK!

Brigit might not be on official police duty now, but at home she was never off watchdog duty. Her superior ears had heard the rumble of the delivery truck coming up the street and the soft squeal of the brakes as it stopped in front of their house. Megan was in the kitchen putting dishes away and Frankie was in her bathroom taking a shower. It was up to Brigit to let the unsuspecting humans know that a uniformed man in a truck had invaded their turf and was heading across the yard with a box to deliver and possibly other, as yet unidentified, nefarious intentions.

She ran to the front door, where she could smell the man on the other side of it and hear the sound as he dropped the package on the welcome mat. *Plop.* She scratched at the inside of the door and spoke again, this time as a warning to the man that if he tried any funny business she'd put a stop to it right away. *BARK-BARK-BARK!*

Megan walked out of the kitchen. "Cool it, loud-mouth."

Brigit didn't know exactly what the words meant, but surely they had to be an expression of gratitude for her faithful service. She wagged her tail.

"Stay," Megan said, ruffling her ears as she opened the door to get the package.

Brigit hoped it might be a pair of new shoes she could gnaw on. For some reason, Megan had been storing her shoes on the top shelf of her closet where Brigit couldn't reach them. *Grr.* She wasn't sure why Megan was being so stingy with them. After all, she had several pairs.

But what was in the box was even better than new shoes. It was a new bone! Just for Brigit! And three cans of her favorite treats!

Yippee!

She spun in a circle, yapping and wagging her tail to express her doggie delight. She also changed her mind about the delivery guy. He wasn't a threat. He was welcome to invade their turf with treats and toys anytime.

Megan fed her a couple of the treats—*yum!*—and gave her the new bone to chew on. As Brigit lay on the rug testing her teeth on the bone, Megan tried a new fabric harness on her. She lifted Brigit's right front paw, then her left, as she slid the device onto Brigit, lifting her center to snap the clasp closed and running a finger around the edges to test its fit.

"Looking good, pretty girl," Megan said, giving her neck a two-handed scratch.

Brigit wasn't sure what "pretty" meant, but she knew

"girl" was another name for her. Megan had all sorts of nicknames for Brigit. *Brig. Briggie Boo.* She sometimes even called Brigit *Baby.* But today she seemed to be trying on a new name for size. *Britney.*

Britney was close enough to her usual name that the dog had responded when Megan first said it this morning. Given that Megan had rewarded her with a "good girl" and a belly rub, she'd continued to respond to the name all day, earning more "good girls" and more belly rubs.

Seth and Blast came over and they all ate dinner together, then Megan and Seth did that thing where they put their mouths and bodies against each other and wrapped their arms around the other, an activity Brigit had come to realize meant affection among humans. Blast gave Brigit a canine sign of affection and subordination by licking at her mouth as they left. Blast wasn't the toughest dog around, a total beta, but Brigit liked him anyway. She was alpha enough for both of them.

As Brigit and Megan settled into their bed Sunday night, the dog could sense that her partner was both excited and nervous. She liked the excited part. When Megan was excited it often meant that they were in for some fun, maybe a search or a track or a chase. Brigit loved to search buildings, loved to track. And chases? Those were the most fun of all. But the nervous? She didn't like that. When Megan was nervous it often meant that there'd be a loud sound that would hurt Brigit's ears or a mean person who might try to hit them. Brigit didn't like being hit. Her first owner had hit her a lot, most often with an open hand, but he'd kicked her on occasion, too. He'd been an asshole. Megan had never hit her. Megan only petted and stroked and scratched her. And for that, Brigit would do her best to keep Megan safe.

At the moment, there were no suspicious smells or sounds coming from outside their house. Nothing for her to worry about. She stretched her legs, draped her head over Megan's thigh, and closed her eyes.

THIRTEEN
BANKING ON IT

The Dealer

First thing Monday morning he logged in online, typing the bank account number and hitting the enter key.

There it was. A deposit in the amount of half a million dollars. It had hit his account just this morning.

He was relieved. He was even a little thrilled.

But, most of all, he was terrified.

FOURTEEN
BACK TO SCHOOL

Megan

Early Monday morning, I put extra curl in my hair and loaded on the makeup, using liquid liner to add wings to my eyes. I dressed in a purple Horned Frogs T-shirt, white shorts, a pair of sandals, and an excess of jewelry. I'd dug out my backpack from my college days and filled it with spirals, ballpoint pens, and my personal laptop. I'd also filled two suitcases with casual gear, jewelry, and makeup, as well as some towels and bedding. A beach bag contained Brigit's food, treats, bowls, and toys.

I stepped into the living room with my bags, set them down, and twirled in front of my roommate. "How do I look?"

Frankie frowned. "Like the reason I decided not to go to college."

Being big and athletic and boyish, Frankie had never fit the mold of the popular girlie girl in high school. Though too afraid of her to make fun of her to her face, the mean girls had talked smack behind her back in the way girls do at that age in an attempt to make themselves feel better about themselves. Ironically, the talk only made each girl wonder what was being said about her when she wasn't around. Were her hips too wide? Her nose too big? Her clothes too yesterday?

"I just hope Brigit and I can pull this off," I said.

"You've taken down a bomber and a murderer. A drug dealer will be nothing."

"Thanks for the vote of confidence."

Frankie picked up her cat and put Zoe's face next to hers, moving the feline's paw as if the cat were a puppet. "Zoe and I will miss you two, though. Won't we, Zoe?"

Zoe replied with a *mew*. I wasn't sure whether that was a yes or a no, but I chose to believe it was a yes. More likely it was *a put me down or I'll scratch your eyes out*.

"We'll miss you, too."

"On the bright side," Frankie said, returning Zoe to her spot on the back of the couch, "with you gone I'll have the place all to myself and I won't have to eat any quinoa or kale or organic food."

I took the jibe about my cooking in stride. "If you change your mind, there's plenty in the pantry and fridge."

"And that's where it will stay."

I rounded up Brigit, and Frankie helped me load our things into her Juke. Frankie dropped me and Brigit by the W1 station on her way to the fire academy.

After wrangling my things out of the cargo bay, I gave her a hug. "Thanks for the ride."

"Be careful," she said, her eyes now clouded with concern despite the assurance she'd given me earlier.

"I will." Or at least I'd be as careful as I could be under the circumstances. Going undercover meant I couldn't wear my Kevlar vest or keep my gun and baton in easy reach at my hip. I'd be relying on my wits more than my weapons.

As she drove off, I headed inside with my partner in tow and aimed straight for Detective Jackson's office, tapping my knuckles on the door frame. *Rap-rap.*

She waved me in, then reversed direction once I'd stepped inside, indicating for me to close the door behind me. "Good morning, Officer Luz." She picked up a manila envelope from her desk and held it out to me. "Or should I say Morgan Lewis?"

"Morgan Lewis," I repeated, trying the name on for size. I took the envelope from her and sat down to peruse the contents. The first thing I discovered was a new cell phone and charger. I turned the phone on to discover some contacts had already been entered. "Aunt Jackie?"

"That's me," Detective Jackson said. "Detective Bustamente is listed as Uncle Buster."

Hector Bustamente was another seasoned investigator in W1 who often let me help on his cases. It was nice to know the two of them were only a call away in case things went south.

Also inside the envelope was a Texas driver's license with the same photo that appeared on my real license. The name on the license read Morgan Elizabeth Lewis. The address was on a county road in Perryton, Texas. Having never heard of the place, I looked up at her. "Where's Perryton?"

"Panhandle," she replied. "Just a few miles south of the Oklahoma border. It's a town of around nine thousand people. We gave you an address out in the country. It's unlikely you'll run into anyone on campus from Perryton, but if you do, the fact that you lived in the sticks would explain why your face wouldn't be familiar to them."

I nodded and perused the background information sheet provided. Per the page, my father worked in the local oil industry as some type of executive. My mother, a homemaker, had homeschooled me. That would explain why my photograph wouldn't appear in any high school yearbook. I'd allegedly attended a community college in Amarillo, the largest city in the panhandle, before applying for a transfer to TCU. Morgan Lewis was an only child. Oddly, I felt sorry for my fictional self. While my real self had often been irritated by my four siblings, who often borrowed my things without asking and left their wet towels on the bathroom floor, I knew life would've been dull without them. Growing up so isolated must have been very lonely for my fictional alter ego.

"Try to avoid talking about yourself too much," Jackson said. "That'll make it less likely you'll have to make something up and be caught contradicting yourself."

I nodded. No worries there. Given my childhood stutter, I'd learned not to say much about anything. Besides, in my experience, most people were much more interested in talking about themselves than learning any deep and meaningful information about anyone else. College kids, who were at the peak of their self-interested phase of life, would only want the basics. *What's your name? What's your major? We look the same size. Can I borrow that cute top?*

"Only the campus police and the top-level administrators will know you're a cop," Jackson continued. "To the professors and other staff, you'll be just another student. Keep that in mind. The registrar's office is expecting you this morning. They'll get you a student ID and direct you to the housing department to get your dorm assignment."

"Registrar's office. G-got it." I continued to dig around in the envelope and pulled a set of keys from the bottom. The fob attached to them told me they were car keys. "What am I driving?"

"Twenty fifteen red Jeep Renegade. It's in the lot out front."

"Nice ride." It would fit right in at TCU, where the majority of the student body came from wealthy families and could afford nice cars.

"Be sure to bring it back it one piece."

"I'll do my best." I slid the keys into the pocket of my shorts. "Did you find out anything yesterday?"

"Little bit. I spoke with Colby Tibbs and the friend from out of town. Her name's Shae. Both said that Ashleigh White had gotten the Molly from someone else—they're not sure who or how—and they'd each paid Ashleigh for a single pill. They said she's not regularly a dealer, though, that she'd bought the drug for them, and I'm inclined to believe them." The detective leaned forward in her chair, intertwining her fingers on her desktop. "Ashleigh's family has lawyered up and her attorney says that, barring an immunity deal, she's pleading the Fifth. I'm going to check with the prosecutor and see if we can't work something out. But in the meantime we've got to keep moving on this."

Our business concluded, I stood. "I'll be in touch once I learn something."

She looked up at me, her gaze pointed. "I hope you're a fast learner, because lives are in your hands, Officer Luz."

The lifeless eyes of Miranda Hernandez flashed in my mind, and I swallowed hard to force down the strain now choking me. "I'll do my best, Detective."

"Say cheese!" called the female student working the camera in the registrar's office.

I smiled at the camera, opening my eyes wide, hoping to make myself look more youthful on my student ID. There was a *click* as the camera snapped my pic.

A moment later, the card printed out and the student handed it to me, still warm. "Here you go."

I looked down at my photo. Not bad. My class schedule, on the other hand, was horrible. One of my classes was at eight o'clock every morning. *Ugh.* I'd decided to major in political science, with the alleged intention of going on to law school one day. After all, as a law enforcement officer, I knew a lot about criminal law already and had taken a number of government classes in my undergraduate studies in criminal justice at Sam Houston State University in Huntsville. I figured studying political science would be relatively easy for me, and give me the most free time to do my real work—*tracking down a drug dealer*—while still providing some new intellectual fodder for me to ponder.

The girl glanced around to make sure her supervisors weren't looking, and whispered, "Let's make an ID for your dog, too. You said her name was Britney, right?"

I gave her a grin and nodded. "Sit, Brit," I instructed my partner.

The girl aimed the camera down at Brigit and snapped another pic. The printer whirred again and spat out another card. The girl handed it to me, smiling conspiratorially. The student ID featured the name Britney Lewis alongside Brigit's photo. If Brigit's performance during K-9 training was any indication, she'd make the dean's list here.

The girl reached over to a stack of parking decals and handed a numbered decal to me. "Put this on your back windshield. Make sure you only park in the designated student areas or you'll get towed. The university cops are Nazis when it comes to parking." She rolled her eyes.

"I appreciate the warning." Though I did not appreciate the dig at law enforcement. Cops and lawyers had a lot in common. Nobody liked them until they needed them.

"One last thing." The girl reached under the counter for a copy of the extensive student handbook. "Some light reading."

I took the handbook from her. "C'mon, girl." I gave Brigit the signal to follow me and raised a hand in goodbye to the girl behind the counter. "Thanks!"

We ventured on to the housing department, where a gray-haired woman programmed my ID to give me access to my new dorm room. She returned the ID to me and gestured to the handbook tucked under my arm. "You'll find the residence hall rules in the handbook. It's the usual commonsense stuff. No smoking. No space heaters. Quiet hours from ten P.M. to ten A.M. Administration can search your room at any time if they have reason to believe there's a safety risk or criminal activity taking place, so no funny business, young lady."

She gave me a stern look, preemptively reprimanding me for an offense I had no intention of committing. Looked like I was pulling off this college kid act pretty well.

"Thank you," I told the woman. "I'll behave."

With that, Brigit and I moved our new Jeep from the visitor parking area to the student parking lot and headed over to our dorm, getting lots of looks and smiles from our fellow students as we made our way across the campus. Brigit's pink-painted toenails and the big bow I'd added to the new pink harness took the edge off her, making her appear more friendly than ferocious. Looked like Detective Jackson was right about the whole hiding-in-plain-sight thing. Some of the students even stopped and asked if they could pet Brigit. To her delight, I let them. She could be ferocious when she needed to be, but she was well socialized and friendly, too.

As we walked, I considered how I would approach my investigation. Often, the key to figuring out *who* had committed a crime was figuring out *why* a person would do it. With drug dealing, the *why* seemed fairly obvious.

Money.

Lots of it.

Quick.

In this case, the motive might also reveal the person behind the dealing. Any student spending a lot of unexplained cash would be a potential dealer. Conspicuous consumption could provide a clue. Unfortunately, given that TCU was a private university with tuition costing four times the rate at the state schools, students by and large came from wealthy families. It might be difficult to tell how much of the money being spent was daddy's money, and how much the student had earned via dealing Molly. Another problem was, who didn't like money? And lots of it? Quick? Heck, wasn't that the reason people bought lottery tickets? I'd certainly have my work cut out for me on this case.

I rolled my suitcases into the dorm, located the elevators, and wound my way down the hall until I found our room on the second floor. I ran my new ID through the skimmer and the door unlocked with a *click*.

We stepped into the room. Nobody was inside. Looked like my roommate was out at a class, or maybe studying at the library. Her bed, which bore a faded Hello Kitty bedspread—*ironically, I hoped*—was made, and her desk and dresser were neat. Several textbooks sat on her bookshelf, including one entitled *Exploring Chemical Analysis* and another called *Microbiology with Diseases by Body System*. Ew. The books, along with her poster of Bill Nye in cartoon form above the words SCIENCE RULES, pegged her as a premed major. Yep, the bedspread had to be ironic.

While Brigit sniffed her way around the room, sticking her nose under and between pieces of furniture, I unpacked my clothing, hanging some in the small closet on my side of the room and stashing the rest in the dresser. I made my bed with the twin sheets I'd bought yesterday, topping it with the girlie striped comforter, the pillows, and the oversized teddy bear Seth had bought me. Brigit jumped onto the bed and settled down to watch while I continued to make the place our own. I tacked my Thor poster to the wall over my bed where Chris Hemsworth could keep watch over me as I dreamed.

Moving on into the bathroom that connected our room to the one next door, I hung a hand towel on the rack by the sink and stashed my shower caddy, which contained my shampoo, conditioner, shower gel, and a razor, underneath it. My toothbrush and toothpaste joined three other such sets on the shelf mounted beside the sink.

The sound of the door opening in the bedroom met my ears, followed by a high-pitched shriek, and a *BAM* as the door was slammed shut. "What the hell?" a girl's voice cried from outside the door.

"Sorry!" I called, rushing to the door.

Brigit hopped down from the bed to join me. I opened the door to find a girl with honey-colored hair pulled back into a ponytail. The wide blue eyes and gaping mouth told me that opening the door to find a big, furry beast inside had freaked her out. Who could blame her?

I stuck out my hand. "Hi, I'm Morgan." I angled my head to indicate Brigit, who stood beside me, wagging her tail. "This is my service dog, Britney."

The girl ignored my hand and gave her head a good shake, as if forcing the information into place in her mind. "You're my new roommate?"

"Yep. I just transferred in. Britney is a seizure warning dog. I have epilepsy." *Shh!* I admonished myself, remembering Detective Jackson's warning. *Only offer information when it's asked for!* My nervousness had me flapping my gums.

The girl shook her head again, though this time it was in disbelief. "First I get a druggie, and now a dog. I'm cursed when it comes to roommates."

She shoved past me into the room.

I looked down at Brigit, who looked back up at me, her brow furrowed as if asking *Why didn't that girl pet me?*

Because she's a bitch, I replied in my mind.

The girl plunked down at her desk. "Make sure you clean up her fur. She better not pee on the rug or lay on my bed or I'll file a complaint. And I don't want her sniffing around my stuff, either."

Too late for that. Of course I didn't tell the girl that.

I closed the door. "So," I snapped back. "I guess we won't be braiding each other's hair, then?" She ignored me, instead stuffing ear buds into her ears.

"C'mon, Brit," I said, rousing my dog. "Let's go buy our books."

On my way down the hall, I kept an eye out for faces from the Facebook printout. A redhead named Ruby Rathswohl had appeared on both Miranda Hernandez's and Ashleigh White's friends lists. While Ruby had regularly posted on Miranda's page, which told me the two were likely close friends, she'd made only one comment on Ashleigh's page and it had been several weeks ago. I'd squinted at her picture, willing the girl in the static image to open her mouth and tell me if she was the one I'd seen with Miranda at Panther Pavilion. I was fairly certain she was. With any luck, maybe I'd spot her on campus.

A natural introvert, I forced myself to be friendly and

outgoing, summoning my former baton twirler persona and acknowledging those we passed with smiles and greetings. "Hey!" "How's it going?" "Great earrings!" *Ugh. Being sparkly is exhausting.*

Brigit eyed me suspiciously. She knew me well, and this was *not* me. I mean, I could be fun and light, but I generally had to get to know people first before opening up. That was something Seth and I had in common, though he was a much harder nut to crack than I.

We made our way out of the dorm and across the campus. With Brigit wanting to stop and explore every bush and greenbelt and post, it took forever to reach University Drive. But it gave me time to read the posted flyers. A bagel place nearby was running a two-for-one special after eight on weeknights. The A Cappella Society was recruiting singers for an upcoming performance featuring the hits of the Beach Boys. Wednesday night, senatorial candidate Essie Espinoza would be having a rally on campus. No way would I miss that, especially now that I was purportedly a political science major.

We reached the intersection, waited for the light to change, and crossed along with a crowd of students, making our way to the strip center across the street that housed the bookstore, a pub, and an assortment of eateries offering cheap food options.

We sauntered up and down the aisles of the bookstore, looking for the required textbooks for my Political Psychology and Campaigns and Elections classes. Finally, we were at the counter buying a couple of books that seemed to weigh twenty pounds apiece and were

priced higher per ounce than gold or cocaine. Having
no credit card in the name of my alias, I paid in cash.

"Here's your change," the clerk said, counting it back
to me. "Have a good day."

"You, too." My backpack felt like an anvil on my
back as we left the store. Out on the sidewalk, I looked
down at my partner. "Hungry, Brit?"

A guy walking by snorted in laughter. I'd become so
used to talking to Brigit as if she were human I didn't
think twice about it anymore.

We headed back to the dorm, aiming for the cafeteria. Fortunately, the dining hall offered several options,
from more traditional meals with vegetable sides to
casual offerings like pizza and burgers and sandwiches.
I took a spot in the sandwich line.

The guy in line ahead of me turned around. He was
attractive in a cute, boyish type of way. He had light blue
eyes, pale skin, and soft, curly black hair cut short, like
a poodle who'd just come home from the groomers.
The fine hairs on his upper lip and chin area said he
was trying his damnedest to grow a beard, yet wasn't
man enough to pull it off just yet. When he spotted fur
in his peripheral vision, his gaze went from me down
to Brigit. "A dog!" He tilted his head to read the words
SERVICE DOG imprinted on the side of her vest. "Is it okay
to pet her?"

"Sure. She'd like that," I said. "But thanks for asking
first."

He bent down and gave Brigit a good two-handed
rubdown before standing again. "I've got a Boston ter-
rier back at home. We call him Paulie, after Paul Re-
vere." He pulled his phone out of his back pocket and

showed me his wallpaper, which featured a photo of the dog. "I miss 'im so much."

"Anytime you need a fix," I said, "you can find her in room two twelve."

A grin played about his mouth. "I'll keep that in mind."

Sheesh. I'd inadvertently come on to the guy, hadn't I?

He cocked his head as he eyed her. "She kind of looks like a police dog."

Uh-oh. Was he feeling me out figuratively after having just felt Brigit out literally? I wasn't sure. But suspicious or not, he needed to be convinced she was not a K-9 officer. "All shepherds look that way, I guess," I said with a shrug. "But Britney is much too sweet to ever be a police dog." I cupped her chin in my hands. "Aren't you, girl?"

Brigit wagged her tail as if to confirm my statement. *Yep, I'm a sweetie, all right.*

When the line moved forward, the guy in front of me placed his order. The male clerk assembled the sandwich with quick precision, plunked it down on a plate, and handed it over the counter.

"See ya," the guy said to me before walking away.

The clerk turned to me. "What can I get ya?"

I moved up to the counter. "I'll have the veggie s-sandwich," I told him. "My dog'll have one with pastrami only."

"Dog?" The clerk leaned forward to peer over the counter. Seeing Brigit standing next to me, drooling and smacking her lips, he added a heaping pile of sliced meat to her sandwich roll. "Here you go," he said, sliding the tray onto the counter.

"Thanks." If only my roommate could be so nice.

I took the tray and glanced around the room, mentally sorting through the Facebook friend pics in my mind, trying to identify anyone who might have been among them. Finally, I spotted a platinum blonde who looked vaguely familiar. I made a beeline for her table, where she sat with another blonde, though the other girl's hair was more corn silk colored.

I stopped next to their table and threw myself on their mercy. "Hi," I said, feeling awkward. "I'm brand-new here and I don't know anybody. Would it be okay if I join you?"

The two exchanged skeptical glances until corn silk spotted Brigit and her face brightened. "Sure!"

I'd been worried that bringing my partner along on this investigation might hamper me, but instead I realized she could open doors. The other students might seem ambivalent about me, but everyone seemed to want to meet Brigit. I suppose I shouldn't be surprised. We'd recently arrested a substitute teacher after a chase that ended in the high school's cafeteria during lunch. After taking the guy down in front of the students, Brigit had become so popular she'd been nominated for prom queen.

I slid into a seat at the table. "I'm Morgan, by the way," I said, introducing myself to the girls.

"April," said corn silk.

"Jasmine," said the platinum blonde.

April hiked a thumb at Brigit. "Is that one of those emotional therapy dogs?"

Way to get personal, huh? "No," I told the girl. "I

have epilepsy. She's trained to tell when I'm about to have a seizure."

"Really?" she replied. "Wow, that's amazing!"

"Yeah." I stroked Brigit's head. "She can tell before I can that one is coming on. That way I can make sure I won't fall and hurt myself."

"What's her name?" Jasmine asked.

"Britney." Brigit looked up at me when I said the name. *Good dog.* She was a natural at this undercover business.

Jasmine whipped out her cell phone. "My family has a poodle." She held up her phone. On the screen was an apricot poodle sitting in a kitchen sink, looked dejected, a pile of bubbles on the poor thing's head. "Her name is Mango."

"She's adorable."

Not to be outdone, April pulled out her phone and showed me a photo of two tuxedo cats. "That's Leonardo," she said, pointing at one of them, "and the other one is Clooney."

No need to ask her where the names had been derived.

Knowing that nothing wins a pet owner over more than showing interest in their dog or cat, I gushed, "They're so cute!"

She looked back at her phone and smiled. "They are, aren't they?"

As we ate our lunch, the conversation turned to standard getting-to-know-you topics. I kept my answers short and simple, always turning the conversation back to the two of them. Halfway through my sandwich—

Brigit had already wolfed hers down—I managed to lead the discussion in the direction of Miranda Hernandez.

I took a sip of my drink. "My roommate said that the girl who used to live with her had some type of drug problem and that her parents forced her to withdraw. I think she said the girl's name was Miranda something? Hernandez, maybe?" Of course my roommate had said nothing of the sort. Heck, she'd hardly said two words to me, and the words had been snide and insulting. But these girls didn't need to know that my information had actually come from the Fort Worth Police Department files.

April said, "I heard she committed suicide."

I faked a gasp. "Really? That's awful."

Jasmine dipped a French fry in ketchup. "That's what I heard, too. She overdosed on heroin, I think."

Blurgh. I'd hoped these girls might be able to give me some information, but so far all they had was *mis*information. I suppose I shouldn't have been surprised. That's how the rumor mill worked, after all. Things got misinterpreted or blown out of proportion or misstated as it moved along. Still, maybe there was a chance I could steer them back on track.

I toyed with my straw. "I thought it had something to do with Molly."

Jasmine tossed the fry into her mouth. "Molly who?"

Clearly, I was barking up the wrong tree here.

Jasmine's phone chimed and she tapped the screen to turn off the alarm. "That's my reminder to get my ass to class." She stood. "See y'all later."

As Jasmine left the table, April finished the last of

her burger and stood, too. "Nice meeting you, Morgan. See you around."

"Bye." Alone with Brigit now, I polished off my sandwich, tossed my trash in the garbage can, and the two of us went in search of Scharbauer Hall.

FIFTEEN
CANINE COED

Brigit

Brigit's day was going great!

First Megan gave her a new comfy bed to sleep on, then she took her on long walks back and forth across the campus and let her sniff everything in sight, then she fed her a sandwich loaded with dead animal. And she'd been petted, stroked, scratched, and rubbed by packs and packs of people.

Brigit loved college!

Now they were in a room with a lot of seats facing the same direction, and most of those seats were filled with people in their sexual prime. The hormone levels nearly overpowered the poor dog's nose.

A woman standing at the front of the room continued to speak. She'd been talking for quite a while now, but had said none of the words Brigit liked. She hadn't said "walk" even once, let alone "treat" or "play." It was all *blah-blah-blah*. She was like a high-strung Chihuahua, *yip-yip-yipping* but saying nothing of importance.

Might as well take a nap. Brigit lowered her head to her paws and closed her eyes. *Yep, college is awesome.*

SIXTEEN
NEGOTIATIONS

The Dealer

"We buy a lot of your products," the Dealer said, his grip tight on his phone as if he could force the man on the other end to comply with his demands. "It's time for you to buy some of ours."

The man had the nerve to laugh. *Bastard*.

"Show me something you make better and cheaper than ourselves," the man replied in imperfect English, "maybe then we buy from you."

SEVENTEEN
SNIFFING FOR SUSPECTS

Megan

Back at the dorm that afternoon, I heard the sink running in the bathroom. Given that my roommate remained seated at her desk studying with her earbuds firmly in her ears, totally ignoring me, it had to be one of my suite-mates.

I walked to the door that led to the sink area and stepped inside, closing the door behind me.

The girl's dark hair was cut in a short, choppy style that looked ridiculously cute on her. She was petite, with delicate features and long eyelashes. Her gaze met mine in the mirror. "Hey, there," she said. "You the new suite-mate?"

"That's me," I said. "My name's Morgan."

She turned to dry her hands on a towel. "I'm Paige McQuaid."

"It's great to meet you. I just moved to Fort Worth and I don't know many people here yet."

Her lips curved in a self-assured smile. "Well, you've met the right person. I know *everybody* around here."

I returned the smile. "Good to know." Already, I could peg Paige as the queen bee type, an alpha female, the kind of confident, powerful girl who could be your best friend or your worst enemy, or sometimes even both at the same time.

My roommate's voice cried out from our room. "Don't leave me alone with this dog!"

I rolled my eyes.

Paige tilted her head. "You've got a dog in there?"

"Yeah." I waved a hand. "Want to meet her?"

"Definitely!"

Paige followed me into my room and I motioned for Brigit to come over. She hopped down from the bed and stretched on the rug.

"Her name's Britney," I said.

Paige dropped to her knees and put her hands on either side of Brigit's neck. "Hello, Britney! You look like a sweetie pie."

A dog lover? Paige and I were going to get along just fine. One look at the bliss on Brigit's face as Paige scratched and petted her and it was clear my partner felt the same way.

Paige looked up at me. "How'd you get permission to have a dog?"

"I have epilepsy," I said, the lie rolling off my tongue more easily with each iteration. "She gives me a warning when I'm about to have a seizure."

"She can tell that?"

I nodded. "Apparently I give off signals that even I don't notice. But she can."

"Cool." She released Brigit and stood. "My roommate and I were about to go to dinner. Wanna come with?"

"That would be great." I motioned to the back of my roommate, who had yet to turn around. She had yet to tell me her name, too. "Should we invite her?" I whispered.

Paige's face contorted in a grimace. She stuck out her tongue and shook her head.

I formed an "okay" sign with my thumb and index finger. *Message received.* I grabbed my ID card and Brigit's leash and we headed back through the bathroom to Paige's room on the other side.

Lounging on one of the twin beds was a girl with mocha skin and bronze hair cut in a sleek, angular style. Paige pointed to her roommate and me in turn. "Morgan, Alexa. Alexa, Morgan." She then pointed down to Brigit. "That's Britney."

Alexa sat bolt upright, a broad smile jumping to her lips. "A dog?" She tossed her history book aside, rolled off the bed, and came over. "It's okay if I pet her, right?"

"She'd love it."

She reached out a hand to let Brigit sniff her and, when Brigit looked up at her in approval, ran her hand over the dog's head and neck. "She's so soft and shiny!"

"It's her shampoo," I said. Of course I left out the additional fact that I, too, used the peach-scented flea shampoo on my own hair to keep it just as soft and shiny. In fact, I'd scrounged one of Frankie's empty shampoo bottles out of the recycle bin and filled it with the flea shampoo to bring here. Couldn't have these girls figuring out my secret. It would be too embarrassing.

Paige stepped to the door. "Morgan's going down to dinner with us. C'mon, Alexa."

Something flickered across Alexa's face, something

that told me she didn't much appreciate her roommate speaking to her in the same way I spoke to my dog. That could be the problem with queen bee types. They were great leaders, but they tended to talk down to their subjects. A split second later, though, the smile was back on Alexa's face and we were out the door.

I ordered Brigit to stay at a table we chose near the window, grabbed an unsweetened tea, and fixed myself a salad at the dining hall's salad bar. Paige and Alexa joined me at the table a moment later, both of them carrying slices of pepperoni pizza and cups of soda.

Paige eyed my meal as she set her plate down on the table, her cell phone next to it. "You some kind of health nut?"

"I guess you could say that," I replied.

"Not me," she said. "I run on pizza and truffle fries."

"They serve truffle fries here in the dining hall?" I asked.

Paige scoffed. "I wish."

Zzzzt. Paige's phone sounded with an incoming text, the screen indicating someone identified as Chaoxiang had sent her a message. She picked up her phone, smiling softly as her gaze ran over the words on the screen. She used her thumbs to type in a quick reply, pushed the button to turn her phone off, and returned it to the table, taking a bite of her pizza.

As we dug into our dinner, I asked the two what they were studying.

"Political science," Paige said.

"Me, too!" I said. "Were you planning on going to Essie Espinoza's rally Wednesday night?"

"Only to check out the competition."

Competition? "What do you mean?"

"I intern at Senator Sutton's local office."

Impressive. Also, cause for concern. If she'd been with his entourage at the Fourth of July event, she might have seen me there and eventually recognize me and Brigit as the K-9 team who'd been up on the stage.

"Wow," I said. "How'd you get a job in a senator's office?"

Alexa chimed in now. "Is it called a job if it's unpaid? Or is it called volunteering?"

Paige cut a raw look at her roommate. "Hardly any internships pay anymore. Students do them for the experience, not the money." She turned back to me now. "I got the *job*," she said, emphasizing the word, "because my grades are really good. I've made the dean's list every semester so far."

I broached the subject in what I hoped was a subtle manner. "Senator Sutton's the politician who spoke at Panther Pavilion last week, right? At the Fourth of July event?"

"That's him," she replied. "My parents know him from the club."

"The club?"

"Timarron Country Club," she said, "in Southlake."

Southlake was one of the most exclusive Fort Worth suburbs, sitting about twenty miles northeast of the city. The average home price hovered just under nine hundred thousand dollars. In Texas, where houses were relatively inexpensive compared to the rest of the country, that kind of money got you an awful lot in the way of square footage and custom upgrades and gates to keep out the riffraff.

"Is that where you're from?" I asked. "Southlake."

Paige's mouth full of pizza now, she merely nodded in return.

"Did you go to Panther Pavilion on the Fourth to hear Senator Sutton speak?" I mentally crossed my fingers that she'd tell me she hadn't been there.

"No," she said. "I have better things to do on my day off than hang around with my coworkers. They're all like forty or fifty years old and the only thing they want to talk about is their kids or their lawns or their arthritis."

Relief relaxed me and I felt my shoulders loosen of their own accord. "Interning for a senator must still be exciting, though, getting to work on big issues and meet important people."

"Meh," she replied. "I had way more fun working the purse counter at Macy's last summer. All of the exciting stuff happens in his Washington, D.C., office. His local office handles all the routine work. They've got me responding to his e-mails. People only write in to bitch about things." She mimicked his constituents. *"Social Security doesn't pay enough for me to live on. All these wars cost too much. China's taken all of our manufacturing jobs, do something about it."* She rolled her eyes. "Get a life, people."

With that kind of attitude, she might have been better off majoring in something other than political science. In fact, I wondered how she'd chosen her major and asked as much. "So you're majoring in poli sci why, then?"

"That's a good question." She plucked a pepperoni off her pizza. "I couldn't make up my mind when I started college so I took one of those aptitude tests. It told me

I'm a people person and suggested I go into public service, nursing, or sales. Blood makes me squeamish, so nursing is definitely out, but sometimes I think maybe I should change my major to marketing. There's so many restrictions in politics. You can't say this, you can't do that." Another eye roll. "Ugh!"

Her rant complete, she stuck out her tongue and dropped the pepperoni on it as if it were a communion wafer. I was tempted to give her an "amen." Instead, I steered the conversation onto a more relevant topic, for me, anyway. "My roommate said something about the girl who lived there before me doing drugs?"

Alexa cringed. "Yeah. She took some bad Molly."

Paige plucked another pepperoni off her pizza. "I don't think the Molly was bad. I think she just didn't know how to prepare for using it."

Aha! So this girl knew something about the drug. "Prepare for it?" I repeated. "What do you mean?"

She waved the pepperoni around. "You know. Like making sure she was hydrated and all that."

"Does that help? Drinking water?"

"Supposedly," she said. "I mean, I don't do that kind of thing, so I can't personally say. But you hear stuff."

What do you hear? I wanted to ask. *And from who?* But I knew I had to be subtle or risk giving myself away. "Do a lot of people here do Molly?"

Paige shrugged. "As much as any other college, I guess. Most people just drink if they're looking to party."

"Do you drink?" I asked.

Paige and Alexa exchanged glances before Paige answered for them. "We're only nineteen. We're not old enough to drink." She punctuated her words with a snort. "So of course we do it!" She laughed out loud now.

Alexa joined her. "What's the harm in a beer or two?"

"Or ten," Paige replied, which led to more laughter.

"Where do you get it?" I asked.

"Parties, mostly," Paige said.

"Do you go to a lot of parties?" I asked.

"Pretty much every weekend," Paige said, slightly smug with pride at her popularity.

"Take me with you sometime?" I pleaded. "I'd love to have some fun and meet people."

She cocked her head. "Guys, maybe?"

"Sure," I said. "If you know any cute ones." A twinge of guilt puckered my gut. If I went to any parties with these girls, I'd be sure to wear the granny panties Seth had foisted on me.

"Speaking of guys," Paige said, her gaze shifting to somewhere behind me and narrowing, "there's Logan."

I turned to see a ginger-haired boy heading our way, a smile on his face. With his chiseled features, nice build, and preppy dress, he looked like he'd stepped out of a J. Crew ad.

"Not bad," I said, wagging my brows.

Paige's lip curled back in disgust. "Before you take off your panties, you should know he spent spring break with hookers in Vegas. He brought home crabs and herpes as a souvenir."

I gagged on my drink and was still coughing when Logan stepped up to the table.

"Hi, ladies," he said, his voice oozing sex as he shamelessly looked me up and down. "Who's your new friend with the dog?"

"Morgan," Paige snapped before I could respond. "And she doesn't date diseased losers like you, so fuck off."

Despite the harsh language, Logan remained unfazed, even chuckling. "Such dirty talk for such a pretty girl. You give Senator Sutton blow jobs with that mouth?"

"Ew!" If I'd had my police baton with me, I probably would've hit the guy on reflex.

Logan eyed Paige intently. "You know you want me, Paige. When will you just admit it?"

She scoffed. "What part of 'fuck off' did you not understand?"

He chuckled again, taking us all in with his sweeping gaze. "Later, ladies."

Once he'd stepped away, Paige let out a groan. "I can't believe I ever had a crush on that loser."

I cast a glance his way as he aimed for the pizza counter. "You did?"

"Beginning of freshman year," she admitted. "Before I realized what a man-whore he is."

As we continued eating, I glanced around the room, noting a girl with wavy red hair. *Could she be Ruby Ruthswohl, the girl I suspected had been with Miranda Hernandez at Panther Pavilion?* It was possible. She was about the same size as the girl I'd seen and looked similar to the photos of Ruby I'd seen on Facebook. She was dressed casually in jeans, a tank top, and flip-flops, with a trendy and expensive Kate Spade backpack-style purse on her back.

"Do either of you know the redhead by the soda machine?" I asked. If they did, I could ask whether they'd ever seen her with Miranda.

They both glanced toward the girl.

Alexa shook her head in response.

Paige said, "No, I don't know her. Why?"

Yeah, Morgan. Why? "She looks sort of familiar. I thought maybe I knew her from somewhere. She might be in one of my classes." I changed the subject again. "Are y'all staying in the dorm this fall, too?"

"I am," Alexa said.

"Not me," Paige replied. "No offense, but I'm tired of sharing a room and bathroom. I'm going to start looking for apartments soon."

Honestly, I couldn't blame her. I knew from experience that dorm life could get old pretty quickly. You had no control over your space, little privacy, and all manner of roommate issues ranging from dirty panties on the floor to theft of laundry money. Plus, having lived in Southlake, she'd likely had a large bedroom and bath all to herself growing up.

We chatted amiably for the rest of the meal before Paige begged off to go meet a study group and Alexa excused herself to do some reading for her literature class. I decided to take Brigit on a sniffing tour of the dorm and identify rooms on which she alerted to drugs. The campus police could give me the names of the students in the rooms, enabling me to narrow down my search for the Molly dealer. Of course Brigit and I would have to be careful that it wasn't obvious we were doing a drug sweep.

I started on the first floor, waiting until the hallway was clear before leaning down to whisper in her ear, issuing her the order to scent for illegal drugs. She put her nose to the ground and began sniffing around the bottoms of the doors as I led her down the hall. Unfortunately, she wasn't exactly quiet as she sniffed. *Snuffle-snuffle-snuffle. Snuffle-snuffle.*

I was ten steps past a door when it whipped open behind me. I looked over my shoulder to see a shirtless boy sticking his head and shoulders out the door.

"That noise was a dog!" he called back to an unknown person inside the room.

"Sorry!" I said. "She likes to sniff. We're new here and she's checking everything out."

He looked from Brigit to me, squinting as if trying to figure out what health issue I suffered from that allowed me to have a dog in the dorm. "Is that dog one of those emotional therapy dogs?"

"No," I said. "She alerts me to impending seizures. I have epilepsy."

"Oh," he said. "Cool." He raised a hand in good-bye before shutting his door.

We continued on. Brigit failed to alert at any of the doors. Looked like the first floor was clean.

I entered the stairwell and led Brigit up to the third floor, figured we'd tour our own floor last before heading back to our room. She alerted on two doors on the floor, sniffing around the threshold and sitting down in front of them. I made a quick note in my phone of the room numbers: 306 and 313. The fourth floor appeared clean, but she alerted to a door on the fifth: 518.

Rather than going back to the stairwell at the far end of the hall, I took the elevator down to the second floor, making my way up and down the hall with Brigit. Though she sniffed at each door along the hall, she alerted on none of them. I gave her a "good girl" and a liver treat and led her back to my room. As I ran the key through the skimmer, she sat and stared straight ahead. I glanced down at her, then did a double take when I realized she was giving her passive alert again. *Holy crap! Could my rude roommate be the dealer?*

EIGHTEEN
QUITTING TIME

Brigit

Brigit wasn't sure why they seemed to be living in this large building now, sleeping in a different bed and eating their meals in a noisy dining hall rather than their quiet kitchen. But a change of scenery was always fun. There were lots of new things to hear and smell and see.

While she could scent drugs all the time, and sometimes alerted on them even without Megan specifically asking her to, she'd been too distracted by all the new things to give any alerts before. But after dinner, Megan had directed her to put her nose to work, so she had.

Mostly she'd smelled sweaty sheets, the scent of students having sex, and all kinds of fragrances intended to mask a human's natural scent. Perfume. Cologne. Body wash. Shampoo. Deodorant. She'd never understand why humans fought their natural smells. You wouldn't catch a dog trying to mask its scent. Dogs were a proud yet simple species.

When they'd returned to the room they now shared with the girl who had yet to pet Brigit, the dog gave her passive alert as asked. For some reason, though, Megan took her off task when they stepped inside the room.

The other girl was seated at her desk, working on her computer. She cast a glance at Brigit, and the dog noticed the flash of fear in her eyes. She could also smell the fear pheromones the girl was giving off. Poor thing. She was afraid of furry creatures. Brigit would have to show her that she had nothing to fear but fur itself.

NINETEEN
SHOPPING SPREE

The Dealer

That half million dollars wasn't going to spend itself. He'd have to give it some help.

Of course he didn't want his spending to be too obvious. People might start asking questions, poking around. But he'd been given that money for a reason, he'd taken a huge risk accepting it, and he'd be damned if he wasn't going to put it to good use.

TWENTY
FOR A GOOD TIME, CALL MOLLY

Megan

Monday evening, my idle curiosity got the best of me and I got online and performed some quick personal research. I'd read between the lines of what Paige had said at lunch, that her parents knew Senator Sutton from their country club. I had an inkling their connection might have played a role in Paige's landing the internship. Sure enough, I discovered that Richard and Suzanne McQuaid had contributed the maximum amount to each of Senator Sutton's campaigns over the past years. They'd also contributed tens of thousands to political action committees, though none of those funds went into Sutton's coffers. Unlike many politicians in Texas, whose largest contributors were oil and gas companies. Sutton refused contributions from special interests. It was one of the reasons he was so respected.

Though hiring the daughter of contributors seemed to fly in the face of his slogan—"The Best Representation Money Can't Buy"—Alexa had a valid point. If the internship was unpaid, it was more like volunteering, right? For all I knew he had a whole slew of unpaid interns slogging away in his office and at his campaign headquarters. And if Paige had a high GPA and good job references, she shouldn't be prevented from getting an internship just because her parents had donated money to Sutton's campaign. She should simply be given the same consideration as any other applicant.

My roommate only left our room Monday night to brush her teeth and use the facilities in the adjoining bath, so I hadn't been able to have Brigit search the room and show me where the drugs were hidden. But at least I'd finally learned my roommate's name.

After I'd turned off my desk lamp around eleven, I'd said, "I know you aren't happy about having a dog in the room, but we're stuck with each other so we might as well do our best to get along." *At least until I have to possibly arrest you for selling drugs.* "You haven't even told me your name, you know."

Still bent over her textbook and chemistry homework at her desk, her leg pumping up and down with nervous energy, she exhaled sharply. "It's Emily."

"All right," I said. "That's a start. Good night, Emily."

A few seconds later she issued a reply, speaking so softly I could barely hear her. "Good night, Morgan."

Tuesday morning, I woke a few minutes after six. It took me a few hazy seconds to realize the bed didn't feel familiar. Also missing was the familiar warm, heavy body pressed up next to me.

I sat up in the dim dawn light peeking through the miniblinds and scanned the room. Brigit wasn't lying on the rug. She wasn't on the tile by the door, either. Nope, she was curled up on Emily's bed, tucked in the V between my roommate's legs, her head draped over Emily's calf.

This isn't good.

As quietly as I could, I slipped out from under my covers and stood. On hearing the movement, Brigit opened her eyes partway, but blatantly ignored my hand motioning for her to get down from the bed and closed them again. *Darn dog!*

What now? I couldn't very well call her name or I'd risk waking Emily. The last thing I needed was her freaking out again.

I tiptoed across the rug, bent down, and puckered my lips, aiming a stream of breath at Brigit's face to get her attention. She opened her eyes again, but unfortunately so did Emily.

My roommate sat bolt upright, jerked her covers up to her chin, and shrieked at the top of her lungs. "Aaaaaah!"

Brigit stood on her bed, took a moment to yawn and stretch, then hopped down.

"I'm so sorry!" I told Emily. "She must've climbed onto your bed during the night."

Tears had formed in Emily's eyes and she panted like a dog, her breathing loud in the otherwise quiet room. *She doesn't dislike dogs. She's terrified of them.* For a potential drug dealer, the girl was quite a wimp.

I clipped Brigit's leash onto her collar and ordered her to sit. "Emily," I said, kneeling next to her bed. "I promise you there's nothing to be afraid of. Britney is a very well-behaved dog. She wouldn't hurt a flea."

It was true. Mostly because I made sure she didn't have fleas. Criminals, on the other hand? Heck, yeah, she'd go after those with incredible determination and ferocity. But I couldn't very well tell Emily that, especially since she might be one of those criminals we'd be going after.

Emily gulped as a tear escaped and ran down her cheek. "Promise she's nice?" she asked meekly.

"I promise. How about if I bring her over and you can pet her? Would that help?"

She bit her lip. "I don't know."

I'd learned from experience that the only way for a person to overcome her fears was to face them. "Can we try?"

Emily's gaze went from me, to Brigit, and back again. Her eyes were still wet and wide, bloodshot, too, from lack of sleep, but, finally, she nodded.

"Come here, Brit," I said, patting my leg.

Brigit came over and sat as instructed, wagging her tail as if to encourage Emily to trust her. Slowly, tentatively, Emily reached out a hand and gave Brigit's head a single pat. Brigit responded by giving Emily's hand a long lick with her tongue.

"See?" I said. "She's not so bad."

Emily held up her dog-slobber-moistened hand. "That was sweet and disgusting at the same time."

"Sweet and disgusting," I repeated. "That's dogs in a nutshell." With that, I threw a robe on over my pajamas and slid my feet into my slippers. "I need to take her out. We'll be back in a few minutes."

I rounded up the roll of poop bags and stuck them in the pocket of my robe along with my ID card and cell phone. As quietly as possible, I led Brigit out of the dorm and over to the far side of a green space so she could relieve herself. Fortunately, at this early hour, only a couple of maintenance workers were out and about on the campus, so I didn't embarrass myself. I unclipped Brigit's lead to give her some freedom, and took advantage of the moment to contact the university police department.

"She alerted on rooms 306, 313, and 518," I told the male officer who answered. "She also alerted on the room I've been assigned, the one Miranda Hernandez lived in, but I haven't had a chance to search it yet. My roommate hasn't left the room since my partner alerted. As soon as we're alone, I'll see what we find and let you know."

"Great," he said. "In the meantime, I'll get officers over to those rooms to see what they find."

Brigit had gone number one, and was now popping a squat under a large live oak tree. *Good.* I wouldn't have to worry about her needing to go in the middle of my morning class.

While my partner dropped her load, I left a voice mail on Detective Jackson's phone at the police department, telling her what I'd told the campus police. With any luck, they'd find a huge stash of Molly in one of the rooms, identify the student as the dealer who'd sold to Miranda Hernandez and Ashleigh White, and Brigit and I could move back home. Of course, depending on what I found in my own dorm room, it could turn out that Miranda herself was the dealer and that she'd had a bad reaction to her own product. Still, despite the fact that all sorts of people were dealing drugs these days, I had a hard time believing a young woman with such an innocent face could be a drug dealer. Call it instinct. Or maybe call it naiveté. It was possible my instincts were nothing more than wishful thinking and that her face had looked so young and innocent only because she'd been unconscious.

Having finished her business, Brigit turned her attention to the tree, sniffing around its base and peering up into its branches, probably hoping to see a squirrel to chase. I whipped out the roll of bags, pulled one off the end, and scooped up her droppings, tying the bag closed.

"C'mon, Brigit!" I called, grimacing when I realized my blunder. *Britney,* I reminded myself. *She's Britney now.*

I looked around for a trash can, but none caught my eye. Rather than take the bag of poop into the lobby to dispose of it, I figured the considerate thing to do would be to toss it into the big metal bin behind the dorm. I circled around the back of the building and tossed the poop onto the top of the bin, which was nearly full. The bag landed with a soft *plup.*

When I turned to go, I discovered the red-haired girl from the dining hall coming toward me, a white garbage bag in her hands. She looked down at her cell phone as she walked, multitasking. She looked up on hearing my footsteps, her feet faltering for a split second and her face showing surprise on seeing someone else out here so early. As she approached, she gave me the standard, "Hey."

"Hey," I said in reply. It took everything in me not to ask, *Were you the girl with Miranda Hernandez at Panther Pavilion?*

Brigit and I returned to our room to find it empty. The

sound of the shower running in the bath told me that Emily was bathing.

Now's our chance.

I gave Brigit the order to search for drugs. She lifted her head and put her nose in the air, sniffing. Rather than moving to Emily's side of the room, my partner stepped over to my bed and hopped up on it, still scenting the air, her nostrils twitching. She stepped from my bed onto the taller desk, her paws sliding on the flat surface. As I stepped over to make sure she wouldn't slide off and hurt herself, she reared up onto the bookcase bolted to the wall over the desk and stretched her head up as high as she could. *Sniff-sniff.* She froze in that position.

Above the bookcase was a small metal slatted air vent held to the wall with screws. *Are the drugs inside the vent?* I had neither the time to remove the vent, nor the tools to do so at the moment. It would have to wait until later.

As I spooned canned food into a bowl for Brigit, the shower stopped running. I gathered up a pair of clean underwear and a bra so I could be next in the shower. When Emily returned to our room, I traded places with her, taking Brigit with me, instructing her to lie on the mat until I was done.

When I was finished, I returned to the room to find Emily dressed and checking e-mails on her computer, her knee bouncing up and down as usual. The girl had so much nervous energy, was wound so incredibly tight, it was a wonder she didn't fly into a million little pieces. After sliding into a pair of jeans, sandals, and a short-sleeved peasant blouse, I applied my makeup and twisted part of my hair onto my head in a messy but stylish pile, holding it in place with a clip. Ready, I turned to my roommate. "Want to get breakfast?"

She glanced up from her computer. "Okay."

I took my backpack with me so that I could head straight to class from the dining hall. Emily brought hers, as well. Downstairs, I rounded up a banana, a bowl of oatmeal, and a glass of orange juice. Emily met me at the table with a tray bearing three cups of coffee, along with greasy hash browns and bacon, early death on a plate.

I eyed the mugs. "*Three* cups of coffee?"

"And that's just for starters," she said, raising a mug and taking a gulp.

I sipped my juice. "Do you have an eight o'clock class, too?"

"Yeah. My other one is at three."

Good to know. That would give me a couple of hours later this afternoon to look in the vent.

I eyed her across the table. Her eyes were puffy and she had huge, dark bags under them. Her skin seemed paler, too. She appeared not unlike some of the drug addicts I'd dealt with on the job. "Are you feeling okay, Emily?"

"I'm fine," she said. "Just a little tired is all." She tossed back a big gulp from one of the mugs. "I'm the first one in my family to go to college. I'm here on grants and an academic scholarship. I'm trying to maintain my 4.0 average, but these summer classes are killers."

She spoke the truth. When professors had to cram a full semester's worth of material into four or five weeks, the pace was nothing less than frantic. It was bad enough with my political science courses. I could hardly imagine what it would be like to take two chemistry classes with their required additional labs in a summer session.

Her comment about the grants and scholarship caught my attention, too. The fact that she qualified for grants meant she came from a family of modest means.

"Did you get a full ride?" I asked.

"I wish," she replied. "The scholarship pays for half, the grants cover some of the rest. I have a part-time job at the rec center on campus. But I've had to take out a student loan, too. I only hope I'm not still paying it off when I'm fifty."

She wasn't the only student with that concern. Still, her financial straits made me wonder. Just how far was she willing to go to finance her education? I'd heard about a college student in Florida who'd pocketed thirty grand a week from sales of MDMA. Several students at the University of California–Santa Cruz, including sorority girls, had also been busted for dealing the drug. And that was just the tip of the iceberg. Would those worries about student loan debt cause Emily to resort to dealing Molly? *Hmm* . . . I'd keep an eye on her, see if any evidence presented itself.

"Alexa and Paige seem nice," I said, changing the subject. "Do you know them well?"

"Not really," she said. "Miranda used to hang with them some, but I'm not really the party-girl type."

Yeah. I'd picked up on that when she'd stayed up studying until the wee hours of the night. But the fact that she was a serious student didn't mean she wasn't selling Molly. Smart dealers didn't use their own product. It was a quick way to end up addicted and broke and in deep with people who wouldn't think twice about breaking your kneecaps with a crowbar.

Still, I wasn't entirely convinced she wasn't using drugs of some sort. Maybe something she thought would give her a competitive edge, help her focus. She wouldn't be the first college student to abuse Ritalin or Adderall. Short of searching through her things, I had no way of knowing if she had those types of drugs in our room. In order to maintain probable cause and avoid an unconstitutional search, Brigit was trained only to alert on illegal substances. In fact, when some states had legalized pot, dogs who'd been trained to sniff for marijuana had been rendered useless as drug detection dogs in those states.

I ate a spoonful of my oatmeal. "I wonder where Miranda got the Molly," I asked, carefully watching Emily's reaction. A dealer would realize I was asking where I, too, might score. An innocent person would think it was an innocent question.

Though she shrugged nonchalantly, she seemed to be carefully watching me, too. "It's probably not hard to find."

What does that mean? College kids could be somewhat cryptic.

She glanced down at Brigit, who was staring at the stack of bacon and drooling. "Can I give her a slice of bacon?"

"I'm sure she'd love it."

"Will she bite my fingers?"

"Not if you toss it."

Emily picked up a piece of bacon and threw it up into

the air. Brigit rose onto her hind legs and adeptly snapped it into her mouth on its way down.

"She's quick," Emily noted.

"And always hungry." I poked at my oatmeal with my spoon. "What was Miranda like?"

"What do you mean?" Emily asked.

I shrugged. "Well, I know she did drugs. But did she do a lot of them? Was she street smart?"

Emily snorted. "Street smart is the last word I'd use to describe Miranda."

Now it was my turn to ask, "What do you mean by that?"

"This may sound mean, but she came off as, like, a twelve-year-old. Coming to college was her first time away from home other than a few sleepovers. She said her parents would never even let her go to summer camp. They called her constantly to check in. It was really annoying. She even cried her first night in the dorm."

Poor girl. I doubted Emily had done anything to make her roommate feel more comfortable. If anything, she'd probably made her feel worse.

Emily gave me a pointed look. "What's with all the questions about Miranda?"

Uh-oh. Had I been too obvious? I raised a nonchalant shoulder. "Just curious."

Luckily for me, Emily let it go.

When we finished our breakfast, we turned in our dirty dishes at the appropriate window and headed out into the lobby.

"Need to use the restroom?" Emily asked.

"Might as well." I'd had a big glass of orange juice and it was a long time until class would be over.

We stepped into the public restroom off the foyer. I parked Brigit outside a stall and headed inside. When I turned around, I froze. There, on the back of the door, among a variety of graffiti and next to the standard *If you sprinkle when you tinkle,* someone had written FOR A GOOD TIME, CALL MOLLY (817) 555–2567.

This message was not so cryptic, at least not to someone in the know. I whipped my cell phone from my backpack and, when a loud toilet flushed, snapped a pic. Quickly, I returned my phone to my bag.

Had Emily steered me into this bathroom on purpose? I had no way of knowing for certain. But with the two of us having discussed Molly only minutes before, it was difficult to write things off as mere coincidence.

I finished my business, washed my hands, and retrieved Brigit's leash. Emily and I walked out of the restroom and exited the dorm together, parting ways on the front steps.

"See you later!" I called.

"Yep!" she called back.

I debated my options. A big part of me—the impatient part—wanted to duck between some bushes and call the number right now. Another part of me—the smart part—realized I should probably run things by Detective Jackson before taking any action. After all, this investigation was hers to manage. I was merely a willing minion tasked with collecting information or evidence.

As I headed to class, I texted the photo I'd taken in the bathroom to the detective, along with a message. *Found this written in lobby restroom. Next step?*

A minute later I received a reply. *Call the number. Set up a buy.*

Ok, I texted back. My hand a little shaky, I dialed the number. On the first ring, the call went to voice mail. "Hello," a voice said. It was either a low-pitched female voice or a high-pitched male voice. Given that the speaker seemed to have used one of the voice-changer apps to disguise his or her voice, it was impossible to tell. "Molly can't get to the phone. Send her an e-mail at funtimemolly@gmail.com." The recording went on to spell out the e-mail address. There was no invitation to leave a message at the beep, so I didn't.

Using my phone, I logged in to the e-mail account I'd set up for my alter ego. After discussion with Detective Jackson, we'd decided to use an address that would not identify the account holder as my alter ego, Morgan Lewis. The fact that I was asking questions around the dorm might already have raised suspicions, no matter how subtle I was trying to be. If I openly identified myself in the e-mail, that could be the icing on the cake if the dealer thought I'd come to the dorm undercover, looking to make a buy. Better to remain anonymous. I'd chosen a generic e-mail address, the word "bluebonnet" in honor of the state flower, followed by three random numbers.

I mulled over what to say in my message to *funtimemolly.* Hmm. I was totally out of my element here. Finally, I decided to go with: *Would like to meet up with you by this weekend, Molly.* That would leave the ball in their court as far as how they wanted to handle the deal. And if it turned out that the message on the bathroom wall was truly for a girl named Molly, it would sound innocuous enough.

I texted Jackson to inform her what I'd done.

Good work, she texted back. *I'll trace the phone number.*

Having done what we could for the time being, Brigit and I continued on to class. Though it was only five minutes before the lecture was scheduled to start, we were among the first to arrive. Looked like early classes plus summer session led to a lot of late arrivals. I took a spot near the back of the room where I'd be less conspicuous.

A horde of students poured into the room right as the wall clock turned to eight. Many, both boys and girls, wore baseball caps in an attempt to hide the fact that they'd woken up too late to comb their hair. The abundance of wrinkled clothing said that many of their outfits had been worn yesterday and retrieved from floors in a rush this morning. One boy walked in, shamelessly dressed in what were clearly pajama pants given that they were made of flannel and bore cartoon superhero images.

Brigit lay at my feet, napping, as the lecturer launched into a comparison of elites versus activists. While I found the subject fascinating, my partner clearly did not. At one point she began to snore, drawing the attention of students around me and more than a few snickers until I nudged her awake with my toe. She looked up at me bleary-eyed as if to ask *What did I do?*

As the class went on, I looked around at the students. Though only a few years younger than me, they looked like children. My years since college, the things I'd seen while on the police force, they'd aged me well beyond my years. As a cop, I knew things they'd never know, should never have to know. Things nobody should ever have to know.

I wondered who among them had never tried drugs and never would. Who among them had tried drugs once or twice out of curiosity or peer pressure. Who among them regularly used drugs. Who among them had become addicted and would spiral out of control until they ended up in jail, rehab, or a coffin. I hoped there were few of the former and none of the latter, though I suspected the large class held some of each type.

Two hours later, the lecturer wound things up and the class ended. I led Brigit back to the Jeep and drove to my house, which was only a mile and a half from the university, yet far enough that few, if any, students lived in my neighborhood. Leaving Brigit in the car, I hustled into the house, grabbing a Phillips head screwdriver from the kitchen junk drawer and a pair of disposable gloves from under the sink. After giving Zoe a quick scratch under the chin, I returned to the car.

We returned to the campus. As we approached the dorm, I spotted two campus policemen talking with a male student outside. The strained look on the boy's face told me he was in trouble. *Did they find something in his room? Is he the dealer I've been looking for?*

Seemed I had a lot of potential suspects, but no concrete conclusions. Until I did, until whoever was selling Molly to these kids was behind bars, I had to keep working.

I slinked around behind the student, trying to be as invisible as possible as I entered the dorm. Hooking a left, I led Brigit into the girls' restroom. Forgoing the stall I'd used that morning, I ducked into each of the others. The back door of each one bore the same message and phone number. *FOR A GOOD TIME, CALL MOLLY (817) 555–2567.* I wondered if the same message appeared in the boys' restroom.

I took the stairs up to the second floor, passing five boys in the stairwell and exchanging friendly "heys." Emily wasn't in our room, but I couldn't take a chance on checking the air vent yet, not until I was certain she was in class. I stashed the screwdriver in my desk drawer and glanced at the clock. It was straight up eleven. On the early side for lunch, but given that I had a one o'clock class and had eaten an early breakfast, I figured I might as well head down to the dining hall.

I went into the bathroom and knocked on the door that connected to Paige and Alexa's room. "Paige?" I called. "Alexa? Want to go to lunch?"

There was no answer. Looked like they were out. At least with a dog for a partner, I was never alone. I clipped Brigit's leash back on her and downstairs we went.

In the cafeteria, I looked around for familiar faces. I saw April and Jasmine, but given that they'd been no help the day before, I didn't see any point in sitting with them. I gave them a friendly wave, and fixed myself another salad at the salad bar. Brigit got another meat-only sandwich.

Glancing around the room, I spotted the curly-haired boy who had been in line in front of me before. He caught my eye and smiled, angling his head to indicate the seat across from him. I had to admit I was flattered, even though I had no intention of pursuing anything with this boy given that Seth and I were in a committed relationship. Still, what could it hurt to flirt a little? It's not like anyone would know and, after all, I was only doing my job here. The guy might have known Miranda or Ashleigh or Colby, might have known who sold them the Molly.

I led Brigit over to his table and sat down. "Hi," I said, giving him a smile.

"I'm glad you came over," he replied, smiling in return and extending a fisted hand across the table to greet me. "My name's Hunter, by the way."

I gave Hunter a fist bump. "I'm Morgan." I ruffled Brigit's neck fur. "My dog here is Britney."

He reached down a hand toward my partner. "Can you shake, girl?"

TWENTY-ONE
SHAKE, RATTLE, AND ROLL OVER

Brigit

Could she shake? Of course Brigit could *shake*. She could also *sit, lie, speak, roll over,* and *play dead.* She was no slouch, no silly lapdog who could only blink its eyes and look cute. She was a master performer. And that didn't even include the things she could do in her police work, like search, track, and take down a suspect.

Shake? Sheesh. Give her a challenge. This was college, after all.

Brigit raised her right leg and held it up in front of her. The boy took it in his hand and moved it up and down. Why humans chose to greet each other in this odd way she'd never understand. Why not just sniff each other's butts, like dogs did? You could tell a lot from a canine anus, like the dog's gender and reproductive status and emotional state. Butts were the faces and Facebook status updates of the dog world.

Brigit hopped up on the chair next to Megan and waited until her partner had torn her sandwich into

bite-sized pieces for her. Yep, Brigit had her partner
well trained.

Megan and the boy talked while Brigit ate the bites
of turkey and bread. When she finished her sandwich,
the boy gave Brigit a couple of his fries. It was nice of
him to share.

After lunch, Megan took Brigit back outside and let
her off leash in a grassy area to pee. A group of students
were playing Frisbee on the long lawn. When the Frisbee sailed over the head of the one nearest her, Brigit
figured she might as well help the guy out. She ran,
leaped into the air, and grabbed the Frisbee between her
teeth. Easy-peasy.

Yep, college was fun!

TWENTY-TWO
JOB DISSATISFACTION

The Dealer

Everyone seemed to be riding his ass today. He'd just finish one call when another would come in on its tail. Why the hell he'd ever gone into this line of work was beyond him.

Oh, yeah. He'd done it because he wanted to be the type of guy people looked up to, someone who helped people, who made the world a better place. A hero. He'd thought the job would give him that opportunity, along with some respect and clout and authority. What a joke, huh? The only thing this job had given him was hemorrhoids.

TWENTY-THREE
CLOSING IN

Megan

I was standing at the curb on University Drive, waiting to cross after my afternoon class, when Derek Mackey pulled up in his cruiser, rolling to a stop as the light turned red. His face puckered in irritation as he reached for the mic on the dash and responded to dispatch. Looked like he was having a hectic day.

Too bad, so sad.

I had to admit, I was enjoying this undercover gig. Besides the change of pace and scenery, it was exciting to get to focus on one big goal rather than being pulled in a million different directions and dealing with minor matters all day. I liked the thrill of being a spy. And I liked that I got to wear shorts and sneakers to work instead of that hot polyester police uniform.

Brigit and I crossed the street in front of the Big Dick's cruiser. He didn't spot us among the students. *Sheesh.* For a guy who also aspired to make detective, he could be darn oblivious.

I took long strides back to the dorm, Brigit trotting

to keep up with me. Inside the room, I pushed my desk chair over to block the door in case Emily came back from class early. The last thing I wanted was for her to catch me searching the air vent.

I grabbed the screwdriver from the drawer, climbed on top of my desk, and reached over the dusty top of the bookcase to remove the screws at either end of the vent. I pulled the cover off. Given that the top of the vent sat only an inch below the ceiling, I couldn't get my head high enough to see inside the air duct. I'd have to stick my hand in. I only hoped I wouldn't be bitten by an errant mouse or spider.

I slid a glove onto my right hand, reached into the duct, and felt around.

Nothing.

Nothing.

Nothing.

Bingo.

I pulled out a small green plastic bottle. The lack of dust on it told me it had been placed in the vent not too long ago. The printed label on the outside identified the contents as vitamin C capsules, but I didn't buy that for a second. The bottle might have once held vitamin C, but now it held five small white capsules that had to be Molly.

I reached down, stuffed the bottle into my backpack, and stood back up to screw the vent into place again. My immediate mission accomplished, I plopped down on my bed to think things over.

Had the bottle been full of pills, I'd say we'd caught our dealer and the case was closed. But with only five pills in the bottle, it looked more like I'd happened upon Miranda's personal secret stash. *Hmm.*

Rather than risk being caught taking the bottle to the police department on campus, I texted Detective Jackson for guidance. *Found five pills in air vent in my dorm room. What should I do with them?*

A couple of minutes later, she sent a reply. *Bring them to the station. Make sure you're not followed.*

I did as ordered, keeping a careful eye on my rearview mirror to make sure I wasn't being followed. As an extra precaution, I parked my telltale red Jeep in the lot of a fast-food place a block down from the station and circled around the backs of the buildings where it was less likely I'd be seen.

Derek's gleaming black pickup caught my eye as I passed through the parking lot. The truck was his pride and joy. He'd decorated the thing with a pair of rubber truck nuts that hung from the trailer hitch in the back. Clearly, he was overcompensating.

Something about the truck looked different, though. What was it? It took a moment for me to figure it out. *The rims.* The truck bore a set of shiny new chrome rims. They'd probably set Derek back a grand or more, a significant sum for public servants like us. But, like they say, the only difference between men and boys is the size—and in this case the *price*—of their toys.

It crossed my mind that the street value of the drugs that had disappeared, the ones I'd confiscated from Graham Hahn and given to Derek to take into evidence, approximated the value of the rims. But surely if Derek were dirty, he'd have the sense to hide it better, wouldn't he?

I found Detective Jackson at her desk and handed

her the bottle of pills. "What do you think?" I took a seat and signaled for Brigit to sit beside me.

The detective unscrewed the top and peered inside. "If this is vitamin C, I'm Beyoncé." She slid the bottle into an evidence bag, using a fine-point marker to fill out the form on the side to document the chain of custody. "I'll send this to the lab. They can check it for prints and tell us for sure if it's Molly."

I had little doubt the lab would confirm our suspicions regarding the pills, but we'd need their results in order to go forward with arrests. Of course that assumed we'd eventually figure out who to arrest. We weren't there yet. If there were any fingerprints on the bottle other than Miranda's—*Emily's, perhaps?*—those prints might prove useful.

"Did you get a response to your e-mail yet?" Jackson asked.

I'd checked my account several times since sending the message to *funtimemolly* this morning, but it couldn't hurt to take another look. I pulled up the account on my phone. *Nope. No response.* "Still waiting. What about the phone? Any news there?"

She held up a sticky note on which she'd jotted some information. "It's one of those cheap burner phones, a basic Samsung bought at a Dollar General store. Service is paid through a TracFone airtime card."

In other words, "The phone and the buyer are untraceable, then."

"The buyer, maybe," Jackson agreed. "There's no remaining security footage from the time the phone was purchased. But the phone? We can ping it. Of course we'll need some hard evidence that we aren't chasing a rabbit first."

"Some proof that the owner of the phone is selling Molly."

"Exactly. Once you get a response to that e-mail, forward it to me and shoot me a text. If it looks like funtime Molly is selling, we'll ping the phone."

While landlines provided emergency dispatchers with a firm origination point for incoming calls, mobile phones did not. For years, law enforcement had been able to use triangulation to narrow down a cell phone's location by testing signal strength from the three closest towers. Given the greater number of towers in highly populated urban areas, it was somewhat easier to locate a phone in cities than in more remote areas where the towers were more spread out.

Still, the technology wasn't as precise as needed, especially in emergency situations. Given that an estimated seventy percent of calls to 911 came from cell phones, and that young, injured, or emotionally rattled callers might not be able to give the emergency dispatcher an accurate location, the Federal Communications Commission had pushed for regulations requiring technology in new phones to provide Enhanced 911, or E911, capabilities. Just as aviation officials could narrow in on pings emitted from downed aircraft, law enforcement could now narrow in on pings emitted from cell phones and trace them with much higher accuracy.

The Fort Worth Police Department owned a portable cell phone tracking system called KingFish to help locate and identify priority offenders. When the department purchased the system a few years ago, the ACLU had raised concerns about privacy and probable cause. The department had assured civil rights advocates that the system would be used only after obtaining the proper search warrants.

"By the way," she said, "those dorm rooms Brigit alerted on last night? The university police found small amounts of weed in the two on the third floor. The boys were processed and released. First-time offenders. The two are friends. They took a hiking trip to Colorado earlier in the summer and bought the marijuana there using one of their older brother's driver's licenses."

The patchwork of state drug laws was making it easier for people to get their hands on pot. As this instance illustrated, much of the product was bought legally but then transported into states where marijuana use was prohibited.

"What about 518?" I asked.

"Nothing was found in the room."

"Huh."

I knew a person was never supposed to say never, but Brigit's nose was never wrong. There might have been no illegal drugs in the room when the police searched it this morning, but there'd been something in the room last night when Brigit alerted on it. No doubt in my mind.

"These are the girls who live in 518." The detective pulled a printout from a manila folder and slid it across her desk for me to take a look.

I picked up the page. On the left side was a photograph of a girl with fair skin and long hair so straight and pale it was nearly transparent. I didn't recall seeing her around the dorm. When my eyes moved to the right, my lungs gasped in air. Smiling up at me from the

page was the redhead with the wavy hair I'd seen at Panther Pavilion, Miranda's friend. "Ruby Rathswohl lives
in 518?"

"Yes, indeed," the detective said, her expression wry.

"I ran into her really early behind the dorm. She was
taking a bag of trash out to the Dumpster."

"Or disposing of evidence," Jackson replied, arching
an accusing brow. "Keep an eye on that little redhead."

"I'll do my best."

Our mutual update complete, I bade Jackson farewell
and returned to the dorm. Emily was back at her desk,
working on homework, a frozen microwave dinner on
the desk beside her, steam rising from the sauce-
smothered entrée.

I laid my backpack on my bed. "You're not eating in
the d-dining hall, I take it?"

Rather than respond verbally, my roommate merely
picked up the plastic tray that held the food as if that
were the answer. *Talk about moody.* Emily could benefit from a chill pill. Then again, maybe pills were the
reason for her erratic mood swings. Paranoia and
depression were side effects of many illegal substances.
Then again, she'd called her former roommate a "druggie" and seemed disgusted by drug use. Was she just
prone to mood swings?

Rounding up Brigit, I ventured into the hall and
knocked on Paige and Alexa's door. A moment later, Alexa answered.

"You two want to grab dinner?" I asked.

"Paige is out," she said, "but I'll go. I just need to put
on some shoes." She waved me into the room.

As she sat on her bed and buckled her sandals, I glanced around the space. The side that belonged to Alexa was neat and tidy, her bulletin board featuring numerous candid photos of her with family and friends, including several of her with Paige. On the opposite side of the room, Paige's bulletin board was also covered with candid snapshots, though her space was much less neat. Her bed was rumpled, clothing lay draped over the back of her desk chair, and several pairs of shoes were scattered haphazardly about the floor. Still, the risk of tripping aside, a little mess never really hurt anyone and, besides, I'd seen much worse.

I turned back to Alexa. "Have you and Paige been friends for long?"

She stood. "Since our sophomore year of high school," she said. "We were on drill team together."

"I was—" I stopped myself just in time. I'd been about to say I'd been a twirler with my high school band. *Yikes!* I could've blown my cover. "Always jealous of girls who could dance," I improvised. "I've got two left feet."

"It's not about the feet. It's about the hips." She whipped her hips around, performing a little spin maneuver and chuckled. "See?"

"Not bad."

Alexa, Brigit, and I took the stairs down to the dining hall, where we joined April and Jasmine for dinner. Unfortunately, while chatting with the girls was entertaining enough, the meal did nothing in terms of advancing my investigation.

Rather than stay in my room after dinner, I opted to take my textbooks and laptop down to the study lounge on the first floor. Since it had comfy sofas and large tables, a number of students chose to study or work on group projects there. The wide, open doorway would also provide me a vantage point from which to keep an eye on the comings and goings of others in the residence hall.

I plopped myself down in an overstuffed chair, kicked off my shoes, and rested my feet on the coffee table. Brigit lay down next to the chair, in a corner. I pulled her chew bone out of my backpack and handed it to her so she'd have something to do.

After completing the assigned reading for my political psychology class, I took a selfie with my textbook and sent it to Seth along with a message that read *Do I look smarter?*

A moment later a *ding* told me he'd replied. I consulted the screen to find his message. *You can give me an education anytime.*

"What are you smiling about?" asked a friendly male voice.

I looked up to find Hunter staring down at me. I pushed the button to turn off my phone. "Kitten videos on YouTube. I treat myself to five minutes of mindless entertainment when I finish my homework."

He swung his backpack down from his shoulder and dropped it onto the coffee table with a *plunk*. "Mind if I join you?"

"Sure." It could give me another chance to see what he might know about Colby Tibbs, Ashleigh White, Miranda Hernandez, and whoever might be selling drugs in the dorm. I'd hoped to raise the subject at lunch, but after he'd shaken Brigit's hand he'd received a text and immediately excused himself.

He unzipped his backpack and pulled out a laptop before easing back onto the couch and propping the computer on his thighs.

"What are you working on?" I asked.

"American history," he said. "I've got a paper due on the Bay of Pigs invasion by Friday."

"That seems soon," I said. "The semester just started."

"Every week of summer school is like three weeks in a regular semester." He glanced down at Brigit. "It's sort of like counting time in dog years."

On hearing the word "dog," she stopped gnawing her bone and paused to listen, tilting her head and pricking her ears.

Hunter laughed and reached out to ruffle her head. "You're a smart girl, aren't you, Britney?"

Funny how so much human communication with dogs involved asking them questions they had no hope of answering.

"Are you a history major, then?" I asked.

"No," he replied. "Engineering. But I didn't dare take an engineering class in the summer. It would've kicked my ass."

Always good for a person to know their limitations.

As Hunter returned his attention to his computer and began typing, so did I. I logged in to my e-mail account. Surprise! *Funtimemolly* had replied to my message. I leaned in eagerly to read the response.

Get a PO box for delivery and send me the address. $40 each. Tape cash to bottom of the trash can in the bathroom at Tio's Taco Stand on Vickery. E-mail me after you've left the cash.

I knew the place. It sat only a mile or so northwest of

the campus. Tio's Tacos was a small mom-and-pop Mexican restaurant, a mere hole-in-the-wall, really, but insanely busy given its great food and "so low they're loco!" prices. I stopped in on occasion for a bean burrito, though I always avoided the lunchtime rush hours, when they'd have a takeout line extending out the door.

Funtimemolly's response told me several things. First, the response told me that the message on the bathroom wall was indeed targeted at students looking to buy Molly. Second, the message revealed how the exchanges were taking place, via a drop site and post office box rather than in-person transactions. It was an unusual yet clever arrangement, one that would make it much more difficult to identify and nail the dealer. In many cases, dealers were nabbed after police caught a customer with drugs and the DA offered a reduced sentence in exchange for information that would lead to the dealer's arrest. By delivering the drugs through the mail rather than in person, the dealer ensured that his or her customers couldn't identify their source even if they wanted to. Finally, the response told me that while it would require some craftiness to identify this shrewd and surreptitious dealer, we were nonetheless a step closer to catching the culprit than we had been only seconds before.

I replied to the e-mail. *Got it. I will leave $ tomorrow.* After responding to the e-mail, I forwarded it along with my reply to Detective Jackson. She could have one of the department's tech specialists take a look, see if they could determine what IP address the dealer's message had been sent from. Given that an IP address is unique to the network connection used to send the message, they might be able to use the information to identify the dealer. Of course an IP address could fairly easily be hidden if the sender used a proxy server or a service such as Tor, which sent messages through a network of virtual underground tunnels via servers operated by volunteers. Journalists had used the service to communicate with whistleblowers and dissidents who didn't want to risk arrest. The system could also be used in reverse, to circumvent censorship settings and allow a user to view blocked content. Not that I understood how any of it actually worked. Technology was like magic to me. Still, I knew the detective would also need to get a court order to force the Internet service provider to identify its client, and that the response could take several days. I wasn't counting on the e-mail leading anywhere right away.

I looked up to find Hunter eyeing me intently. "What?"

"Just thinking," he said.

"About what?"

"About whether I should ask you out."

I laughed. When he said nothing further, I said, "Well?"

He gave me a coy smile. "Still thinking about it." With that he returned his attention to his computer screen.

I scoffed in indignation, though I had to give the guy credit. He knew how to flirt, to get a girl on the hook and play with her. He'd never reel me in, of course. I decided to take advantage of the moment to see if I could pry any information out of him, assuming he had any to pry free. "I heard something about the campus police finding weed in the dorm today."

"Weed?" he said. "That's nothing. There's a guy on my floor who ended up in the hospital last weekend.

They say he took bath salts or something. He hasn't come back yet."

He must have been talking about Colby Tibbs.

"Bath salts?" I said, though I knew that information was off. "Whoa. Where'd he get something like that?"

It was Hunter's turn to scoff now. "It's not hard," he said. "You just go to a party or club and start asking around, eventually someone will come to you."

He might have misidentified the drug that had taken Colby Tibbs out of commission for the time being, but he certainly seemed to know how things got done. Was Hunter simply street smart, or had he seen these deals in action? Might he know who was selling drugs to the kids in our dorm?

As long as we were on the subject, it couldn't hurt to press further, could it? "Are you speaking from experience?"

He simply stared at me for a moment before replying. "What you're really asking is whether I do drugs."

It was a statement, not a question. I wasn't entirely sure how to respond, so I said nothing, cocking my head and raising my brows in inquiry.

Alas my brows did not get the response they sought. He stared at me another long moment before speaking. "I better get back to my paper."

TWENTY-FOUR
SWING AND A MISS

Brigit

Brigit woke to Megan gently shaking her. She peeked her eyes open just enough to see that the window was still dark. *Screw this.* If Megan wanted to get up in the middle of the night, she could leave Brigit out of it.

Megan shook her again, harder. Without opening her eyes, Brigit emitted a low growl. *Grrr.*

Megan put her mouth to the dog's ear and whispered, "Treat?"

Well, now. That changes everything

Brigit opened her eyes and climbed down from the bed. Megan clipped her leash to her collar and quietly opened the door to their room, slipping into the hall and closing it softly behind them.

After Megan fed her a liver treat, they went down the stairs and into the dimly lit lobby. Two girls and a boy still worked at a table in the lounge, while another boy slept on the couch, his arm thrown back over his head as he snored. They didn't seem to notice Brigit and her partner crossing the foyer.

Megan led her across the open space, pausing before a door and opening it slightly, putting her ear to the crack to listen. *Poor humans and their inferior ears.* With Brigit's superior hearing, she could tell there was nobody in the restroom. She could tell that one of the sinks was dripping, though. *Drip-drip-drip.*

Megan led her inside, ducking into each of the toilet stalls. While the ladies' room they'd been in earlier today had been relatively clean, the scent of urine was very strong here, especially around the floor of the urinals. Male humans were like male dogs, aiming their stream in the general direction of a urinal or tree trunk and not much worrying whether they hit their target.

A few seconds later, Megan led her back into the foyer. As long as they'd come down, Brigit figured she might as well relieve herself, too. She pulled Megan in the direction of the front doors.

After crouching in the bushes flanking the front steps of the building, Brigit felt much better. She and Megan returned to their dorm room, where Megan slowly and carefully ran her ID card through the skimmer. The resulting *click* was as loud as a bark in the silent hallway.

Megan opened the door and they slunk back into the room.

Emily sat up in her bed. "Can't you two be more quiet?" she hissed.

TWENTY-FIVE
SLEEPLESS NIGHTS

The Dealer

He couldn't sleep.

He was too frustrated.

Too anxious.

Too . . . *conflicted*.

He climbed out of bed and walked over to his dresser, gazing at his dim reflection in the darkness. Though his face looked the same, he hardly recognized himself these days. Had he taken the wrong risks? Made the wrong decisions?

Who had he become?

TWENTY-SIX
SOMETHING TO RALLY AROUND

Megan

The lower student population in the summertime meant that not all of the rooms in the residence halls were needed. A few of the buildings were closed for the summer, some of them undergoing repairs and updates. But others remained open for business.

On my way to class Wednesday morning, I ducked into one of the other residence halls that had remained open for the summer. My gaze scanned the lobby, looking for the ladies' room. *There it is.* I led Brigit over and pushed the door open to step inside.

A girl stood at the counter, fluffing her hair and applying lip gloss, but other than that, the room was empty. I sat Brigit down by the wall, ordered her to stay, and stepped into a stall.

On the back of the door was some random graffiti.
C+D.
Why do I suck at calculus?
A talentless doodle of the horned frog mascot.

Sure enough, among the musings and doodlings and professions of love was the same message I'd seen in my dorm. *FOR A GOOD TIME, CALL MOLLY (817) 555-2567.*

When the girl left, I checked the other two stalls. Both of them contained the same message. The handwriting appeared to be the same as that on the walls of the women's restroom in my dorm. The writing I'd seen in the men's room at my dorm had been different, though, indicating more than one person was involved, perhaps one male and one female.

I rounded up my partner and we left the hall. A quick detour into another dorm confirmed that the dealer had placed ads in this residence hall, too.

As we made our way to our morning class, I pondered the significance. Was it coincidence that all of the kids who'd succumbed to the drug lived in the same dorm? Had they obtained the drug at or around the same time, ended up with a bad batch, while other students had obtained a purer product? There was no way of knowing. At least not yet. Still, it had me wondering whether our assumption that the dealer had a connection to my dorm was incorrect. On the other hand, at least my presence on campus had led me to finding the "ads" and put us that much closer to shutting down the illicit activity.

I continued on to my poli psych class, taking a seat in the back as usual. A male student down my row kept nodding off during the lecture, his chin nearly reaching his chest before his head would jerk back again. A shame really. The topic was actually quite interesting.

Between classes, I drove the Jeep to the closest post office that provided PO boxes. It was on Eighth Street, only a five-minute drive from campus.

I waited in line behind a modern-day Mother Goose, a woman in her sixties with five young children in tow, three girls and two boys. The two boys shrieked and hid behind the woman when they saw me step up with Brigit. The two older girls stared. The toddler on the woman's hip reached down with her hand, but was too high to touch my partner.

The woman turned around, her eyes going from me to Brigit. "Beautiful dog," she said.

"Thanks." I beamed though, really, any credit belonged to Brigit's biological mother, whoever she might be. The only thing I'd done was make sure the dog was kept well fed and well groomed. I had nothing to do with her DNA. That wasn't going to stop me from feeling proud of my furry partner, though.

While one little boy tentatively peeked out from behind the woman, one of the others looked up at her. "Can we go to the park, Granny?"

"As soon as we're done here," she replied, reaching down and using her thumb to wipe what appeared to be peanut butter from his cheek.

It was weird to think that one day I'd be a grandmother, regaling my grandchildren with bedtime stories of busting bombers and burglars and drug dealers. That random thought led me to wonder who their grandfather would be. Would it be Seth? *Hmm . . .*

I was crazy about the guy. Or at least as crazy about him as I'd let myself be about anyone. A smart woman kept her head, maintained control, right? And now, at this phase in life, my primary focus was my career. Still, Seth and I had agreed to be exclusive, and he'd been slowly opening up to me, letting me close. He was good to Blast, getting up early to take him for walks and to the dog park when surely Seth would rather sleep in. That selflessness and sacrifice was a sign he'd be a good father one day. He'd dropped out of high school to join the army and thus escape his cold and distant grandfather, but Seth's lack of education did not translate into a lack of intelligence. He understood the science of bomb technology better than most people could ever hope to, and he was a whiz with anything mechanical, whether it be cars, assembling a doghouse, or fixing a toilet that wouldn't stop running. So, yeah, maybe. Maybe I could see growing old and gray with him.

"Can I help you?" The counter clerk's voice brought me out of my reverie.

I stepped up to the counter. "I need to rent a PO box."

"What size?"

Uh, gee, big enough to accommodate a small quantity of illegal drugs? Of course I couldn't say that. "A small one will do."

"All right." He pulled a form out from under the counter and held it out to me. "You'll need to fill out this application and show me your identification."

I picked up the pen that was chained to the counter and quickly filled in the blanks on the form, using the name and address on my fictitious driver's license. When I was done, I handed the completed form back to the man along with my license. It occurred to me that submitting false information on an official U.S. government document was a federal criminal offense, but surely there'd be some accommodation for local law enforcement working undercover.

He verified my identification, and I paid for a six-month rental in cash. Our transaction complete, I slid the receipt into my wallet and took the two long, golden keys he offered. "Thanks."

I headed back into the main lobby and located my box. It was at the bottom of the row, requiring me to crouch down to test the keys. Yep, they worked. *Good*.

I pulled up my e-mail account on my phone and sent the dealer a message with my new PO box number, and stating that I was on my way to leave my payment as instructed.

Having secured a post office box, I drove to Tio's Taco Stand. On the way over, I noted two men standing on the platform underneath a billboard, using rollers on long handles to apply a new vinyl facing to the sign. As they unfurled the artwork, a five-foot-high image of Senator Sutton's grandfatherly face smiled down at me. No doubt his campaign manager had chosen this location to counteraffect Essie Espinoza's billboard across the street. The two candidates smiled at each other across four lanes of traffic in a virtual face-off.

Though it was only eleven when I arrived, there was already a line at the counter and most of the booths and tables were occupied.

At a two-top in the back sat Detective Hector Busta-mente, a plastic card bearing the number 16 on it in a metal stand in front of him. Like Detective Jackson, Bustamente had recognized both my ambition and my willingness to work unpaid overtime and taken me under his wing, letting me assist in earlier cases. Together, we'd figured out who'd been stealing purses and pickpocketing wallets at the stock show and rodeo.

Bustamente was a hefty man with thick lips and little fashion sense. He wore white crew socks with his brown loafers, the socks peeking out from under his too-short navy pants. One of the buttons on his button-down collar had been overlooked, the corner curling up slightly. But what he lacked in appearance, he made up for in brain power.

I realized he was here to keep an eye on the restroom, to try to figure out which of the people using the facilities was picking up the cash. No doubt he'd alternate with Detective Jackson, maybe watch with binoculars from a car across the street to avoid any of the restaurant employees becoming suspicious of him for hanging around too long.

He made no eye contact, continuing to peruse the newspaper, and I walked past. Nobody would ever suspect the two of us were in cahoots.

As I headed down the hallway, I wondered why the e-mail from *funtimemolly* hadn't specified the men's or women's restroom. After all, the same phone number had been written on the stalls in the boys' bathroom in the lobby of the dorm, too. But when I discovered they had only one restroom and that it was a unisex facility, things made sense.

The room was not only in use, but an older, white-haired man was waiting his turn. I stood next to him, jittery with the knowledge that my money drop here today would get us that much closer to identifying and busting the dealer.

I stepped into the small space and locked the door behind me. In the corner, under a towel dispenser, was a large plastic trash can. It was lined with a garbage bag.

Chances are the staff only changed the bag and never actually removed the can from the room. Hence, why the dealer chose this spot as a money drop.

I crouched down and put my hand on the side of the can, tilting it backward against the wall. I peeked underneath. There were no other bills there. I wondered if the dealer assigned this drop point for me only, or if other buyers had left their payments here, too. I supposed there would need to be several drop points or the dealer would risk a buyer coming back later to steal other customers' funds.

I pulled a roll of tape and four rolled-up twenties from my purse, carefully taping them along the inner rim of the garbage can where they wouldn't be as obvious if someone tipped the can. As directed in the e-mail from *funtimemolly,* I sent a reply notifying the account holder that the cash was ready for pickup. My work here done, I left the restroom, passing Bustamente once again as a waitress brought his order to his table. Looked like he'd opted for the enchilada special. *Yum.*

So long as I was out and about, I figured I'd check in on Seth. While working undercover was exciting, I hated that it kept me from my boyfriend, my friends, and my family. It was essentially a 24/7 gig, requiring total personal sacrifice. Well, almost total.

I pulled into the parking lot at Forest Park and found an empty spot near the entrance to the swimming pool. Today was Seth's day off, and he often spent his free time swimming. It was his exercise of choice, his release, his chlorine-scented moment of Zen.

I stepped to the chain-link fence that surrounded the pool area and peered inside. A mother held on to a flopping toddler wearing inflatable water wings. An adolescent boy called, "Marco!", his group of friends calling back, "Polo!" Sure enough, in one of the far swim lanes, a muscular back with an army eagle tattoo arched upward, disappearing a second later under the surface only to reappear an instant later. The butterfly. Seth's best stroke.

I circled around to the back fence, watching and waiting until he swam ten more laps and stopped at the end of the row to take a break. "Hey, you!" I called.

His head turned my way. He scrubbed a hand over his face to sweep away the water droplets and gave me a smile. "Hey, yourself!"

He put his hands on the edge and lifted himself straight up and out, his shoulder muscles and biceps flexing with the effort. The teenage female lifeguard on the stand nearby stared and reflexively mouthed her whistle. As a cop, I had experience with a whistle, too, and could firmly attest that a piece of cold, hard metal was a poor substitute for Seth's warm, soft lips.

Seth stepped over, water dripping from the hem of his green swimsuit. Despite being a serious swimmer, he refused to wear a revealing Speedo. I was glad he kept his privates private. Victoria wasn't the only one who should have secrets.

He hooked his fingers over the chain link and leaned in close. "Kiss me," he ordered, putting his mouth to one of the holes between the wires.

"You're not the boss of me," I said in return, though I kissed him anyway.

"You wearing those ugly panties I bought you?" he demanded.

"Every day." I pulled out the waistband of my shorts to show him.

"Good."

The lifeguard scowled and turned her attention back to the pool, blowing a *tweet* at a boy scurrying along the edge. "No running!" she hollered.

"What are you girls up to?" Seth asked.

I lowered my voice. "We made a cash drop a few minutes ago. We're buying some drugs."

He frowned in concern. "How dangerous is this case, anyway?"

I raised my palms. "Who knows?"

"That doesn't make me feel better, Megan."

"Would you rather I lie to you?" I asked. "Police work is dangerous. You know that. B-but it doesn't look like we're dealing with hardened felons from the street. Probably more like some overgrown juvenile delinquent."

He digested that for a moment before his face softened and he reached a finger through the fence to twirl a lock of my hair around it. "I miss you."

I reached through the metal mesh and put my index finger on his chin dimple, my own way of connecting physically with him. I looked into his green eyes and said, "I miss you, too."

We simply stared at each other for a moment before he spoke again. "My mother wants all of us to have dinner together."

"Really?" I said, lowering my hand. "I'd like that."

Seth's mother had given birth to him when she was only in her teens, and had basically abandoned him with her parents afterward. She'd been in and out of his life since, but never with any consistency. Though I wanted to hate her for how she'd treated Seth, for the attachment issues he suffered as a result, it was hard to fault a girl who'd been a child herself when becoming a parent, especially when the baby's father had not been involved and her own father had treated her horribly. I realized none of that excused what she'd done, but it did explain it.

She'd recently returned to Fort Worth, expressed a desire to reconcile with Seth and to do her best to make amends. Seth had not exactly been receptive, but I'd encouraged him to try. What good could come from hanging on to the anger and resentment?

"As soon as your undercover gig is over," Seth said, "we can make plans."

"That sounds great." I checked the time on my cell phone. "I better get back to campus. I have an afternoon class starting soon."

"Say something brainy," he said, a grin playing about his mouth. "You know how it turns me on."

I racked my brain for a tidbit from my political psychology class. "Polythink syndrome."

"God, Megan," he moaned, resting his forehead on the mesh. "I've never wanted you more."

I gave him another quick kiss, waving as I stepped away.

"Stay in touch!" he called after me.

Early Wednesday evening, Essie Espinoza arrived on the campus amid an entourage of staff, large men dressed all in black who appeared to be private security/bodyguards, and a dozen Fort Worth police officers, including Officer Spalding and the Big Dick.

Something was up. I just didn't know what.

A temporary stage had been erected on a wide green-belt where we students waited to hear Essie speak. Food trucks were parked along one side, their service windows closed for the time being. Along the other side was a table where student supporters were selling T-shirts, water bottles, travel mugs, and window signs bearing Essie's slogan. ESPERANZA ESPINOZA—OUR HOPE FOR THE FUTURE. *What the heck,* I decided. I forked over a ten-dollar donation and in return got one of the travel mugs for my roommate. That way she could take her coffee with her in the morning.

After speaking with a group of university police and school officials, Essie ascended the stage, flanked by Derek and Spalding, both of whom wore mirrored aviator sunglasses, making it impossible to tell where they were looking.

She stepped up to the standing microphone and raised her arms. "Good evening, Texas Christian University!"

The crowd roared in welcome, including both Alexa and Paige, who stood next to me.

"Traitor," I teased Paige.

"What can I say?" She shrugged. "Essie makes Senator Sutton seem like a boring old geezer."

"Maybe you should intern for her instead."

"That's a thought."

From the stage, Essie surveyed the crowd. "I'm glad to see such a great turnout tonight. But in good conscience I feel I must warn you. An hour ago someone called my campaign headquarters. While the caller did not directly issue a death threat, he said that if I continued my campaign he would find a way to stop me."

Whoa. That explained the bodyguards and extra police presence. The crowd murmured in surprise and concern. *Politics is a dirty, dangerous business.*

Essie raised a palm over her head. "Never fear, my friends! *¡No tengas miedo!*" She paused for effect, and when she spoke again her words were slow and deliberate. "Nothing can stop *me*. Nothing can stop *us*. And nothing can stop *progress*. *¡Nada!*"

The crowd's response nearly deafened me. I could only imagine how it sounded to superior canine ears. I reached down and pushed Brigit's head up against my leg, blocking her left ear and putting my hand over her right to drown out the sound.

Essie proceeded to give a rousing speech, one directed squarely at the millennial crowd gathered on the TCU campus before her. "The student loan crisis has risen to epic proportions. You students should not have to mortgage your future to get an education!"

The crowd erupted in supportive noise.

"You deserve the bright futures you've dreamed of!"

We roared again in agreement.

"Tomorrow belongs to you!"

While the crowd applauded and whooped again, I found myself wondering. *If tomorrow belongs to these students, who does today belong to?*

Over the next twenty minutes she continued to speak, touching on the lack of employment opportunities for young people, the need to stop the loss of jobs to overseas labor markets, to create more jobs for Americans, to open Chinese markets to more American goods. She raised the issue of Senator Sutton's proposed China–U.S. Partnership, the bill he'd referred to in shorthand as the CUSP when he'd mentioned it during his Fourth of July speech at Panther Pavilion.

"Unfortunately," Essie continued, gripping the sides of the podium as she leaned into the mic, "Senator Sutton has made no progress on the CUSP. Despite his best efforts, China has adamantly refused to back down from its tariffs on American products." She raised her palms. "Look, Monty Sutton is a nice guy. I'll give him that. But nice doesn't always get things done. It's time to get rid of old ideas and old ways of doing things, and bring some fresh, new ideas to Congress."

Though she hadn't directly called Montgomery Sutton a doddering codger, her repeated use of the word "old" certainly seemed intended to plant that seed in people's minds. Frankly, I found the ploy distasteful. Senator Sutton was no spring chicken, but he wasn't anywhere near being put out to pasture yet, either. Why did politics have to be so ugly? I'd thought Essie Espinoza was different from other politicians, was above the name-calling and backstabbling and mudslinging. Maybe I'd been wrong. Then again, maybe I was overreacting. It's not like she'd come right out and called him a geezer.

I cast a glance at Paige to gauge her reaction. She hadn't seemed to take offense at Essie's stabs at her boss. Given the comments she'd made about her intern job previously, her lack of commitment to Senator Sutton didn't really surprise me.

"Cheap foreign labor has wreaked havoc on our manufacturing sector," Essie continued, "putting factories out of business and Americans out of work. But"—she wagged her index finger—"this isn't all about self-interest. Chinese workers are being exploited by large corporations, forced to work in bad conditions and paid so little they can barely survive. That's not fair, either. Something must be done to protect workers both here in the U.S. and in China. That's why my first order of business as your new senator will be to propose a bold new bill to level the playing field, to impose the same kinds of taxes on Chinese imports here that they impose on American goods in their country. I'm calling this bill the American Tariff Against Chinese Commodities Act, or ATACC. Because our economy is under attack, kids. American jobs are under attack. Human rights are under attack. Your very futures are under attack." She jabbed an outraged finger on the podium. "I'm the candidate who will fight the good fight and win—" She paused for effect before lifting her finger to point at the crowd and crying, *"For you!"*

The crowd roared again.

Essie's speech went on to touch on dark money in politics and the Citizens United case, in which the Supreme Court ruled that the First Amendment prohibited the government from restricting campaign contributions from nonprofit corporations. The ruling opened the door for individuals to secretly funnel money to candidates through nonprofits the donor controlled. "Government should not be for sale to the highest bidder!" Essie cried.

Again, the crowd roared in support.

Still, while Essie Espinoza talked a good line to the public, she was viewed as a rabble-rouser by other politicians. She might prove too polarizing to be effective in Congress. I'd have a lot to think about before deciding whom I'd cast my vote for in the November election.

She ended her speech by crooking her fingers in the horned frog salute and offering a rousing cry of, "Go, frogs!"

Paige, Alexa, and I had been smart enough to stand near the food trucks while the speech was under way. When Essie gave up the mic and the windows opened on the trucks, we were the first in line.

Given that the food was gratis, I would've expected the servers to scrimp. Instead, they were generous, loading so much melted cheese onto the tortilla chips that they were more soup than nachos. After getting our free food, I sat on the grass, Brigit lying in front of me, Alexa and Paige to either side.

Paige shoved a cheese-and-bean-covered nacho into her mouth and moaned in bliss. "Mmm. These nachos are so good!"

"Good enough to make you switch teams and vote for Essie?" I asked, licking a bit of salsa from my thumb.

"Maybe," Paige replied with a grin.

"Ugh," Alexa said. "Asshole at two o'clock."

I looked up to see Logan approaching, a heaping paper plate of cheese-drenched nachos in his hands. Without invitation, he dropped to the grass next to us. I was tempted to ask if he'd taken care of his crab problem. Didn't want one of the critters crawling out of his shorts and making its way over the lawn in my direction. I found myself reflexively shifting to put my legs under me and lift my nether regions higher. If a crab wanted to make its home in my crotch, it was going to have to put forth some effort to get there.

"You can leave now," Paige told him.

"You can't tell me what to do," Logan replied with a

grin, "it's a free country. Essie said so herself." He
gestured to the elevated stage at the front of the green-
belt where Essie remained, speaking with school officials, probably chancellors and provosts, whatever those
were.

Paige rolled her eyes.

Movement near the stage caught my eye. Essie Espinoza appeared to be leaving now, her entourage, surrounded by blue uniforms, moving en masse toward their
cars, which were parked in a restricted zone beside one
of the nearby buildings. Before Essie could slip into an
SUV, Trish LeGrande scurried up, followed by her cameraman. Rather than her trademark pink, Trish was
dressed in TCU purple tonight. Appropriate, given that
she was an alum, having earned her master's degree in
journalism here. She managed to slip that personal tidbit into interviews and reports on occasion. But who
could blame her for being proud? That same journalism
program had produced the well-respected journalist
Bob Schieffer.

Logan's gaze spotted Trish, too. "That reporter has a
great rack."

The words were out of my mouth before I could stop
them. "God, Logan! You're such an ass."

He merely laughed in return. "I've been called
worse."

I'd bet he had. Deservedly, too.

"I want to hear the interview," I told the group. When
none of them made a move to come with me, I said, "I'll
be right back."

Leading Brigit on her leash, I stepped over to listen.
I didn't have to worry about Derek or Officer Spalding

outing me. Spalding was a professional and wouldn't do anything to inadvertently out a fellow officer working undercover. As for Mackey, heck, he hardly acknowledged me when I was in uniform working alongside him. No need to worry about him paying any attention to me now.

Trish stepped into place next to Essie, and the cameraman began to roll.

Trish smiled at the camera. "I'm here at my alma mater, Texas Christian University, where senatorial candidate Esperanza Espinoza held a student rally this evening. Would you say tonight was a success, Esssie?" Trish tilted the microphone toward Essie.

"I certainly would," Essie said. "We had a huge turnout, bigger than we could have ever expected."

How much of that turnout was for her and how much was for the free nachos was debatable. College kids could be bought off cheaply and easily.

Trish held the mic to her own mouth again. "Polls show that you've gained on Senator Sutton and that the two of you are neck and neck, but your detractors say that you lack Monty Sutton's experience and influence, especially when it comes to foreign relations. How would you respond to that?"

When the mic angled her way again, Essie offered a patient smile. "I'd say that we've seen the results when things are done the same old way year after year. Congress has stagnated, and little, if any, real progress is being made. It's time for some fresh faces and fresh ideas in Washington, D.C."

Both apparently happy with the sound bite, Trish

thanked the candidate and Essie slid into the passenger seat of the SUV.

I returned to my place on the grass, watching as the motorcade headed out. Officer Spalding pulled his cruiser onto University Drive and flipped on his lights, stepping back out of the car and raising a hand to keep oncoming traffic at a halt while the politician and her staff pulled out in their vehicles. Derek was the last to leave, rolling out in his cruiser and hooking an illegal U-turn to head north.

An elbow drew me back to the conversation taking place around me.

"What?" I asked, looking from Alexa to Logan to Paige, unsure which of them had addressed me.

"Club Bassline?" Alexa said. "Friday night?"

The thought of going to a loud nightclub packed wall to wall with people and being jostled all night sounded like hell. So, naturally, I replied with, "Sounds like fun. Count me in!"

TWENTY-SEVEN
QUESO ME MUCHO

Brigit

Drips of nacho cheese seemed to be everywhere. On people's legs, on the grass, on the sidewalk, on the plates people had left behind. Brigit must have died and gone to heaven!

As Megan led her away, the dog did her best to catch every bit, whipping her tongue out to clean a knee here, lick a plate there. The unexpected treat more than made up for the loud noise she'd had to endure. *Yum, yum, yum!*

TWENTY-EIGHT
CROWD SOURCE

The Dealer

Essie Espinoza had drawn a huge crowd. He had to give her that. The food trucks had been a brilliant idea. Nothing brings out college kids like free food.

He punched the gas and drove off, but even with the windows down to clear the air the scent of spicy peppers pursued him.

TWENTY-NINE
PINGED

Megan

As I walked back to the dorm with Paige and Alexa, an attractive Asian boy approached from the opposite direction. His hair swept up and over in dark spikes made shiny with hair gloss. He wore jeans and a casual tee, one hand clutching the strap of the backpack slung over his shoulder, the thumb of the other hooked around a belt loop. He lifted a chin in acknowledgment to Paige, and she raised a hand in return.

"Who's that?" I asked under my breath. "He's hot."

Behind Paige, Alexa cringed and shook her head, making a cutting motion with a bladed hand and silently mouthing the word "no." *Oops.* Looked like the guy was an off-limits subject. Of course Alexa's warning had come too late.

"Chaoxiang?" Paige said, frowning. "Yeah, I guess he's hot. But don't waste your time. I think he's got a girlfriend."

Before I could ask how she knew the guy, whether he lived in our dorm, my phone jiggled in my pocket. I pulled it out and checked the readout. *Aunt Jackie.* My pulse picked up.

Had Detective Bustamente identified the dealer picking up my payment at the taco stand?

Would Brigit and I be able to move back home?

"I gotta take this," I said to Alexa and Paige. "See you later."

As they continued on, I pushed the button to accept the call. "Hi, Aunt Jackie." I stepped away from the flow of foot traffic on the sidewalk so no one could overhear my conversation. But just in case, I figured it couldn't hurt to speak in code. "Did you or Uncle Buster take out the trash?"

"What the hell are you talking about, Officer Luz?"

So much for code, huh? "Did you figure out who picked up the cash I left under the trash can?"

"No," she said. "Hector said there were so many people in and out of that bathroom they might as well put a revolving door on it."

Rats.

"He had a dash cam running on his car," she added. "He parked on the street where he could pick up all the license plates of cars going in and out of Tio's lot. I'm going to review the footage and see if I can trace any plates to convicted or suspected dealers."

"I hope something turns up."

"Me, too," she said. "In the meantime, we've pinged the phone."

My heart rate rocketed. "Where is it?"

"On the TCU campus. We've been able to narrow its location down to the main library. That's as precise as we could get."

"That's fantastic!"

"Head on over there ASAP and see what you can find out," Jackson directed. "Let me know who you see there."

"I'm on it." I thumbed the button to end the call, turned toward the library, and set off in a hurry, Brigit trotting along with me. This case could be over soon. Maybe even tonight. God, I'd love to be back in my own bed, to have my bedroom all to myself rather than sharing the space with an emotional time bomb like Emily.

As I approached the building, my excitement began to fade. Not only did the library have a large footprint, it was three stories high. When Detective Jackson had said they'd narrowed things down, I'd expected things to be easy. This search would likely be anything but.

When I went inside and glanced around, my hope faded further. Dozens of people moved about inside the space, and a steady stream of students made their way in and out of the building. If the library was this bustling in summertime, I could only imagine what it was like in the winter when the student population was much higher. Finding the person with the cell phone I'd called wouldn't be as hard as finding a needle in a haystack, but it wouldn't be a cinch, either.

I decided my best course of action would be to survey the place, see if anyone looked suspicious. I made my way past the main information desk and around the first floor, walking slowly past the line of group study rooms. The outer wall of the rooms was glass, allowing passersby to see inside.

Some of the rooms contained small groups of students ardently bent over their books and notes, while others contained larger groups of students kicking back in the chairs, their feet up on the table as they chatted and laughed. Those latter groups had clearly met up here to socialize rather than study.

As I glanced into the last room, a flash of red hair caught my eye and my feet stopped moving of their own accord.

Ruby Rathswohl.

She sat at the table, a hand in her hair as she stared down at a textbook, a pen poised in her other hand to take notes in the open spiral in front of her. In the room with her, sitting on the opposite side of the table, was a tall boy with brown hair, quite possibly the boy I'd seen her with at Panther Pavilion. Also in the room were another boy and girl who didn't look familiar to me.

When the boy I didn't recognize looked up and caught my eye, I realized that I had not only been standing there too long, but that I was gaping. *Some undercover agent I am, huh?* I forced a smile and a wave and continued on, turning to make my way back into the stacks.

I stopped between the shelves to process this information. Ruby Rathswohl, the girl I was more and more certain had been with Miranda Hernandez when she'd collapsed on the Fourth, was here in the library. The boy sitting across from Ruby looked very similar to the boy who'd also been with Miranda on the night she collapsed. The person who was selling Molly, whose number I'd obtained from the bathroom stall, was also here in the library.

Coincidence?

Or clue?

I decided I'd push my luck and find out. I waited a few minutes, found a vantage point between the shelves from where I could peek through a two-inch break between books and see into the study room, and pulled out my cell phone to dial the dealer's number.

I watched Ruby carefully as the phone rang, but she made no move to go for a phone, continuing to look at her textbook and chew on the end of her pen. The tall boy made no telltale movements, either.

Hmm . . .

Just as it did last time, the call went to voice mail after a single ring. I jabbed the button on my phone to end the call.

Had Ruby or the boy ignored the call?

Had their phones been on silent?

There was no way I could know for certain. And until I did, I had to make sure I'd explored all of the possibilities.

I slid my phone back into my pocket and stepped out of the stacks, continuing around the space with my partner, checking things out on the first floor. I carefully eyed the students I passed to see if they were familiar faces from the dorm. While one or two others rang a bell, many did not.

We took the stairs up to the second floor and slowly made our way around, weaving up and down through the stacks, looking over the shoulders of the people sitting at the study carrels. Well, I looked over their shoulders and Brigit instinctively sniffed at their backpacks and legs. One boy had somehow smuggled a plate of soggy nachos past the front desk, but violating the no-food policy hardly made him a criminal.

As Brigit and I headed up from the second floor to the third, a voice from above called, "Hey, Morgan."

I looked up to see Hunter coming down the stairs, taking them two at a time, his backpack slung over one shoulder. With his boyish good looks and loose-limbed style, I half expected him to break out in some boy band song and do a sliding side-step dance move.

I stopped on the landing. "Hi, Hunter."

"Got some studying to do?" he asked, hopping to the landing with both feet together.

"Unfortunately."

He leaned to the side and checked out my empty back. "Where are your books and stuff?"

Yeah, Morgan. Where? "I'm doing research," I said. "I need to take a look at some primary sources." *Primary sources?* I'd pulled that out of my metaphorical back end, hadn't I?

"Oh," he said. "What are you researching?"

Fortunately, there was no need to reach again into my back end. Essie Espinoza's speech provided me with fresh fodder for an answer. "Campaign financing."

"That seems to be a hot topic."

"I guess that's why the professor is making us write about it." *Go, Megan, go!*

He gazed at me a moment before asking, "So, what are you doing this weekend?"

Was he planning to ask me out? If he was, how could I let him down easy? Or should I go out with him and pick his brain on our dormmates? I wasn't sure how to handle things, so I opted for telling the truth. "Paige and Alexa and I are planning on going to Club Bassline Friday night."

"Club Bassline." He gave me a soft smile. "Maybe I'll see you there."

"That would be great." *I can teach you what it's like being a grown-up.*

"Later." He continued down the stairs, virtually skipping now.

I ascended the next flight, guilt tugging at my heart. I was leading the poor kid on, wasn't I? But what choice did I have? I had to play my part to the best of my ability, and flirting with boys was part of the role.

As I ventured onto the third floor, something dawned on me. *What if Hunter is the dealer?* God, I hoped not. He seemed like a nice guy. It would stink if he turned out to be involved in drugs.

Forcing the thought aside, I circumnavigated the third floor. There were far fewer students on this level, only a handful scattered about. Most looked older, like seniors or maybe graduate students.

Taking a seat at an empty study carrel, I texted Detective Jackson. *Ruby Rathswohl is on first floor but didn't respond when I called phone again. Not seeing anyone else suspicious. Is phone still in library?*

I'll check, the detective replied.

I glanced around as I waited. A boy had his head down in a study carrel nearby, snoring softly as he took a nap. A girl at a table nearby bobbed her head to music coming through her earbuds as she highlighted a passage in a textbook.

Jackson's reply came back. *Still there.*

There was nothing I could do but make another round, right? Of course I had to do it without raising suspicions.

As quietly as possible, I led Brigit around the floor again. Nobody caught my eye. We descended to the second floor and looped through the stacks, checking everyone out. As we circled the last shelf, a honey-colored ponytail on a girl in the back corner caught my eye. *Is that Emily?*

My focus moved down to her backpack: the black-and-white-checkered print and the mismatched thread where a hole had been patched told me that, yes, the girl in the corner was indeed my roommate. Her cell phone peeked out of the back pocket of her shorts.

I shrank back before she could see me. Had she been in the library when I'd made my first run-through? It was possible I'd missed her. She could have been in the restroom, or moving about on another floor.

I sat down on the floor as if looking at the books on the bottom shelf and peeked over the tops of the row while dialing the dealer's number on my phone. When the phone rang, Emily shifted slightly in her seat, but did not take the phone out of her back pocket. I'd heard no sound of her phone ringing, and I was too far away to tell whether her phone had vibrated in her pocket. Maybe her movement had nothing to do with her phone.

I tried the number again, but she remained still this time. *Hmm . . .*

Frustrated by the lack of definitive evidence so far, I ventured back down to the first floor and slunk through the stacks until I reached the spot from where I'd spied on Ruby and the brown-haired boy earlier. While the other boy and girl were still in the study room, Ruby and the boy who'd been sitting across from her were gone. There were no telltale backpacks in the seats they'd vacated, and nothing on the table to indicate they planned to return.

I rounded the entire first floor to see if they'd simply relocated, but saw no sign of the two. I texted Detective Jackson again. *Ruby and boy are gone now. Has phone moved?* If so, it would point to one of them as being the dealer.

It was several minutes before Jackson replied. *Phone still in library.*

Blurgh! I wanted to toss up my hands in frustration. *Who here in this library right now has that damn phone?!?*

I decided to try a different tack and wait outside the library. I led Brigit outside and took a seat on a bench nearby. I phoned Jackson to let her know my plan. "I'm sitting outside the library now. I was afraid I'd look suspicious if I kept walking around. Can you let me know when the phone moves outside the library?"

"Sure."

I sat there for what felt like forever, the sun setting and the night growing dark, and still there was no contact from Jackson. I got up and walked Brigit around a grassy area within view of the library doors. I sat down in the dark under a tree with her and listened to the rhythmic chant of the crickets. *Chirp-chirp-chirp.* Still there was no contact from Detective Jackson.

While the library schedule posted on the window indicated it was open twenty-four hours during the fall and spring semester, it closed at nine in the summer, reopening in the early morning. At nine, the lights dimmed, first on the third floor, then on the second, then on the first. The last remaining diehards filtered out into the night, none of them spotting me and Brigit watching from across the way. Other than Emily, none of them looked familiar. Still there was no contact from Jackson telling me the phone had moved. I wasn't sure whether to try to follow any of these students or not. If so, which one? I had no idea. A couple of people I recognized as the front desk staff came out, locking the door behind them.

I texted Jackson. *Library just closed. Everyone seems to have left the building.*

She texted back. *KingFish says phone is still in library.*

How could that be? Was the dealer a night janitor? Or had Ruby or Emily or whoever the dealer was left the phone behind by accident?

I sent her another message. *What should I do?*

Get some sleep, she replied. *We'll figure this out tomorrow.*

I roused Brigit and we headed back toward the dorm. Emily was still awake and working on chemical equations when we entered the room. Though I greeted her with a "Working hard, I see," she either ignored my comment or didn't hear me with her earbuds in. Regardless, she failed to greet me, apparently in one of her bad moods again.

I washed my face, brushed my teeth, and put on my pajamas. Climbing into bed, I rounded up my laptop from the desk, sat facing Emily's back so that she couldn't see my computer screen, and opened a new document. Over the next few minutes, I pulled my scattered thoughts together and set about making an inventory of my list of potential suspects and the evidence both against them and in their favor.

Suspect #1: My roommate Emily.

Evidence against her: mood swings and appearance indicate possible drug use. She directed me into women's bathroom in lobby of dorm where I found Fun Time Molly's phone number. The vitamin C bottle found in air vent could belong to her. Fingerprint confirmation is pending. She was in the library when the dealer's cell phone was pinged there. She could use some extra money.

    Evidence in her favor: 4.0 GPA. Would this make her too smart to get involved in drug dealing?

Suspect #2: Ruby Rathswohl.

Evidence against her: She was likely the girl with Miranda Hernandez at Panther Pavilion. Brigit alerted to drugs in her room. Though no drugs were found in a later search by campus police, she could have moved or sold them in the interim, or taken them out to the trash. Like Emily, she was in the library when the dealer's cell phone was pinged there.

    Evidence in her favor: None.

Suspect #3: Ashleigh White.

Evidence against her: She sold pills to her visiting friend and Colby Tibbs, though they have both stated they believe the sales to be isolated cases rather than a regular business for Ashleigh. She has refused to cooperate with police unless given immunity deal.

    Evidence in her favor: She was not in the library when the dealer's phone was pinged there.

Suspect #4: Miranda Hernandez.
Evidence against her: She used Molly on the Fourth of July. She could have sold Molly to Ashleigh White before the Fourth.

Evidence in her favor: She was not in the library when the dealer's phone was pinged. By all accounts she is not worldly enough to know how to run a drug operation.

Suspect #5: Hunter.
Evidence against him: He'd told me that drugs were easy to get, that all someone had to do was start asking around and a source would appear. He wasn't forthcoming about whether he used drugs himself. He was in the library when the dealer's phone was pinged there.

Evidence in his favor: Brigit did not alert on his dorm room. He's too cute to be guilty.

Okay, yeah. I realized cuteness had nothing to do with whether or not the guy might be a drug dealer. But I simply couldn't see it. I hoped my judgment wasn't being clouded by the fact that he had a crush on me, which was flattering.

Suspect #6: Logan.
Evidence against him: Has a rumored lack of moral integrity, along with crotch critters.

Evidence in his favor: He's said nothing to indicate he does or sells drugs. Brigit did not alert on his dorm room. He was not in the library when the dealer's phone was pinged there.

Honestly, I wasn't sure why I even put Logan on

the list. While he was guilty of being a general sleazebag, there was nothing else that pointed to him being a drug dealer. Still, something about him got my senses tingling, and not in a good way.

Suspect #7: Graham Hahn

Evidence against him: I found drugs on him at Panther Pavilion the day Miranda Hernandez collapsed.

Evidence in his favor: He has no apparent acquaintance with any of the victims.

I realized that the evidence in Hahn's favor, which Detective Jackson had initially thought to be important, seemed less relevant now. While he might not have much direct interaction with lowerclassmen, now that we knew the dealer was using cryptic bathroom messages, a secret cell phone, and e-mail and post office boxes to run the operation, the lack of direct contact no longer seemed to exonerate him.

Part of me wondered whether I should add Paige McQuaid to the list. She seemed worldly, and had shown some knowledge about Molly when she'd talked about the importance of users staying hydrated. Of course she'd also stated that she didn't use Molly and that she only knew what she knew because she'd "heard stuff." But Brigit hadn't alerted on Paige and Alexa's room, and neither had been in the library when the cell phone was pinged there, so I felt comfortable leaving her off the list. After all, what college kid hadn't heard something about drugs?

My homework completed, I saved the document for later reference, turned off my computer and desk lamp, and turned over to go to sleep, leaving my roommate to burn the midnight oil.

THIRTY
NIGHT LIGHT

Brigit

Something was wrong with their roommate.

Unlike other humans, she seemed to be nocturnal, like a possum or a bat. While Brigit couldn't tell time, of course, she knew by instinct that it was the wee hours of the night. Why Emily still had her light on, the dog had no idea.

As Brigit watched from the foot of Megan's bed, Emily popped a white pill into her mouth and washed it down with water from a plastic bottle.

Emily might want to stay up all night, but the dog sure didn't. Brigit turned to face the wall and put her paw over her eye to block out the light.

THIRTY-ONE
TRUMPED

The Dealer

He'd tried to negotiate, to barter a deal. He'd rationalized. He'd reasoned. He'd pleaded. Hell, he'd begged. And he'd failed. Miserably.

After all his arguments, all the guy would tell him was, "I'll think about it."

Think about fucking yourself, he was dying to say back. Donald Trump would have said it.

Maybe it was true, after all, that nice guys finish last. Hell, he hadn't been able to finish at all last night. She'd finally said, "I've been done for ten minutes now. Can we call it quits?"

Maybe she should go fuck herself, too.

Then and there, he made a vow to himself. He'd do whatever it took to get ahead. No more playing by the rules. And no more playing nice.

Hell, the whole world could just go fuck itself.

THIRTY-TWO
IMMUNITY, IMPUNITY, IMPURITY

Megan

Halfway through my class Thursday morning, my phone jiggled with an incoming text. It was from Detective Jackson. *Call me*.

Unfortunately, the interruption would cause me to miss the remaining discussion about polarization in American politics. But fortunately, the room was a large one with a back door that enabled me to quietly slip out without causing too much disturbance.

I held Brigit's leash close as we stepped through the door, and closed it as quietly as possible behind me. Knowing my conversation with Jackson could be overheard in the hallway, I hurried down the corridor and three flights of stairs, dialing the detective as I exited the building.

She answered as I hurried over to a quiet place near a row of bushes.

"We worked out the immunity deal with Ashleigh White," she said.

"Did she identify the dealer?"

"Unfortunately, no. She got her Molly the same way you are, by calling the number she found in the bathroom and having the drugs sent to a PO box. She said they came in a small padded envelope."

"Does she have the envelope?" If so, it could be dusted for prints.

"She threw it out."

Dammit! "What about the return address?"

"She doesn't remember there being one on the envelope."

"What about the postmark? Could she tell where the drugs had been mailed from?"

After all, for all we knew there could be more than one person involved here. One person could be handling the money pickups, while another could be handling the delivery of the drugs.

"She said she didn't think to look. Kids these days don't get much snail mail. They hardly know where to put a stamp, let alone know that they can tell where a package was mailed by the postmark."

I exhaled in frustration. "So she gave you no new information?"

"A little. She said that her drop point for the cash was in the family bathroom at Chisholm Trail mall. She was told to tape the money underneath the countertop."

I was familiar with the mall, which sat within the boundaries of the Fort Worth PD's W1 Division. Brigit and I had nearly been blown to smithereens by a bomb there.

"The mall management is getting us a copy of the security-camera footage from the outer hallway. Of course there's no footage from inside the room. It may take a few hours, but I'd like you to come take a look. I'll text you when I've got it. You can review Hector's dash cam video then, too. We weren't able to identify anyone from it, but maybe you can."

"It's a plan. Any luck with the IP address on the dealer's e-mail?"

"Our tech guy confirmed that your e-mail came from an IP address associated with the TCU library."

"That means the dealer has to be a student or staff member. So we're definitely on the right track, right?" Given that TCU was a private university, access to the library was only granted to those with a student or staff ID.

"It certainly looks that way," the detective replied.

"What about the cell phone?"

"We've pinged it several times this morning. It hasn't moved. I'm beginning to think that whoever it belongs to isn't carrying it around with them."

"You think they left it in the library?"

"Possibly."

I thought that tidbit of information over. "That would point to a staff member, too, wouldn't it? If a phone were just lying around in a public area, someone would probably pick it up and turn it in to lost and found or keep it. But a staff member could have a cell phone plugged in at their desk and nobody would think twice about it."

"It would seem that way," the detective said, "but I won't be convinced until you've checked all the public areas. The phone could be plugged in behind a potted plant, or tucked behind a copy machine. Who knows?"

It was my job to know. Or at least to try to find out. "I'll go back and take a close look around."

"If you find the phone," she said, "leave it in place for the time being. We don't want to risk alerting the dealer if he comes to check on it."

"Got it."

"One more thing," she said. "Ashleigh had a second pill in her purse. She's turned it over to us. The lab is going to run it, see what else might have been in it besides MDMA. They can also compare it to the pills you found in the air vent and see if they appear to be from the same supplier."

With that, we ended the call.

I made a beeline for the library. The building was even busier today than it had been the night before. I slunk around, surreptitiously checking out all of the outlets. While most were on the walls, a few of the beams contained outlets as well, while others had been installed in the floor and covered with flat plastic inserts to protect them.

When I reached the bank of copy machines on the first floor, I set my backpack down on the floor next to them and pretended to riffle through it while I leaned forward and glanced behind the copiers. The three plugs in the twin outlets were attached to cords that ran to the machines. Nothing unusual here.

I continued around the space. In a couple of spots, students studying had plugged their laptops and cell phone chargers into outlets near them. Nothing unusual about that, and given that they were being obvious about it, no red flags were raised.

I led Brigit up to the second floor and we did the

same. I looked around to make sure no one was watching me before checking behind the single copier on this floor. *Nope. Nothing.* More cell phones and laptops openly plugged into outlets, their owners working in close proximity.

Like last night, the third floor was significantly less populated than the others, only a random student here and there, types who looked less sociable and/or more stressed out and had come to this floor for the relative peace and quiet. I meandered around and checked every outlet. *Nope. Nope. Nope.*

I'd found nothing. *How can that be?*

A student bent down and removed a book from a bottom shelf in one of the stacks, making me realize that there could be more outlets on the walls behind the books. The other outlets were placed about a foot high on the wall, give or take an inch or so. That would put the outlet's height just under the second shelf.

I cruised the room again, kneeling down at each row of books that was set against a wall. In the far back corner my eyes spotted something plugged into an outlet behind a tall, thick hardback. *Paydirt.*

I pulled out the book, an extensive treatise on the history of art in the Ottoman Empire, and peeked behind it. The thin cord ran down from the plug and disappeared under the bookshelf. I reached my hand behind the books and felt around. Sure enough, my fingers found something hard and rectangular that had to be a cell phone.

Rather than contaminate the evidence with my prints, I left the phone there and replaced the book, making a mental note of its location so I could return just before closing time to remove it.

I glanced up and around to see if there were any security cameras here that might have recorded the person plugging the phone in. Unfortunately, there were none. To be expected, I supposed. The dealer had taken pains to place the phone in a discreet place. He or she would have been smart enough to check for video cameras.

I stood and led Brigit down the stairs and outside. Despite the dark thunder clouds that had begun to gather in the sky, the heat was as bad as ever. Worse even, because it was moist and humid, smothering the city like a wet blanket. It took only a minute of walking for my skin to break out in sweat and Brigit's tongue to loll out as she panted.

We returned to the dorm for lunch. I sat with Jasmine and another girl, today indulging in a pasta salad rather than a green salad for the sake of variety. As we ate and chatted, a loud *crack* of thunder came from outside. Brigit whimpered and attempted to climb onto my lap. It was hard to blame her. Last spring, she and I had been caught in a tornado that flipped our squad car over.

"It's okay, Britney," I reassured her. "Everything's going to be fine."

"Poor thing," Jasmine said. "You think some pizza would make her feel better?"

As if she understood she'd been offered people food, Brigit's ears perked up and she looked from Jasmine to me. "Okay," I told Brigit. "But only a little bite."

Jasmine offered Brigit a piece of crust with some

sauce and cheese on it. The dog scarfed it down in three seconds flat.

Another crack of thunder told me the weather had gotten worse. It also told me I should round up my umbrella from my dorm room.

I slid my ID through the skimmer and went into the room to find Emily sitting on her bed, staring into space and looking dazed.

"Are you okay?" I asked.

"I feel a little dizzy."

"Lie down," I told her, worried she might keel forward off her bed.

She obeyed, lying down with her head on her pillow and closing her eyes.

I stepped over beside her bed. "Should I call someone? Take you to the clinic?" There was an on-campus medical office for minor issues.

"I'll be fine," she said.

I stared at her for a moment. My concern led me to be blunt. "Did you take some kind of drugs, Emily? Like an ADHD med or speed or something?"

Her eyes flew open. "You think I'd do something like that?"

Her tone dripped with insult and moral outrage. I could only imagine how much more insulted and outraged she'd sound if she knew I suspected her not only of taking drugs, but also selling them to her fellow students.

"I've only known you for three days, Emily," I said in my defense, "and during that time you haven't exactly opened up much. How should I know what you would or wouldn't do?"

She threw her arm back to cover her eyes and lay quietly for a moment. "I've been a bitch, haven't I?"

Of epic proportions. Still, I'd seen glimpses of the vulnerable human under the prickly exterior. I'd soften things a bit. "A little," I agreed. "Can you tell me why?"

Her arm still hiding her eyes, she began sobbing then. "I'm so tired! I've been working nonstop and I can barely keep up." She gulped. "This is so hard!"

Drama. One of the things I'd detested about college. Yet, I felt for Emily. She'd been putting forth way more effort than anyone else I'd seen.

"Give yourself a break," I told her softly. "You can only do so much."

A few seconds later she calmed. "Maybe I just need a nap."

"Good idea."

My phone pinged with an incoming text from Detective Jackson. *Got the footage. Come on over.*

"I have to go," I told Emily as I slid the phone into my pocket. "But promise me you'll contact the advisor or the front desk if you need help getting to health services."

"I promise," she said.

Rounding up both my umbrella and my partner, I stepped out of the room and hurried down the hall, eager to see who I might recognize from the mall security recording and Detective Bustamente's dash cam footage.

One look out of the glass doors of the lobby told me it was raining cats and dogs outside. I opened my umbrella—*shnap!*—and wrapped Brigit's leash around my hand, pulling her close to my leg. I led her out onto the covered steps at the front of the dorm. Another crack of lightning lit up the sky, followed by a loud rumble of thunder, followed by Brigit plunking her butt down on the concrete and refusing to budge.

"Come on, girl!" I called cheerfully, patting my leg with the hand that held the leash.

She gave me a look that said I must be crazy if I thought she'd "come on" in that weather.

"Be a good girl," I told her.

The look of disdain remained. She had no interest in being a good girl if it meant she'd have to venture forth in this monsoon.

I played the only card I had left. "Treat?"

Even that didn't seem to motivate her. I finally had to use both hands to pry her rear end up from the cement and use my mean voice to get her to come along.

I jogged as fast as I could to the parking lot and loaded my partner into my Jeep, feeding her three liver treats before climbing in myself. Great. The car smelled like wet dog. *Yick.*

I drove to the W1 station, once again parking a half block down and circling behind the businesses to enter the building. By the time I reached the door, my feet were soaking wet, my shoes *sklurch-sklurch-sklurching* as I made my way down the hallway.

Jackson looked up as I stopped in her doorway. "Heard you coming." Her gaze moved down to my furry counterpart. "Smelled you, too."

"Sorry," I said. "Not much I can do about it."

"Heads up," Jackson called.

When I looked up, she tossed me a thumb drive. When I failed to catch it, Brigit tossed me a look of disgust that said *I could've caught that.* I fished the drive from the floor under the wing chair where it had landed.

"That drive has both the dash cam and mall footage on it," Jackson said. "Take it with you and have a look-see."

"How many hours of footage are there?"

"Ten hours of dash cam," she said. "Bustamente rolled from the time Tio's opened at eleven in the morning until it closed at nine last night. He checked the restroom right before closing last night and the money was gone."

In other words, the dealer had picked up the funds some time yesterday.

"We've got three full days of footage from the mall," Jackson added. "Chances are the money was picked up the first day. The dealer probably wouldn't want to risk someone else finding it and taking it. But I had the mall management give us the additional footage just in case."

Even at four times the usual speed it would take me two and a half hours to review the entire dash cam footage. Chisholm Trail Mall was open from ten A.M. to nine P.M., providing eleven hours of footage each day, thirty-three total, over eight hours' worth at quadruple speed. *Blurgh.* While the other kids in my dorm would be binge-watching their favorite television shows on Netflix, I'd be scouring footage of a parking lot and a hallway outside a restroom. But if I did the work without complaint, showed my dedication to the job, it could only help my career. So I'd suck it up like the dutiful police officer I was.

"By the way," Jackson said, "I made a call to the cell phone and sent an e-mail to *funtimemolly* this morning. The response told me to leave my cash under a trash can at a Texaco gas station on Berry Street. The one that's just a couple of blocks from the university. I'm sending one of the rookies over there in plainclothes to make the drop this afternoon. The station has both interior and exterior cameras, and I'm going to put eyes on the place, as well."

"Another dash cam?"

She nodded. "I put it in a beater car that's been left in the impound lot for three months. We left the car at the back of the gas station's lot. It looks nothing like a law enforcement vehicle, and the station's got an attached repair shop so it shouldn't raise any suspicions being parked there all day." As she turned back to her paperwork, dismissing me, she said, "Let me know if you recognize anyone."

"Will do."

THIRTY-THREE
RAINING CATS AND DOGS

Brigit

Large raindrops pelted Brigit in the face as she and Megan ran back to the car. While Brigit enjoyed a nice swim in a lake or river or swimming pool, especially on a hot day, Brigit hated rain. It was like being poked at random by dozens of wet fingers.

The only thing worse than rain was being forced to take a bath. All that peachy-smelling shampoo. *Ew.* Every time Megan bathed her Brigit ran right outside and rolled in the grass and dirt. She'd much rather smell like the earth than fruit.

When Megan opened the door to their new car, Brigit hopped inside. Why weren't they driving their usual cruiser? Brigit had spotted it sitting in the parking lot at the police station. Brigit liked riding in the cruiser. It had a nice flat space in the back just for her, and she didn't have to try to balance herself on a seat that wasn't made to canine specifications. Like this one, for instance. She turned five times, trying to find a comfortable angle before finally giving up and flopping down sideways.

THIRTY-FOUR
FOR SALE

The Dealer

The shame made him feel tainted. Regret gnawed at his insides like a starved, rabid rodent.

He'd sold out.

Traded his self-respect for a few measly dollars.

It had been an impetuous, stupid decision. And he hated himself for it.

He only hoped that, in the end, it would prove to have been worth it.

THIRTY-FIVE
BINGING

Megan

On the drive back to the campus, I swung by the post office to check my PO box. It was probably too soon for the dealer to have sent any drugs to me, but it couldn't hurt to check. As expected, the box was empty.

As I started the engine in the post office parking lot, I glanced at the clock on the dashboard. If Brigit and I hurried, we could make our afternoon class. While I wasn't worried about Morgan Lewis's grade, I was concerned that skipping classes and leaving early too many times could blow my cover. Best to play the part as closely as I could.

We made it to class in the nick of time. Looking around the room, I spotted an unusual number of empty seats. Looked like many of my classmates had used the downpour as a convenient excuse to skip class. A bad decision, given that the professor decided to surprise us with a pop quiz. Those who'd skipped today would earn a big, fat zero that they'd have to work hard to overcome.

After class, I went back to my room. Emily snoozed

and snored in her bed, dead to the world. I kicked back
on my bed and booted up my laptop, situating myself
so that Emily would not be able to see my screen if she
happened to wake up.

I slid the flash drive Detective Jackson had given me
into the USB port and pulled up the dash cam video
from the day before. An image of the parking lot at Tio's
Taco Stand popped up, the readout in the bottom corner indicating the date and time—yesterday at 11:37
A.M. I played the dash cam video on ten-times speed
until it showed me entering the restaurant. Once I'd left,
I slowed it down to quadruple speed. When I realized
that was still too fast to get a good bead on the people
coming and going from the restaurant, I slowed it even
more, watching it at double speed.

The traffic in the lot picked up, cars driving in and
out, people traipsing into and exiting from the restaurant. On high speed, the effect was somewhat comical.
A man with two bags of takeout in his hands tripped
over an uneven spot on the sidewalk in front of the restaurant and stumbled, frantically swinging the bags and
somehow managing to regain his balance only to drop
his keys when he reached his car. A strong and unexpected breeze lifted the skirt of a woman on her way in
the door, treating me to a view of her lower buttocks and
polka-dotted panties. A group of birds hopped along the
roof, swooping down on occasion to pick at an errant
tortilla chip someone had dropped on the small outdoor
patio at the end of the building.

An hour in, I hadn't spotted anyone who looked familiar and Emily began to rouse, eventually sitting up.

I glanced over at her. The bags under her eyes were

less dark and puffy, and her skin had a healthy pink glow. "Wow," I said, giving her a friendly smile to let her know I was only teasing. "You look almost human again."

She stretched out her arms and smiled back. "I feel almost human, too." Her nose crinkled as she sniffed the air. "What's that moldy stench?"

"Britney," I said. "Sorry. That's what wet dog smells like."

She hauled herself out of bed and headed for the bathroom. "Wanna grab dinner downstairs?"

"Sure." I tugged the flash drive from the port, closed my laptop, and slid both back into my backpack.

As we entered the dining hall, my eyes scanned the space. There was no sign of Paige, Alexa, Logan, Hunter, Ruby, or Ruby's as-yet-unidentified brown-haired male friend. I did spot April, however, and introduced her and Emily. The three of us sat together to eat our meals.

It was barbecue night. I'd filled a plate with sides for myself and sliced brisket for Brigit.

April scooped up a forkful of baked beans. "How are your classes going?"

I tore a piece of brisket in two and fed one half to my partner. "Pretty good. We had a pop quiz in my campaigns and elections class today. I think I did pretty well. There was only one question I wasn't sure about."

"I'm having trouble in calculus," April said. "I just don't get it. It's like my brain has hit a wall and can't go any farther mathwise."

Emily perked up. "I used to tutor in calculus when I was in high school, and I could use some spending money now. Would you be interested?"

"For sure!" April said. "How much do you charge?"

"Twelve dollars an hour."

"That's a bargain," April said. "When can we start?"

"I'm free after dinner," Emily said.

"Works for me," April said.

Sounded like the arrangement would be a win-win.

When I'd finished my potato salad, cole slaw, and beans, and Brigit had licked my plate clean, I excused myself from the table. "I'm going to the library. See y'all later."

Fortunately, the afternoon storm had blown over and, while the walkways were still wet, at least no rain was falling from the sky. Brigit and I headed to the library. First, I made a surreptitious sweep by the dealer's hidden cell phone. *Yep, the charger is still plugged in.*

I ventured down to the first floor, finding a perfect table where I could put my back to the wall and hide my computer screen from passersby, while keeping an eye on the elevator and stairwell to monitor the comings and goings.

I was another hour into the dash cam video when Alexa entered the library alone. She didn't spot me hidden in the corner, walking directly to the elevator and pushing the up arrow button. When the car arrived, she stepped inside and pushed a button.

Before the doors closed, a male student climbed on with her. "Could you push two, please?" he asked.

His question told me that Alexa had pushed the button for the third floor. Was she merely going up there to study? Or was she checking on the cell phone? Could she be the dealer?

To avoid detection, it would be better if the dealer accessed any voice-mail messages remotely. Text messages could also be forwarded elsewhere if the dealer had downloaded autoforwarding software. Given that the dealer had placed the phone in a public place to avoid being connected to it, he or she seemed to be exercising caution. Still, maybe the dealer thought that putting the phone in the library was enough caution. Maybe the dealer occasionally checked on the phone here. After all, I had been able to access the phone with little risk given that it was behind a bookcase at the back of a quiet floor.

Hmm . . .

I decided to go in search of Alexa, see what my suitemate was up to. Maybe I'd catch her in the act of checking the phone and this case could be put to rest tonight.

I left my empty backpack on the table to signal anyone who might be interested in the table that I planned to return. Hugging my laptop to my chest, I tiptoed up the stairs, leading Brigit, exiting onto the third floor. While I didn't catch Alexa in the act of checking the hidden cell phone, I did catch her in the act of sticking her chewed bubble gum under the study carrel where she sat. Not a criminal offense, but perhaps it should be. *Ick.*

Fortunately, Alexa didn't spot me here, either. I led Brigit back down to the first floor and resumed my review of the dash cam footage. The time stamp ticked by at the bottom of the screen, but nobody looked familiar. 4:28. *Nobody.* 5:06. *Nobody.* 6:01. *Nobody.* 6:35. *Wait . . .*

A young man exited the front door of Tio's. He wore a baseball cap and sunglasses, typical of someone who was trying to hide their identity. With his head and much of his face covered, I couldn't tell much about him. His

T-shirt and jeans weren't anything unusual. He had his car keys in one hand, the thumb of the other hooked around his belt loop. The skin on his arms was light brown, indicating he could be Latino, as were many of Tio's customers.

I paused the frame and leaned in, squinting at the image. The quality was poor. To be expected, given that dash cams were intended primarily to capture larger images of traffic stops and high-speed chases where quality wasn't so much an issue. Besides, higher quality meant higher cost. It was a trade-off.

Hmm . . . Something about the guy rang a vague bell, but I couldn't place him. I started the video up again and watched as he sauntered out of camera range.

I went back to a few minutes before, searching for the footage of when he entered the restaurant. Unfortunately, I couldn't get a good look at him going inside. His image was obscured by a group of people who'd hung around just outside the door, having a postdinner chat. All I could see was a hat bobbing up and down behind them and the door of Tio's swinging open as he entered.

I made a note of the exact time stamp of when he appeared. It could be something. Then again, it might be nothing. Maybe he only looked a bit like someone else I'd seen. Besides, I knew from my criminal justice studies how unreliable eyewitness testimony could be. A person who'd been shown photos of potential suspects might later identify one of them in a lineup simply because their mind subconsciously connected the person in front of them with a photo they'd been shown. Lighting could make a huge difference. Skin, hair, and eye color looked very different in a well-lit setting than it did in a dim one. Plus, there were only so many different ways a person could look. Unless they had a distinguishing mole or scar or birthmark, they'd likely fall into one of two or three dozen types. The news was full of men who'd spent years in prison, some on death row, due to faulty eyewitness identifications, only to be later proven innocent by DNA evidence. Still, it was a potential lead, however weak it might be.

As the evening ticked away, I watched the rest of the dash cam video. A group of young men, some of whom wore TCU attire, had dinner at the restaurant, though none of them seemed particularly familiar.

When I was done reviewing the dash cam footage, I pulled up the security video from the mall. Brigit stood and pawed at my leg, letting me know she needed to take a potty break. I took her outside, where she relieved herself at the base of the closest tree, standing and kicking her legs out behind her afterward as if wiping her paws.

We returned to the library, where I began to review the mall tape. The camera was positioned at the end of a hallway and aimed at the three adjacent doors that led to the men's room, the ladies' room, and what was labeled as a family restroom. The mall seemed quite busy. One look at the calendar on my phone and I realized why. The drop date was a Saturday.

As the morning wore on, traffic continued to pick up, mothers with children in strollers taking their children into the more accommodating family restroom. Shortly before noon, a young man and woman came up the hall. They glanced around before the guy grabbed the girl's hand and pulled her, head tossed back in laughter, into the restroom, closing the door behind them. It was clear what they were going into the room for. They were answering a different call of nature, relieving themselves in a different way.

Three minutes later, the door opened slightly and the girl peeked her head out. When the coast was clear, they both stepped out into the hallway and scurried away from the scene of their crime of passion. *Three minutes.* Clearly the guy was a rookie.

At the height of the lunch rush in the nearby food court, there was a flurry of activity at the restrooms. A crowd of people came down the hall, one at the back wearing a knit cap. A hipster, no doubt. Who else would wear a hot winter hat in the height of a Texas summer? He also wore a pair of dark shades. Like the potential suspect I'd seen in the dash cam video, he had light brown skin. *Hmm . . .*

While the males and females split left and right, the hipster tried the family restroom. Discovering it in use and locked, he ducked into the men's room next door. Shortly after a father exited the family restroom with his two young sons, the hipster came out of the men's room and tried the door to the family restroom again. Finding it unlocked now, he slipped inside.

While I'd noticed some people went into the restroom alone, probably for the additional privacy it offered, why hadn't the guy waited in the hallway to use the room? Had he not wanted to remain in view of the security camera any longer than necessary?

A minute later, the guy came back out of the room and strode quickly down the hall. Was he the same guy I'd seen at Tio's Taco Stand? He could be. But he could also be someone else entirely. Just as the dashboard camera provided grainy, low-resolution images, so did the security camera. Yet something told me the two young men could be one and the same.

I made a note of the date and time stamp for this footage also, and texted the information to Detective Jackson so she could take a look for herself.

Yawning, I continued through the footage. Over the top of my computer screen, I saw Alexa step off the elevator and head out of the library. Had she accessed the cell phone while she'd been up on the third floor? I wish I knew. Seeing Seth at the pool and enjoying his kiss had only reinforced what I was missing out on by working this undercover case. Good food. A bedroom and bathroom of my own. Nookie. Seth and I would have to make up for lost time once this investigation was complete. Still, I wondered whether I should add Alexa to my list of suspects.

I turned my attention back to my computer. I'd just begun looking at the following day's recording an hour later when a voice came over the loudspeaker. "Attention, students. The library will be closing in fifteen minutes. If you have materials you would like to check out, please bring them to the circulation desk now. Thank you."

That was my cue. I turned off my computer and stowed it in my backpack. A light shake of Brigit's shoulder was all it took to rouse her from the floor. She and I headed up the steps to the third floor. I saw only one person there, a student who appeared to be around my real age, in his mid-twenties, probably a grad student.

He was packing up his things so there was no need for concern.

I slunk down the back row with Brigit and crouched down, pulling out the book about Ottoman art. Quickly, I retrieved a disposable glove and clear plastic bag from my backpack. After putting on the glove, I reached behind and under the shelf, felt around until I found the phone, and pulled it out, disconnecting it from the charger. One glance at the screen told me it had at least one fingerprint on it. *Yes!* I only hoped it wasn't mine from when I'd felt around for it last time.

I slipped the phone into the plastic bag and dropped it into my backpack along with the glove. As we stood, the library staff issued a five-minute warning over the loudspeaker. *No need to nag,* I thought. *We're on our way out.* Together Brigit and I hurried to my car to take the evidence in for fingerprinting.

Would the techs find a match?

THIRTY-SIX
GET MEOWT OF HERE!

Brigit

When they returned to the dorm room, the girl who lived on the other side of the room, the one Megan seemed to call Emily, hissed at them from her chair at her desk. "Shhh!"

Brigit was a smart dog, and she could tell by the tone and cadence and volume of a person's voice, as well as their scent, what type of mood they were in. Emily had seemed happier the last couple of times they'd been around her, but now she seemed angry again. The girl was like a cat, her moods changing on a whim. Brigit knew cats. She was forced to live with one, a spotted, fluffy one named Zoe. Sometimes Zoe curled up against Brigit and purred. Other times she swiped at Brigit with her claws out, drawing blood. Yep, this girl was as unpredictable as a cat. But at least at the house Brigit had other rooms she could go into to get away from Zoe. Here, there was nowhere for her and Megan to go.

Brigit looked forward to the day when they could have their own bedroom back at the house. They were going back to the house, weren't they?

THIRTY-SEVEN
SCREWED OVER, AND OVER AGAIN

The Dealer

"We've decided to go another way," the prick told him.

"What do you mean?" the Dealer asked, glad they were speaking by phone so the prick couldn't see the confusion and rage on his face. After all the risks he'd taken, the negotiating he'd done, was this bastard backing out on him?

"We don't think you can get the deal done. We've got other options now. Better options. We're going to explore those."

The Dealer exploded. "Why don't you explore your asshole, you son of a bitch!"

The prick laughed. "No need to get nasty. No one needs to know what's gone on between us. We'll keep our mouths shut if you'll keep yours shut, too."

We? "Who the hell is *we*?" the Dealer demanded. Only the two of them were supposed to know about their arrangement. But it was too late. *Click.* The prick was gone.

THIRTY-EIGHT
DANCE MOVES

Megan

Friday morning, I rolled over in bed. The room was surprisingly bright given that it had to be earlier than five-thirty. I'd set my alarm to go off then.

I lifted my head and glanced over at the alarm clock on my desk. The face was dark, no LED digits illuminated. *What the—?* Sitting bolt upright, I grabbed my phone from the desk and checked the time on the device: 6:43 A.M.

Shit!

I was supposed to have met up with Jackson at the station at six-thirty to get the dealer's phone so I could return it to its spot under the shelves in the library promptly when the building opened at seven. *Why hadn't my alarm gone off?*

I leaped out of bed and threw on a pair of shorts, a T-shirt, and a pair of tennis shoes.

Though I'd tried to be as quiet as possible, Emily nonetheless woke. She sat up. "Why are you in such a rush?"

"I've got a paper due at eight this morning and I need to print it out at the library. I set my alarm but it didn't go off for some reason."

She yawned. "Oh. I unplugged it last night. I needed an outlet for my new coffeepot." She gestured toward a small four-cup unit sitting on top of the minifridge. "I bought it with my tutoring money."

I could've throttled her. "Why didn't you unplug your own damn clock!?!"

She shrugged. "It was late. I didn't give it much thought."

I grabbed Brigit's leash. "An apology would be nice!"

She rolled her eyes. "Sorry, jeez."

This inconsiderate bullshit was yet another memory from college I'd hoped to leave behind. I grabbed my backpack and slung it over my shoulder, leaving the room without a good-bye to the self-centered psycho I shared the space with.

I ran down the stairs and led Brigit outside, allowing her to take a quick tinkle in the bushes outside the dorm. It was more than I'd allowed for myself and, believe me, nature was calling loud and clear. When the dog paused to sniff the foliage, I had to urge her along. "C'mon, girl!" We had no time to dawdle this morning.

I sprinted to my car, loaded my partner in the back, and aimed for the W1 station, doing nearly twice the speed limit. Jackson was already in her office when I arrived.

"Any luck?" I asked as I careened into her office, out of breath from rushing down the hall.

She made a show of glancing at her watch. "You were supposed to be here a half hour ago."

"I know. My stupid roommate unplugged my alarm clock."

"You should've activated the alarm on your phone as backup."

I should have. Ironically, I hadn't wanted to irritate my roommate with two alarms going off at once.

She picked the dealer's cell phone up from her desk and held it out to me. "Here you go. There was no match for the prints on the phone. Whoever is selling Molly on campus hasn't been caught doing it before."

Dammit! That meant I'd have to spend more time with my stupid roommate, living in a stupid dorm room. Why I'd wanted to take on this undercover gig I could hardly remember. But speaking of my roommate . . . "Did you get the fingerprint analysis back? On the vitamin C bottle?"

She gave a quick nod. "The only prints were Miranda's."

While this news didn't implicate Emily, it didn't exactly exonerate her, either. She could still have her own stash somewhere. Maybe she had a PO box, too, and left her pills there until she wanted them. After all, PO boxes were accessible twenty-four hours a day, seven days a week.

Jackson handed me another flash drive. "Dash cam footage from the gas station. Take a look and report back." She made a shooing motion with her hand. "Now get back to that library and put that phone back where you found it before you blow this case!"

I turned and ran back out of her office, cursing Emily the entire drive back to the campus. *Stupid, selfish girl.* She'd made me look unprofessional to my mentor. She was lucky I didn't have my police baton with me or I'd give her a nice, solid *whap* with it.

It was 7:42 by the time I put the phone back under the shelf. I'd just returned the Ottoman art book to its place, stood, and taken a couple steps in the direction of the stairs when Emily rounded the end of the row.

"There you are," she said.

"And here *you* are," I snapped. Was she coming to check on her phone? Had she spotted me putting it back? Was she on to me? If so, why not get it out in the open right now? I was sick of her, sick of this case. I just wanted it to be over. I had no weapon or handcuffs with me, but if she was the dealer I'd tie her wrists together with Brigit's leash and take her in anyway.

"Look," she said, a pained expression on her face. "I came to find you because I felt bad about unplugging your clock. I brought you a peace offering." With that, she reached into her backpack and pulled out a banana nut muffin wrapped in a napkin.

"Are you sure that's the only reason you're here?"

She looked taken aback. "What do you mean?"

I gave her a good, long stare, assessing her. She looked more confused than guilty. "Never mind." I took the muffin from her. It was squashed flat and the napkin stuck to it in parts. "Thanks. I've got to get to class now."

I scurried down the stairs, Brigit's nails scrabbling as she tried to keep up. On my way out the front door, I reached over and tossed the muffin into a garbage can. When I turned to push the door open, I saw Emily standing at the bottom of the stairs, her face droopy with hurt. Had I been too hard on her?

"I'm allergic to nuts!" I called across the way, earning me dirty looks from the library staff but at least Emily's face brightened.

I sat in the back corner during my morning class, pretending to be taking notes on my laptop when actually I was watching the dash cam footage from the gas station. The boy from the other videos didn't appear on the screen. But guess who did.

Paige and Alexa.

They drove up to the pumps in Alexa's baby-blue VW Beetle convertible, the top down to enjoy the sunshine. After Alexa started the gas pumping, she did exactly what the warning signs tell you not to do and left the pump running while she and Paige went inside. With the poor quality of the dash cam footage, as well as the fact that stacks of beer and sodas inside obfuscated the interior of the store, I couldn't tell whether the two went into the unisex bathroom. All I could tell for certain was that they emerged with frozen drinks in plastic, dome-top cups.

Had one of them picked up the cash? Or was their visit to the station mere coincidence? The station was the closest one to campus, and catered to student customers, stocking case after case of beer, wine coolers, and hard cider, as well as the usual convenience items like bread, peanut butter, and toothpaste. It would hardly be surprising for a student to stop in. The fact that Alexa filled her tank also lowered my suspicions. She appeared to have come here to fill a need, not just to pick up drug money. Still, it was noteworthy. I texted Detective Jackson and told her what I'd found.

After my morning class wound up, I drove over to check my post office box. *Still nothing.* I wondered if I'd been taken, if *funtimemolly* had kept my money with no intention of giving me any drugs. That would mean I'd spent the week working around the clock for nothing. That would suck. Of course I knew investigative work didn't always come with immediate rewards. In fact, it rarely did. Cases could take weeks, months, or even years before any people were arrested and indictments issued. Call me a blind optimist, but I wasn't going to let a little thing like harsh realities keep me from hoping for a speedy resolution. Nonetheless, I shot off an e-mail to *funtimemolly* asking whether my "order" had been sent yet. Too bad I couldn't track my package like I could when I ordered the latest toys for Brigit online.

I returned to the dorm and sat at a two-person table in the back corner of the dining hall to eat my lunch. I had no interest in company at the moment. I wanted to watch the boys coming and going and see if one of them was the guy from the videos at Tio's and the mall, the one who seemed vaguely familiar. I saw Logan come and go. Ruby and the dark-haired boy who seemed to be joined at the hip. A few other boys I'd come to recognize. But none of them were the guy in the video. Tomorrow I'd spend some time in the dining halls at the other dorms, see if any of the boys there looked familiar.

After eating dinner together that evening, I took Brigit back home. I couldn't take her with me to a loud, crowded nightclub, and no way would I leave her in the dorm with my roommate, the emotional time bomb.

"Don't worry!" Frankie said, scratching that spot at

the base of Brigit's tail that sent the dog into a state of ecstasy. "Zach's coming over to watch a movie. We'll take good care of her tonight."

"Much appreciated," I told her.

On the TV behind Frankie, one of Senator Sutton's new campaign ads played. I hadn't seen the commercial. Emily and I didn't have a television in our room. Few students did. Most streamed the shows on their computers. Besides, I'd been too busy working the undercover case to watch much TV.

As my gaze moved to the screen, Frankie said, "That commercial has played a dozen times today. I could probably recite it by heart."

Airtime, especially in the large Dallas–Fort Worth metroplex, didn't come cheap. Sutton's campaign must have received quite a few contributions for him to be able to afford that kind of play.

The commercial's theme focused on Sutton's skill as a negotiator, and showed him shaking hands after brokering agreements with foreign dignitaries, politicians from other parties, and industry leaders. Unlike Sutton's commercials, which focused on his successes and never even mentioned his competition, Essie's television campaign was subtly malicious, portraying Sutton as a weak, feeble man who had caved on core issues, rather than recognizing his ability to build consensus and make reasonable compromises. While certainly not as blatant as many attack ads, even her minor mudslinging had dampened my enthusiasm for Essie.

I bent down and gave Brigit a good-bye kiss on the snout. "You be a good girl, okay?"

She wagged her tail and gave me a kiss back.

Returning to the dorm, I sorted through the meager selection of clothes I'd brought with me to try to find something appropriate to wear to Club Bassline. *Jeans and a shimmery blouse with sandals? A ruffled knit miniskirt and tank top with heels? Capris with a strapless floral print top and wedges?* I carried my selections through the bathroom. The door to the adjoining room was ajar, lively getting-ready-to-go-out music playing from within, Katy Perry if I wasn't mistaken.

I rapped on their door. "I need help deciding what to wear!" I called through the crack.

"Come on in!" Alexa called. "We'll set you straight."

"Which outfit?" I asked, holding each one up in turn. "This one, this one, or this one?"

Alexa pointed to the floral top. "That's my favorite."

"Ugh, no!" Paige said. "She's wearing the miniskirt and heels."

Alexa frowned at Paige's presumptive veto, but didn't argue with her.

"Thanks!" I said. "I'll be ready in fifteen minutes."

I dressed, applied enough makeup to equip a half-dozen clowns, and floofed up my hair. As I put on my jewelry, Emily returned to the room. "We're going to Club Bassline. Want to join us?"

"Who's 'we'?" she asked.

"Me, Alexa, and Paige."

"God, no!" she snapped. "I'd rather put a fork through my eye."

Gee, Emily. Tell me how you really feel. "Do you have other plans?" I asked. Despite her snark, part of me felt sorry for her. She didn't seem to have many friends.

Or maybe *any*. There weren't a lot of people who would tolerate a volcanic personality like Emily's.

"There's a free movie night in the lounge. I'll probably go down for that."

"All right," I said. "Have fun." *Assuming you're capable of doing so.*

Ready now, I took the shortcut through the bath to Alexa and Paige's room. Alexa wore a cute dress in a deep plum color, along with a pair of gladiator-style sandals. Paige, now dressed in jeans, heels, and halter top that left her shoulders bare, stood from her bed. "You're the designated driver, Morgan. I plan on getting plastered."

Really? Underage drinking? "How do you plan on doing that?" I asked.

She smiled a coy, coral-lipstick-rimmed smile. "I have my ways."

And what are those ways, exactly? I wanted to ask. But I figured I'd act chill and figure it out as the night went on. I was a little miffed that she'd appointed me the designated driver without even the pretense of a vote. She was a fashionable fascist and, so long as none of her subjects objected, she'd continue to reign. As much as I'd like to put her in her place, getting on Paige's bad side wouldn't further the investigation, so I sucked it up and allowed her to treat me like some type of subservient underling.

Ten minutes later, we pulled into one of the parking garages near Sundance Square, the downtown entertainment district. I stopped at the machine, yanked out a green ticket, and proceeded when the arm lifted, finding a spot on the third floor.

We walked a couple blocks over and, as if lured by the throbbing beat coming from inside the bar, stepped into place at the end of the long line outside Club Bassline. The dance club was one of the few venues that allowed patrons aged eighteen to twenty to join their fully adult counterparts, and there were a number of people in line I'd peg as underage. It was past nine by then, and the night was dark, bugs circling under the streetlights. Despite the darkness, it was still relentlessly hot outside. *How many more weeks until fall?*

We chatted as the line inched forward, checking out both the boys and our female competition.

"Check out the girl in the pink dress," Paige said. "Slut, much?"

The girl's tight dress exposed an excess of cleavage and barely covered her butt, but at least she'd worn a pair of footless tights under it. And who were we to judge her, given that we all had our goods on display, too? Funny, the feminist movement had made being a woman so much more complicated. While I didn't envy men their penises, I was jealous of the fact that they didn't have to question everything they did to make sure they were respecting themselves and setting a good example for those who looked up to them. Not that they shouldn't think of these things, but by and large they simply didn't.

As we inched forward, Logan approached with four friends. He was dressed in his usual high-end preppy attire, head to toe in Land's End, J. Crew, and a pair of Sperry Top-Siders. *Could his designer clothing be evidence of drug money?*

"Ugh," Paige said. "Kill me now."

As they continued past, Logan cast a glance our way. "Lookin' good, Paige."

She stared straight ahead, not even deigning to look his way. "Drop dead, Logan."

He responded with a laugh.

Finally, we reached the front of the line.

"I need to see some ID," demanded the bouncer, who had the body and disposition of a WWE wrestler.

We held out our driver's licenses. He checked them and pulled a thick bright red marker from his back pocket. "Turn your hands over." He drew huge *X*s on the back of our hands, which would make it easier for the bartenders and staff to recognize which patrons were underage. "We catch any of you with liquor, you're out on your ass."

"Way to make us feel welcome," Paige muttered.

"You want to feel welcome?" the guy barked back. "Go to church. Now I need twenty bucks from each of you."

Paige gestured to the sandwich board beside him. "The sign says cover is only five dollars."

"That's for adults," he said. "Not the underage crowd."

Paige pulled a twenty from her wallet. "It's not fair."

He snatched the bill from her hand. "Grown-ups spend ten bucks for a mojito. You children pay only three dollars for a Coke. How's that for fair?"

Paige rolled her eyes but stepped inside. Alex and I followed, the drones to the queen bee.

Inside, I suffered a momentary bout of sensory overload. Flashing lights and moving bodies and the smell of alcohol and cologne and a gazillion decibels of techno music overwhelmed me. But a moment later, my senses adjusted and I trailed after Paige and Alexa as they headed for one of the few remaining empty tables in a back corner.

Paige slid onto a stool at the back of the table, while Alexa and I took the stools on either side.

"Alexa!" Paige hollered over the music. "Since Morgan drove you should get the first round."

Again, irritation flickered over Alexa's face but she slid off her stool. I couldn't blame her. Why shouldn't Paige get the first round?

Alexa was a sport, though, and turned to me. "What do you want, Morgan?"

"Sprite!" I yelled at the top of my lungs.

Alexa nodded and headed to the bar for our drinks.

My eyes scanned the place, looking for anyone who might be trouble. Typical cop habit. Fortunately, everyone seemed to be behaving themselves so far tonight.

Alexa returned a couple of minutes later with our drinks, which had been served in red plastic cups rather than the clear glasses the alcoholic drinks were served in. I had to give the bar management credit. They really did seem to be trying to keep kids from getting their hands on liquor.

A moment later, Logan and his friends stepped up to our table.

"Go away!" Paige hollered over the loud music.

Glancing over his shoulder to make sure none of the bar staff were looking, Logan lifted his untucked shirt and pulled a shiny silver flask from his front pocket. It was engraved with his initials in a boxy masculine font. He waved it in front of him. "Sure you're not happy to see me?"

"I am now!" Paige said, grabbing the flask from his hand. She pulled her cup off the table, situated it between her thighs on her stool, and poured a couple of ounces of clear liquid, probably vodka, into her soda.

Though underage drinking was a crime, I couldn't very well do anything about it without blowing my cover. I'd have to let this one pass. At least Paige had the sense to appoint someone more responsible—me—as the designated driver.

She handed the flask to Alexa, who did the same. When Alexa handed it to me, I pretended to do the same, though I put my finger over the spout to prevent any of the liquor from escaping the flask.

"What's in the flask?" I yelled.

"Grey Goose!" he yelled back.

Hmm. Top-shelf stuff. *Did it mean anything?* I handed the flask back to Logan. "Thanks!"

He pointed a finger at Paige. "You owe me a dance for that. I'll be back later to collect."

The place grew increasingly crowded as we sipped our drinks, our gazes roaming around the place. I'd always hated this feeling, of being one of many cupcakes on display in a bakery window, all covered in frosting and sprinkles, hoping they'd be the one a passerby would choose to purchase.

"Woo-hoo!" Paige shrieked, sitting up taller on her stool. "There's Chaoxiang!"

Alexa and I turned to follow Paige's gaze. There, on the dance floor, was the cute Asian boy I'd seen at the political rally on Wednesday, the one who'd texted Paige earlier in the week. The one on whom she obviously had a huge crush. He was dancing with a pale-skinned platinum blonde dressed head to toe in contrasting black. He had some nice moves.

When the song ended and he left the dance floor, Paige slid off her stool. "I'll be back."

Alexa watched as Paige left, then turned to me, rolling her eyes.

I leaned toward her. "What's the story with those two?"

Alexa cupped a hand around her mouth to shout in my ear. "They've slept together a few times, but he won't commit to anything. She won't let it go. She throws herself at him any chance she gets. It's hard to watch."

Looked like Chaoxiang wasn't going to buy the cow, huh? I returned Alexa's gesture, cupping a hand around my mouth to shout into her ear. "How does Paige know him?"

"His father is some big Chinese ambassador or something. Paige met him when he and his dad were at Senator Sutton's local office last spring sometime."

"So Chaoxiang's from China? That's cool."

We reversed positions yet again. "He went to boarding schools on the East Coast before coming here. That's why his English is so good."

As Alexa pulled back, her gaze shifted to someone behind me. I turned to find Hunter walking up. He held out a hand and angled his head toward the dance floor, offering an invitation.

I gave him a smile and took his hand. My insides felt squirmy. I mean, I know I had a role to play here, and it was my duty to do it right, but even if Hunter was over eighteen he still seemed like a kid to me. Besides the *ick* factor, I didn't want to lead the guy on. He was sweet and smart and deserved a nice girl his own age.

He pulled me into the teeming throng and began to move in that loose-limbed way of his, smiling and clearly having a good time. I did my best to match his energy and enthusiasm. As we danced, my eyes spotted Paige and Chaoxiang making their way onto the dance floor across the way.

After three songs, we'd worked up a sweat. "I need a break!" I called.

Hunter nodded. "Me, too!"

We exited the floor, passing Alexa, who was dancing with a guy with one arm raised over his head as if he were hailing a taxi. As we weaved our way back to the table, I spotted Chaoxiang tossing back what remained in Paige's cup. He said something to her and stepped away, heading back through the crowd. By the time we got to the table, Paige was alone and sulking.

"You okay?" I asked.

"No!" she snapped. "Chao's dancing with that whore again." She gestured to the dance floor.

I turned to see her crush dancing again with the blonde and looking like he was having the time of his life. *Ouch.* That had to hurt. I turned back to Paige. "You know he's not the only fish in the sea, right?"

My words had been intended to soothe, but they had the opposite effect. She glared at me with so much fire in her eyes it was a wonder I didn't turn to ash on the spot. Without a word, she grabbed her purse and headed off to the ladies' room.

Hunter took a seat on the fourth stool. "Why do you hang around with a bitch like Paige anyway?"

I laughed. "She is kind of a bitch, isn't she?"

He smiled. "A royal one."

I shrugged. "Just haven't met a lot of people yet."

He looked down into my cup, which sat on the table in front of me. "Need another drink?"

It was half full, but given that nobody had remained at the table to keep an eye on our drinks, I wasn't about to finish it. In the last investigation I'd worked, I'd come across a guy who'd used a date rape drug on several women. The things I'd learned in my police work had made me very cautious. "Another drink? Definitely!"

"I'll be right back."

"I'll come with you."

Hunter gave me that same furtive look he'd given me when I'd questioned whether he used drugs. What did the look mean? Was he annoyed that I didn't trust him not to slip something into my drink? Did he even realize that's why I wanted to go with him?

To allay his suspicions, I forced a smile. "I simply can't live without you, even for a minute."

He shook his head incredulously, but chuckled, too, and turned to go. Before scurrying after him, I emptied what little remained in the other cups at the table into mine and slid them into my purse. I'd drop them off at the police station later and have the fingerprint specialists check to see if any of the prints on the cups matched the ones from the phone.

When we returned with our fresh drinks, both Alexa and Paige were at the table. So was Logan. Paige reached out and slid her hand up and under Logan's shirt, going for his flask.

He laughed and spread his arms wide. "If you want to get in my pants, all you have to do is say so."

Paige yanked the flask out and held it up. "This is all I want."

Logan pushed her arm down and glanced around. "Don't hold it up like that, you idiot! You'll get us thrown out of here!"

Unfazed, she unscrewed the lid and looked around for her cup. "Where'd our drinks go?"

"The waitress must have taken them," I offered.

Paige shrugged, lifted the flask to her lips, and poured the liquor directly down her throat. When she'd emptied the flask, she thrust it at Logan. Her gaze went to the front door and she froze, her eyes flashing with hurt. We all turned to see Chaoxiang and the blonde leaving the club, his arm draped around her shoulders.

"Someone's getting laid tonight!" Logan called. His eyes narrowed at Paige. "Isn't that the guy that you—"

"Shut up!" she screeched. "Shut! The fuck! Up!"

Logan spread his hands again, this time raising them in surrender. "Jesus, Paige! Relax!"

Relax, she did. Logan stormed off and, over the course of the next half hour, Paige grew increasingly mellow. She bought the next round of drinks and smiled and rubbed her hands up everyone's arms and told us how wonderful and beautiful we all were.

"I'm so lucky!" she said. "Y'all are the best!"

Uh-oh. Something weird was going on here.

A guy came by the table and asked Paige to dance.

"I'd love to!" she cried, sliding off her stool.

The guy quickly ferried Paige away to the dance floor.

She returned three songs later with a different guy in tow. She took another swig of her drink and raised it in salute.

He grabbed the cup out of her hand. "What's in there?" Like the guy earlier, he gave the drink a sniff before tossing back a gulp.

Logan returned, apparently having forgiven Paige for silencing him earlier. He sent a pointed look to the guy Paige had brought to the table. The guy took the hint and slipped back into the crowd.

"Let's dance," Logan told Paige.

"Okay," she purred.

Logan led Paige out onto the dance floor, but not until she'd given each of us a hug first. As she went, she smiled and ran her hands over the backs of the people she passed.

The way she was acting, like everyone was her best friend, as if the nightclub patrons were singing a collective chorus of "Kumbahya," made me think—

"Paige is on Molly." Hunter spoke with certainty, his face tight.

"How do you know?" I asked.

"My sister used to use it. She acted the same way. Like everything was kittens and unicorns and rainbows." He looked away as if the memory upset him.

Hmmm . . . What should I make of that?

THIRTY-NINE

THERE'S NO PLACE LIKE HOME

Brigit

There's no place like home! Brigit got to run around in her yard, dig holes, and chase the squirrels. She'd missed doing that. At the new place where she and Megan were living, the dog had much less freedom. Heck, Brigit was even glad to see Zoe, the moody cat. She'd given Zoe a lick across the cheek on her way in, and now Zoe was curled up on top of Brigit, who was herself curled up on the couch.

Brigit wondered if Megan would come back tonight and they'd get to stay here again. She was tired of living in the tiny dorm room. Tired of having to be on her leash all the time. Tired of not getting to run and play and sleep in their big bed.

She felt a vibration as Zoe began to purr from her place on Brigit's back. It was a strange thing, that purring that cats did. But, strange or not, the dog had to admit that the sensation was pleasant. She closed her eyes and enjoyed a moment of Zen.

FORTY
SPENT

The Dealer

He used his cell phone to log in and check the account. The balance was laughably low, the half million long gone. Amazing how easy it was to spend so much money with so little to show for it.

He felt dirty. And tired. And fed up. And exhausted.

It wasn't just the money that was spent. He was spent, too.

FORTY-ONE
NO MEANS NO

Megan

I had little time to contemplate Hunter's revelation before he pulled me back out onto the dance floor.

Logan and Paige danced near us, their moves provocative. Logan slipped around behind Paige and plastered himself to her back, putting a hand on her abdomen and rubbing it up and down, his thumb grazing the bottom of her breast. Paige arched back against him, eyes closed.

My stomach churned. Paige might be snarky and bossy, but seeing her being virtually groped on the dance floor by a guy she despised was making me sick. I knew exactly why she was behaving like this. Seeing Chaoxiang leave with another girl had made her feel sad, and taking the Molly had made her feel uninhibited. But if things with Logan continued to progress, she'd also be feeling itchy in her nether regions and seeing a doctor to get a prescription for Valtrex. The thought that we shared a bathroom was all the more reason for me to do something about this.

Logan put his mouth to Paige's ear and said something. She looked up at him and said something back. When they began to make their way off the dance floor, I grabbed Hunter's hand and we followed them back to the table.

There, Paige reached for her purse. "Logan and I are leaving," she told me and Alexa. "I'll see you back at the dorm."

"No," I said.

Paige laughed. "What do you mean 'no'?"

What kind of friend would I be if I didn't try to stop this? Even though we were only fictional friends, I still felt the need to step in. "You're only leaving with him because you're upset."

She smiled and laughed again. "Do I look upset?"

Alexa tried to help. "How many times have I heard you call Logan an asshole and a jerk?"

Logan didn't even have the sense to be offended. He laughed, too, smirking. "People can change their minds."

When he went to take Paige's arm, I slapped his hand away. "She's on Molly right now. We all know it. You're just trying to take advantage of her."

"It's okay," Paige said, not denying she'd used the drug. "Nobody's taking advantage of anybody. Logan's not so bad, really. I mean, look at him. He's actually kind of hot."

Logan grinned lecherously. "You know it, girl."

I was shouting in Paige's face now. "You're not leaving with him!"

When she merely blinked at me, Logan responded for her. "What she does is none of your goddamn business!"

God, how I wished I had my badge and my gun and

my nightstick right now. My partner, too. I'd take my baton to Logan's backside and let Brigit tear him a new one. Unfortunately, I was armed only with my wits and my words. I looked Logan in the eye. "Unless you want to find yourself facing sexual assault charges, you'll get your sorry ass out of this bar right now!"

That wiped the smirk off his face.

"That's bullshit!" he yelled back. "I'm not forcing her into anything."

Hunter stepped between us. While he was thinner than Logan, he had a couple inches on the guy. "Look, man," Hunter told Logan. "This is getting out of hand. Just go before this gets any uglier."

Logan looked from Hunter to Paige to me. He leaned into my face and snarled. "Cunt!"

His expletive made me want to rip his lips from his face, but at least he walked away then, aiming straight for the doors and leaving the club.

I turned to Hunter. "I could so kiss you right now."

He leaned down, lowering his face to mine and looking into my eyes. "Do it," he said. "I dare you."

I giggled and turned my head.

He put his mouth to my ear now. "Are you refusing because you're not interested? Or are you refusing because you're a cop?"

I stiffened reflexively.

Hunter pulled back a few inches, eyed me, and put his mouth back to my ear. "I knew it."

I grabbed his hand and pulled him toward the door that led to the restrooms. Once we were in the hallway, I looked up at him. "Why would you say something crazy like that?"

"About you being a cop?"

"Yeah."

He smiled. "You mean how did I know? It wouldn't take a rocket scientist to figure it out. But with me being an engineering major that basically makes me a rocket scientist, huh?"

When he saw the irate look on my face, he got down to brass tacks.

"Okay. One," he said, counting on his fingers, "a bunch of kids in the dorm take drugs and end up in the hospital. Two"—he held up a second finger now—"right after that, a new girl moves in with a dog that's supposed to warn her of oncoming epileptic seizures. The dog is a shepherd that looks just like a police dog." He added another finger. "Three, the girl watches everyone in the dorm very closely and asks me questions about drugs." His pinkie shot up now. "Four, the girl who is allegedly an epileptic has spent the entire evening in a bar with flashing lights and hasn't twitched once."

Whoa. He had a point. Flashing lights were known to induce seizures in those suffering from epilepsy. I hadn't stayed in my undercover character well enough. I'd really screwed things up, hadn't I? I should've let Jackson go with one of the rookies rather than insisting she give the job to me.

While I mentally chastised myself, Hunter continued. "Five," he said, holding up his hand with all four fingers and his thumb splayed. "You pulled me over once for speeding. Three or four months ago. You were really nice and didn't give me a ticket, just a warning. I checked out your ass in my side mirror as you walked back to your cruiser. A guy doesn't forget an ass like that." He smiled, his eyes flicking down to indicate my backside. "Plus, I saw your dog in your cruiser that day. She was standing up in the back and wagging her tail."

As much as I wanted to convince him otherwise, I realized any such attempt would be futile. I could only hope he'd kept his conclusions to himself. "Does anyone else know?" I asked him. "Did you mention it to your friends or roommate?"

"No," he said. "I saw what drugs did to my older sister. She used to go to TCU, too, before she started partying all the time and flunked out. She wasted a lot of our parents' money and a lot of her time. It's so stupid. I want drugs off the campus as much as you do."

"So you'll keep this information secret?"

"Hell, yeah, I will."

My body relaxed in relief. "Thanks, Hunter. I really could kiss you now."

He repeated what he'd said earlier, though this time he did it with a soft grin on his lips. "Do it. I dare you."

I stood on tiptoe and gave him a peck on the cheek.

"That's all?" he said. "My tax dollars ought to get me more than that." He shot me a wink and took my hand. "You realize you'll look more legit if you hang with me, right?"

He had a point. "As long as the expectations are clear," I said.

"I'm just trying to build some street cred," he said. "I think I'm the last remaining virgin on my floor."

I gave him a smile. "I bet you're not. I suspect there's more talk than action going on, especially when it comes to guys bragging."

"You could be right."

When the nightclub closed at two A.M., Hunter and his friend walked us back to my car. It was a thoughtful, chivalrous gesture. He'd make some girl a really good boyfriend someday.

Paige frowned. "Logan would never walk a girl to her car," she spat. "I can't believe I almost left with the guy! Did y'all know he has gonorrhea?"

"I thought it was herpes."

"That, too!"

Given that Paige was saying snarky things about Logan again, it was clear the effects of the Molly had worn off. She teetered at several points along the way, still a little drunk, though. Several times one of us had to grab her arm to keep her from falling. Fortunately, though, she was showing no symptoms that would require medical attention.

When we reached the car, Hunter opened the back door and helped Paige in, going so far as to snap her buckle into place. She reached up a hand and stroked his hair. "I love your curls. You're like a tall, sexy poodle."

He took her comment in stride. "Sexy poodle. The words every guy longs to hear."

She gave him a smile. "I bet you don't have gonorrhea or herpes."

"Nope," he said, cutting a look my way. "I'm disease-free."

After he shut the back door, he bent down and gave me a peck on the cheek this time. "See you later, Morgan."

As he walked away with his friend, Alexa and I climbed into the Jeep. She glanced my way from her seat, giving me a knowing smile. "So. You and Hunter, huh?"

"Yeah," I said. "Me and Hunter."

I started the car and circled down to the bottom level. As I took the last turn, Paige moaned and issued a burping sound, a telltale precursor of more to come. "Oh . . . God."

"No!" I cried, slamming on the brakes and jabbing the button to lower the back window. "Not in the car!"

But it was too late. Before I could get the window down far enough for Paige to stick her head out, she'd belched vodka-scented Dr Pepper all over herself and my backseat.

Blurgh.

I looked at Alexa. "Does she do this a lot?"

"All the time," she whispered.

We unrolled all of the windows and, after paying the machine the parking fee, aimed for the dorm. Though I slowed out of habit, the Jeep had no problem with the potholes in front of Flynn Blythe's apartment complex. I wondered if Fort Worth PD had a problem, though. Derek's cruiser was once again in the lot, though this time he wasn't in it. Where was he and what was he doing?

Unfortunately, I could do no investigating for the time being. I had to get Paige back to the dorm and clean out my car.

When we entered their dorm room, Paige began making gagging noises again. Alexa and I led her to the toilet, and I found myself once again holding back the hair of a college student as she puked her guts out. When she'd brought up virtually everything but her spleen, Alexa and I put her to bed, laying her on her side so she couldn't aspirate if she threw up again.

"Keep a close eye on her, okay?" I said. "I'm going to go clean my car and pick up Britney."

Alexa nodded.

Though I could have exited from Alexa and Paige's room, I decided to pop into my room and grab a bottled water from the minifridge. Watching Paige empty her stomach, along with the heat of the night, had made me queasy. Some cold H_2O could help with that.

I walked through the bathroom and opened the door to my room. A lamp glowed from Emily's desk. Her computer was on and the coffee mug I'd bought her sat on the desktop, but my roommate was nowhere to be seen.

Two steps into the room and I tripped over something large on the floor, falling to my hands and knees.

Holy shit!

That something large was Emily!

She lay in a crumpled heap, her eyes closed. I shook her shoulder and screamed her name. "Emily!"

There was no response.

Alexa appeared in the door that led from the bathroom. "Oh, my God! What happened to Emily?"

I put two fingers to my roommate's neck to check her pulse. It was fast and erratic. She seemed to be having trouble breathing, too.

Alexa came into the room and knelt down next to me. "Is she okay?"

I was already dialing 911 and had no time to answer.

The dispatcher's voice came over the airwaves. "Nine-one-one. What's your emergency?"

"I just found my roommate unconscious!" I cried. "Send an ambulance!"

The dispatcher asked several questions in quick succession. Where were we? What was the sex and age of the victim? But then she asked me several questions I couldn't answer. "Has she ingested any drugs, medications, or alcohol?"

"I don't know! I'll look around."

I handed the phone to Alexa while I quickly rummaged through Emily's dresser drawers. I found nothing there. I looked through the purse and backpack on her bed. Nothing. I moved over to her desk and jerked the drawer open. Lying there in the drawer was a package of over-the-counter caffeine pills. Had she been taking these all along? That would explain her jitters and mood swings and sleep problems.

I ran back to Alexa and grabbed the phone out of her hand. "I found caffeine pills in her desk," I told the dispatcher. But were the caffeine pills the only thing Emily had taken?

In minutes, the EMTs arrived. I recognized them immediately. They'd come from Seth's fire station. I could only hope they wouldn't recognize me out of uniform.

No such luck.

As one checked Emily's pulse, the other eyed me. "Meg—?"

"My name's Morgan Lewis," I said, giving him an exaggerated wink to let him know he should play along. "I'm Emily's roommate."

He nodded, still looking a little confused but going with it. "Okay, Morgan. You said you found caffeine pills in her desk?"

"Yes." I handed him the package.

"It would take a lot of these to cause an overdose. But it's not unheard of."

As they loaded her onto a gurney and rolled her out into the main hall I followed them, turning back in the doorway to address Alexa. "I'll be right back. Go stay with Paige."

As the medics pushed the gurney into the elevator, I squeezed into the car with them, having to flatten myself against the cold metal to fit. As soon as the doors closed, I said, "I'm a cop. I'm working undercover. You guys know about all the Molly problems, right? All the kids who've been rushed to the hospital?"

They nodded.

"I worked the one at Panther Pavilion," one of the guys said.

"Is that why you're here?" the other asked in a whisper.

I nodded. "I found some Molly hidden in my dorm room," I said. "I'm not sure if it belonged to the girl who lived there before me, or if it might belong to Emily. There's a chance she might have gotten more somewhere."

"Thanks," they said. "That'll help us figure out what we're dealing with here."

As the doors slid open on the first floor, Emily began to come to, turning her head. "What's going on?"

"I found you on the floor," I said, jogging alongside the stretcher as they wheeled her into the lobby. "You were unconscious."

Her eyes went wide. "What?"

The EMT addressed her as he rolled her out the front doors and down the ramp. "Did you take something? Any medications or drugs?"

"Caffeine," she said, tears forming in her eyes. "I've

got a test on Monday and I was going to pull an all-nighter."

"How much did you take?" the guy asked.

"One an hour since noon," she said.

The EMT glanced at the clock and did the math. "Fourteen pills, then?"

She nodded weakly. "I washed them down with coffee."

My heart twitched in my chest. *I never should have bought her that travel mug.*

"Did you take anything else?" the paramedic asked. "MDMA? Meth? Anything like that?"

"Absolutely not!" she spat. Her disgust sounded sincere.

I put a hand on Emily's arm before they loaded her into the back of the ambulance. "Should I call your parents?"

"Please don't." She squeezed her eyes closed as if to fight her tears, but only managed to force them out. "They'd only worry. I'll be okay."

"I'll come to the hospital," I told her.

She turned her head on the gurney to look at me, a tear rolling from the edge of her eye into her ear. "Thanks, Morgan."

I returned to my room, grabbed my purse, and headed back to my car, which was filled with the stench of regurgitated vodka fermenting on the back floorboard. As disgusting as the odor was, I had to take care of business first. I drove to the W1 station and dropped off the three cups.

The tech slid on a glove before removing them from my purse. "Which cup belongs to who?" he asked.

I'd been in a rush at the club to sneak them into my purse without being spotted and hadn't been able to mark them. "I don't . . . Wait." I'd been about to say "I don't know" when I spotted telltale lipstick stains on the rim of the cups. "The one with the coral lipstick belongs to Paige McQuaid," I said. "The one with the plum lipstick is Alexa's."

The tech jotted the information down before looking back up at me. "And the one with no lipstick?"

"That's Logan's."

"Got it. I'll let you know once we run the tests."

"You'll compare these prints to the ones that were lifted from the cell phone?"

"Of course. I'll let Detective Jackson know the results as soon as we've got them."

I thanked the tech and returned to my car. From there, I drove to my house. Brigit announced my arrival in the driveway by barking her head off at the front window and waking Frankie, who met me at the door.

I cringed in apology as I stepped inside. "Sorry."

She waved a hand. "No worries. How'd tonight go?"

"My roommate's in the emergency room being treated for a caffeine overdose and my Jeep's full of puke."

"Is that good?"

I snorted. "How can an ER visit and a car full of vomit ever be good?"

"I'm assuming it's progress, right? Police work is dirty and messy. You've told me that yourself."

She had a point. It was my point being tossed back at me, but it was nonetheless valid.

"You're right. It's progress." After all, I knew now

that Paige used Molly. I still didn't know whether she was dealing it, too, but I was a step closer to finding out. And I knew now that my roommate wasn't using illegal drugs. She was abusing legal ones. Maybe not a whole lot better, given that she ended up in an ambulance all the same, but at least caffeine caused only short-term adverse effects and didn't leave the user with long-term damage.

I went to the kitchen, where I rounded up a roll of paper towels, a spray bottle of lemon-scented disinfectant, and a garbage bag. I headed back out to my car for puke patrol.

Ten minutes later, the floorboard and mat were as clean as they were going to get and I was high on chemical fumes. I tossed the garbage bag in our rolling can by the garage and returned the remaining paper towels and cleaner to the kitchen. After thoroughly washing my hands, I gave Frankie a hug. "Thanks for watching Brigit tonight. I'm sure she was glad to be home."

"No problem," she said. "Any idea when you might be coming back?"

"Hopefully soon," I said. "The techs are running prints on cups I swiped from the bar. How much longer this will take depends on what they find out."

"Be careful," she said.

"Ironic words coming from a woman who's planning on running into burning buildings for a living."

"I'll be careful, too."

"Good."

FORTY-TWO
EAU DE EW

Brigit

Megan opened the back door of the Jeep and Brigit hopped up into the seat. Immediately, her nose detected odors that had not been in the car when Megan had dropped her at their house only hours before.

There was the acrid, citrusy scent of cleaning spray. Underneath that, there was the scent of liquor and intestinal fluids. She was very familiar with those scents. Her first owner had been a stoner who smoked too much weed, drank too much cheap beer and whiskey, and hung with a crowd of losers just like him. Overdoing it was something they did regularly.

But along with those scents, she smelled the identifying smells of certain people. The two girls who lived on the other side of the bathroom had been in the car recently. But she smelled someone else, too. His scent was faint, as if he hadn't been in the car long, maybe only leaned in or placed a hand on the windowsill. Her nostrils twitched. Yep, she smelled the faint scent of

Hunter, the nice guy who always gave her attention when he saw her.

She wagged her tail. Maybe they'd see him again soon!

FORTY-THREE
THE NUMBERS GAME

The Dealer

He'd been working his ass off, trying to turn things around, and still his numbers weren't as good as they needed to be. His job was on the line. Hell, his *life* was on the line. Because if he lost this job, everything would change.

He'd have no respect.

No authority.

No power.

And without those things, he was nothing.

FORTY-FOUR
FINGERED

Megan

The woman at the desk in the ER waiting room frowned on me bringing Brigit into the space, but relented when I said she was a medical alert dog and issued an implied threat.

"She warns me when I'm about to have a seizure," I said. "If I have to leave her in my car while I wait here, and I have a seizure and get hurt, the hospital could be liable."

I hated to play the liability card, but it was the only one in the deck that would work.

"All right," she relented. "But sit in the corner and keep her away from the sick people."

Given that few diseases were common to both canines and humans, as well as the fact that Brigit had regular checkups and was the picture of perfect health, it was unlikely Brigit would infect anyone. But no sense getting the flustered woman any more riled up. She had her hands full dealing with sick and injured people and didn't need me giving her any more flack.

A few hours later, after the doctors had treated Emily with activated charcoal and laxatives, my roommate was released. She came through the doors that led to the treatment area, her eyes downcast in shame. I stood and walked over to her.

When she looked up, the tears were back. "That was really stupid of me, wasn't it? Taking all those caffeine pills?"

"Even smart girls make mistakes sometimes." Like taking Molly and nearly going home with a crab-infested creep. "But I think maybe you should talk to someone in the university counseling center. You need help dealing with your stress."

"That's a good idea."

We left the ER. It was early morning now, the sun peeking over the horizon. Looked like I'd pulled an all-nighter, whether I'd set out to or not. I couldn't wait to get back to the dorm and get some sleep.

Emily followed me to my car in the parking garage. After she climbed in, she sniffed the air. "Why does your car smell like lemons?"

I cast her a look. "Because it's preferable to Paige's puke."

Her lip curled back in disgust. "She threw up in your car?"

"Yeah."

Emily snorted. "It's been a really fun night for you, hasn't it?"

"There are no words."

She reached over and put a hand on my arm. "Well, I've got a word for you. It's thanks."

"You said that earlier."

She laid her head back against the headrest. "I can't say it enough. You've been really nice to put up with me."

I had to agree with her there.

I slept until one in the afternoon, waking only when Brigit pawed at the side of my bed, letting me know she needed to go out. *Ugh.* I loved my partner with all my heart, but I was feeling darn sick of taking care of others at the moment. *What about me? What about my needs?*

I leashed her up and took her outside, too tired to care that I was still wearing my pajamas and hadn't brushed my hair or teeth.

Hunter walked up as Brigit crouched by a bush. He looked me up and down, fighting a smile. "You look downright scary."

"I'm not surprised. I spent last night cleaning puke from my floorboards and waiting for my roommate to be released from the ER."

His brows lifted. "I'd heard there was an ambulance here last night. It came for Emily?"

I nodded. "She OD'd on caffeine."

"Caffeine?" His brows twisted in confusion now. "Is that possible?"

"Only if you try really, really hard."

"Want to have lunch?" he asked. "After you clean up, I mean. I can't be seen with you looking like that." He gave me a smile to let me know he was teasing.

"All right," I said. "I'll meet you in the dining hall in half an hour."

Brigit and I returned to our room. Emily was still sound asleep, but her breathing was normal and the pulse in her neck appeared slow and constant. I hoped she'd learned her lesson last night. I was pretty sure she had. Drugs were nothing to play around with, and just because something could be purchased over the counter at a pharmacy or grocery store didn't make it safe.

After feeding Brigit a can of dog food and checking my e-mail—still no response from *funtimemolly* on the status of my order—I grabbed a quick shower and shampoo, dressed, and slapped on some makeup. I found Hunter waiting at the entrance to the dining hall. We went in, rounded up some grub, and met at a table in the corner.

He took a sip of his soda and eyed me intently over the table. "You're a wise older woman," he said. "Tell me the secret to getting girls."

"You're sitting with one right now," I told him. "You must be doing something right."

He chuckled at that. "Seriously. Help me out here. What makes a guy irresistible?"

"Okay," I said, sticking my fork in my spaghetti marinara and twirling it. "Honestly? Women are not that hard to figure out or please. How we feel about a guy is only partly about who he is. You're smart and funny and cute, so you've got the initial bases covered."

He sat up straighter, his mouth spreading in a grin and his eyes brightening. "You think I'm smart and funny and cute?"

"Yes." I pointed the loaded fork at him. "But don't go getting a big ego or you'll cancel it all out. Guys who are full of themselves are a total turnoff." I ate the bite of bland spaghetti before continuing. "Besides, that stuff only gets a girl's attention up front. It's not going to keep her hanging around for long. The rest is about how a guy makes a girl feel about herself. Women want to feel special. Pay attention to what makes a g-girl unique, to her particular viewpoints and interests and her positive traits, and find ways to let her know that you've noticed those things, that you appreciate them. And listen. Every girl wants someone who listens."

"Pay attention and listen? That's it?"

"That's it."

"That doesn't sound so hard."

"It's not. Problem is, most guys don't want to put in the effort." I took another bite of my pasta. "Now that I've shared my love lessons, it's time for some quid pro quo. How well do you know Logan?"

"Well enough to know he's a total asshole. The only reason anyone puts up with him is because his parents are beyond loaded and he's always inviting people to their ski condo in Taos or their beach house in South Padre."

"You think he could be dealing drugs?" I asked quietly. "You think maybe he gave Paige the Molly last night hoping it would loosen her up?"

Hunter shrugged. "I can't say. It wouldn't totally surprise me. The guy likes to party. Rumor has it his grades are horrible and that he's on academic probation. I heard he's in summer school to try to get his grades up. We've got some mutual friends from our floor, but I try to keep my distance."

I would, too, in Hunter's shoes. Guys like Logan, who didn't know when to quit, often dragged others down with them.

Alexa and Paige entered the dining hall. Alexa waved to me on her way to get food, while Paige headed straight for our table, plunked herself down in a chair, and laid her cell phone and cheek on the table, closing her eyes. "Make it stop," she whined.

"Make what stop?" I asked.

"The throbbing in my head."

"Take some aspirin," I suggested.

"I did. It hasn't kicked in yet."

If she was looking for sympathy, she wasn't going to find much at our table. She had yet to apologize for hurling in my car.

Her phone vibrated with an incoming text. She sat up and read the message, her face brightening as if she'd been instantly cured of her hangover. "Pool party at six." She looked up at me. "You up for it?"

"Sounds like fun."

We'd be able to cool off and it could give me a chance to question Paige about the Molly she'd taken last night. Had she seen the phone number in the lobby bathroom, made a cash drop somewhere, and gotten the drug via a PO box, or did she have more direct contact with a dealer? Could she, herself, be the dealer? It was possible, maybe even likely. After all, I'd seen her and Alexa go into the gas station where a drop was being made. Of course that fact put suspicion on Alexa, too.

"Who's throwing the party?" I asked.

"One of the girls who lived across the hall last year," Paige said, clicking her phone off and returning it to the table.

Having rounded up some food, Alexa joined us.

"Pool party at six," Paige repeated.

"Awesome!" Alexa said.

We made small talk while we ate. Hunter finished his

burger and headed out, but not until he'd given Brigit a nice scratch under the chin.

"See ya," he said.

When Logan entered the dining hall a few minutes later, Paige ducked her head and shielded the side of her face with her hand in an attempt to hide herself. "What was I thinking last night?"

"You weren't doing the thinking," I said. "The Molly was."

Her head snapped in my direction. "What are you talking about?"

"The way you were acting last night," I said, "it was pretty clear you'd taken some Molly. It's not a big deal."

"Not a big deal?" she spat. "You accuse me of taking drugs and it's not a big deal?"

I raised my palms. "I'm sorry, Paige. I must have misread the situation." *Nope. Didn't misread it at all.* Frankly, her righteous indignation only made me more certain she'd taken the drug.

Her eyes flared, just as they'd done last night when I suggested Chaoxiang wasn't the only fish in the sea. "I was drunk, that's all."

Sure. "Okay. I believe you. Really, I'm sorry. I didn't mean to offend you. It's just that, you know, the group I hung with back in Amarillo did a lot of MDMA. We didn't think much about it."

She stared at me for a moment with the same assessing look Detective Jackson sometimes gave me. I tried to look as sincere as possible. *Yep, that's me! Ecstasy fiend!*

"I'd be happy to drive to the party," I said, hoping the offer would get me back on her good side. The last thing

I needed was her excluding me. The party could present some more opportunities for me to ask questions, gather information.

Luckily, Paige took the bait. "Okay."

I gathered up my trash and stood to go. "I've got some errands to run. Catch ya later."

I tossed my garbage in the can and led Brigit out to my car. Our first stop was the post office. I led Brigit inside as I went to check my PO box. When I stopped in front of the wall of boxes, Brigit put her nose to the ground and sniffed. *Snuffle. Snuffle-snuffle.* While I hadn't ordered her to check for drugs, she sometimes did so out of habit or in an attempt to earn herself a treat, a type of K-9 extra credit. She sniffed at my box and sat down on the tile floor, facing the row, issuing her passive alert.

Looks like my order has been delivered.

My heart pumping in overdrive, I crouched down and slid the key into the box. One turn and it was open, revealing a small padded yellow envelope inside. I removed the envelope carefully, holding it by an edge, and took a look. My alias, Morgan Lewis, was scrawled across the front, along with my PO box address. The return address showed only my PO box number again. The postmark indicated the package had originated in Fort Worth. The package bore four first-class stamps.

I returned to my car and texted Detective Jackson. *Received delivery. Meet at station?*

Her reply came quickly. *I'm already there.*

I should've known. The woman was just as dedicated as I was.

I drove to the station, again parking a block away in a spot that wouldn't be easily visible from the street.

Hurrying Brigit along behind the buildings, I made my way to the station and went inside.

Detective Jackson was on her phone but waved me into her office. As I took a seat, she swiveled the mouthpiece away from her lips and said, "I've got a fingerprint tech on the line." Turning the handset back into place she said, "Uh-huh . . . uh-huh. Okay . . . No need to call her. She's right here in my office. I'll let her know. Thanks for the information."

I was on the edge of my seat. "What did they find out?"

"One set of prints appeared on all three cups—"

"The bartender's?" I asked.

"That's what we were thinking, too," she replied. "The other prints on Alexa's and Logan's cups didn't match the phone."

She hadn't mentioned Paige's prints. That must mean they matched! I jumped out of my seat. "But Paige's did? Her prints matched the ones from the cell phone?"

A smile played about Jackson's lips. "Don't get ahead of yourself, Megan." She motioned for me to sit back down. "It's possible Paige's prints matched."

What? "What do you mean 'it's possible'?"

"Paige's cup had five sets of prints. The ones we believe belong to the bartender, and four others. One of them belongs to Paige. The three others belong to persons as yet unidentified. We aren't sure which set was Paige's. None matched anyone in the system. But, yes, one of them matched the prints lifted from the cell phone."

In other words, whoever owned the cell phone hidden in the library had been at Club Bassline last night and had touched Paige's cup.

"It has to be her," I said. "Doesn't it?"

"But then—" Jackson began.

"Why didn't she show up on the dash cam video from Tio's Taco Stand or on the mall security tape?"

"It's likely—"

"That she's working with someone else?"

Jackson threw up her hands. "Are you asking me those questions, or are you asking yourself?"

"Sorry," I said. "I'm thinking out loud."

"Think back to last night," she said. "Who else drank from Paige's cup?"

Paige had danced with several guys before she and Logan began engaging in foreplay on the dance floor. I recalled her offering her cup to at least two of them.

"A few random guys she danced with drank from the cup," I said. Really, the thing might as well have been a communion wine chalice for all the mouths and hands that had been on it. "I don't know who any of them were. I think they were strangers to Paige, too."

Jackson took the information in. "The fact that the guys were strangers points even more to Paige being the dealer. But in order to arrest her, we'll have to verify that her prints match the ones on the phone. We need to get something that we know for certain has her prints on it and hers alone. You think you can do that?"

My mind went to our shared bathroom, to Paige's plastic bin of hair products and skin products and makeup stashed on the shelf under the sink. I'd seen Alexa dip into Paige's bin on occasion for body spray or lotion. Heck, I'd tried Paige's cherry blossom lotion myself. But her toothbrush was in the bin, too, in a plastic cup. A toothbrush was something nobody else would share.

"What if I get her toothbrush?"

Jackson dipped her head in acknowledgment. "That'll do it. Now show me what you got in the mail."

I carefully pulled the envelope from my purse, again holding it gingerly by a corner. Jackson donned a pair of gloves, picked up a letter opener, and sliced the flap open. Turning it, she dumped out the contents. A small, clear plastic bag fell to her desktop. *Plup.* She picked it up and finagled it between her fingers. "There's two white capsules here. I'll have the lab identify them and check the bag and envelope for prints."

My work there done, I floored it all the way back to the dorm. If the prints on Paige's toothbrush matched the ones on the cell phone, my job would be done. I could move out of the dorm and be back in my own bed tonight. Maybe Seth could be in it with me.

I stepped into the bathroom to find the shower running, the curtain closed, and the air warm and steamy. The mirrors were partially fogged, distorting my image, like an old, faded photograph. Alexa pulled the curtain aside—*swish*—and poked her head out. "What are you wearing to the party?"

Argh! I wanted to scream. I was so close now! But I forced myself to remain calm. "It's a pool party, so my bikini?" I raised my palms. Seriously, wasn't the answer obvious?

"I mean over your bathing suit," Alexa said. "Shorts? A cover-up? A sundress? What?"

It was ridiculous how young women obsessed over what they wore. And why should anyone's outfit be contingent on what anyone else was wearing? Still, I understood the angst. While everyone that age wanted to be noticed, nobody wanted to stick out for the wrong reasons, like an unusual fashion choice.

"Shorts and a T-shirt, I guess," I replied, mentally willing her to close the curtain so I could snatch Paige's toothbrush.

"You guess? You mean you haven't decided for sure yet?"

Oh, for Pete's sake! "I have," I said. "I'm wearing shorts and a T-shirt." *As if it matters!*

"Okay. I'll wear shorts, too." She closed the curtain.

Thank God! I reached down for Paige's toothbrush when *swish,* the curtain slid partway open again.

Alexa's head popped out once more. "Sandals, tennis shoes, or flip-flops?"

It took everything in me not to rip the towel rack off the wall and throw it at her. "Flip-flops."

"Okay." The curtain swished closed.

I hesitated a moment, anticipating another question. When I heard the squeak of her turning the faucet off, I seized the moment, seizing Paige's toothbrush, too. I pinched its bristles to avoid contaminating her prints with my own.

"What are you doing with my toothbrush?" Paige stood at the door that led into her room. I hadn't heard her open it over the squeak of the faucets.

"Sorry!" I said. "I was looking to see if you had any sunscreen and I accidentally dropped it on the floor."

"Ew." She snatched it out of my hand and tossed it into the nearly full trash can. "I'll have to get a new one now." She bent down and rummaged around in her bin, standing with a brightly colored plastic bottle in each hand. "Do you want SPF 15 or SPF 50?"

"Fifty," I said.

She handed me the bottle, returned the other to the bin, and reached down to pull the garbage bag out of the trash can, tying the top in a knot so nothing would fall out. She thrust the bag at Alexa, who'd stepped out of the shower, a towel wrapped around her torso. "Here, Alexa. Take this out when you get a chance."

That same irritated look flicked across Alexa's face, but she took the bag nonetheless.

I held out a hand. "I can do it. I've got some trash in my room that I need to take out, too."

"Great." Alexa handed me the bag.

I returned to my bedroom, where Emily was still sleeping, making up for all those lost hours. I rounded up what little trash we had, dumping it into a plastic grocery store bag, and carried the bags outside, bringing my backpack and Brigit with me. I circled around the back of the building, tossed the bag containing Emily's and my trash into the Dumpster, and ducked behind the Dumpster out of view to shove the bag with Paige's toothbrush in it into my backpack.

Walking as fast as I dared, I led Brigit to my car and returned to the W1 station. Unfortunately, no fingerprint tech was immediately available. A hand-lettered sign on the door said they were out working a scene.

I scurried down the hall to Jackson's office. Luckily, she was still in. I held up the bag. "I've got the toothbrush!"

Her gaze roamed over the bag. "It looks like you've got a bunch of trash."

"That, too," I said, "but the toothbrush is in here."

She waved a hand. "Go give it to the fingerprint gurus."

"I can't," I said. "They're out at a crime scene."

"Oh, right," she said. "There's been an apparent murder-suicide."

And on such a sunny summer day.

She held out her hand for the bag. "I'll get the toothbrush to them as soon as they're back. Keep your phone close. If we get a match we'll arrest Paige right away. Any idea where she might be later?"

I knew exactly where Paige would be later. With me, at a pool party. I shared our plans with the detective.

"Perfect," she said. "Try not to let her out of your sight."

"I'll do my best."

FORTY-FIVE
PARTY ANIMAL

Brigit

Brigit felt like the belle of the ball. Everyone at the pool party was petting her and feeding her junk food and rubbing her belly. She even jumped into the pool and dog-paddled around. It felt good to cool off. She tried to climb onto a floating raft with Megan but something went wrong and all of the air went out of it. That was okay. She was having the time of her life!

FORTY-SIX
BACK TO THE TABLE

The Dealer

He breathed a sigh, though he wasn't sure it was one of relief. After nearly giving in and giving up, he'd rallied. He'd had to use all manner of persuasion available to him, but he'd brought the prick back to the table. He had to. His numbers were down and if he didn't do something it would all be over.

Of course it might all be over anyway. But he wouldn't go down without a fight.

FORTY-SEVEN
MAKING A SPLASH

Megan

The party started out fairly low-key, a dozen people casually hanging out around an apartment pool, having a few beers. Paige and Alexa were among those indulging in a brew or two. I suspected some of the others who were drinking were underage, too, but nobody was getting out of control. I couldn't risk missing a chance to bust a drug dealer by taking in a few children for minor-in-possession charges.

We'd stopped at a grocery store on the short drive over. I bought Paige a new toothbrush and myself a cheap inflatable pool lounge float in a fun lime-green color. It took me fifteen minutes to blow the darn thing up, and Brigit only fifteen seconds to pop it with her claws. *Party pooper.*

As expected, everyone in the group was checking everyone else out. The guys were checking out the girls in their bikinis. The girls were checking out the guys in their swim trunks. The guys were checking out the other guys to see how they ranked in comparison. The girls were doing the same with the other girls, performing mental computations of attractiveness. *Five extra points for big boobs, six-pack abs, or a tight ass. Minus three points for poochy tummy, saggy butt, or back fat. Add two for nice hair or teeth . . .* It was like some sort of sexual attraction calculus.

My nerves were on fire, my senses all abuzz. *Why hasn't Jackson contacted me yet? What's taking the fingerprint techs so damn long? Argh!*

"Morgan! Alexa!" Paige called from her seat on a lounge chair. "Time for a selfie!"

She'd attached her phone to a selfie stick and held it out in front of us, as Alexa slid in on one side of her, me on the other. "Wait. Let's get Britney in the picture, too." She scooted closer to Alexa to leave a space between me and her and patted the spot. "Up here, Britney!"

Brigit complied, hopping into the space. I turned her around to face the camera.

"One, two, three," Paige said, and snapped the shot. *Click.*

We alternated between late-day sunbathing and cooling off in the pool over the next couple of hours. As the day transitioned into early evening, the sun sinking to the west and the lights coming on in the pool and around the complex, more people came out to hang, adding cases of beer and fresh ice to the coolers sitting about. The background music that had been playing became louder and faster, several people moving in place to the beat. Apparently nobody had called the police to complain, probably because the vast majority of the tenants were college kids who were down here by the pool. Any tenants who were not students must have realized they'd signed on for this when they'd signed a lease at a complex so close to the college.

Paige stood on a chair and cupped her hands around her mouth. "Who wants pizza? I'm taking up a collection. Ten bucks each."

I had to give the girl credit. Drug dealer or not, she had leadership skills.

Knowing Brigit would insist on a slice or two, I chipped in twenty bucks for pizza. I sat next to Paige on a chaise lounge turned sideways as she placed the order. Alexa sat on the other side of Paige.

"Send a couple orders of breadsticks, too," Paige said into her phone. "And dipping sauce." When she was done, she looked out over the crowd, a wistful expression on her face. "I'm going to text Chaoxiang. See if he wants to come have some pizza." Alexa started to say something but Paige silenced her with a raised hand. "I don't want to hear it, Alexa! Chao's a good guy. You just don't understand our relationship. We're . . . keeping it casual."

Alexa leaned back, her gaze meeting mine behind Paige's head. She shook her head as if to say, *She's pathetic, isn't she?*

Frankly, drug dealer or not, I felt sorry for Paige. Clearly she had more feelings for the guy than he had for her. It was one thing to have a casual relationship when neither party wanted more, but when one person hoped for something more meaningful it was a recipe for emotional disaster. She was setting herself up for a big heartbreak.

Paige's fingers worked her phone's keypad. When she

finished sending the text, she stared down at her screen as if willing Chaoxiang to respond right away, to show her he cared. As if she realized both Alexa and I were watching her, she slid her phone into the beach bag at her feet, attempting to act nonchalant. "Last one in's a rotten egg!" She stood and ran to the pool, jumping off the side and performing an improvised jackknife. She immediately extended her bent leg upon hitting the water so that her head wouldn't go under and ruin the makeup and hair she'd spent an hour getting just right, probably in the hopes of seeing Chao tonight.

I jumped into the pool, too, as did Alexa and Brigit. After bobbing around for a minute or two, we took places along the side, folding our arms over the edge, resting our heads on our arms, and letting our legs drift behind us. Brigit swam to the steps, climbed out, and lay on the concrete near us, softly panting in the warm evening.

"We should head over to Chisholm Trail Mall tomorrow," Paige suggested. "Since it's after the Fourth, all of their summer stuff will be on sale."

"I can't wait for the winter clothes to come out," I said. "I love boots and sweaters and—"

Paige's head popped up. "There's Chao!"

He'd arrived at the same time as the pizza delivery guy, the two of them making their way up the walk in tandem, the pizza guy rolling a dozen stacked pizzas on a dolly.

Paige was up and out of the water faster than a breeching dolphin. She scurried over to the chair where we'd left our things and quickly wrapped her towel around her waist. Grabbing the roll of bills she'd collected, she returned to the pool and thrust them at me. "Here, Morgan. Pay the pizza guy."

I took the bills from her and eased off the edge and backward into the chest-high water, holding my hands up by my head so the money wouldn't get wet. I walked through the water to the steps, and climbed out of the pool, meeting the pizza guy by the gate. Chao slipped past us to come into the fenced pool area.

"How much do we owe you?" I asked.

"Hundred and sixty bucks," he said.

I counted out the cash. Fortunately, there was enough to cover the pizzas and breadsticks and give the guy a decent tip, too. "Here you go," I said, handing him the wad.

He tipped his hat. "Y'all have fun."

"Thanks. We will."

We had no plates or napkins, but that didn't matter. People ate the pizza right out of the box, using their beach towels to wipe their hands.

Paige and Chaoxiang stood in a corner on the opposite side of the pool. Alexa and I assumed our seats on the lounge chairs. As I ate my pizza, I sent telepathic messages into the universe, willing the techs to finish up their work at the murder-suicide and run the prints on the toothbrush, and for Detective Jackson to send me a text that the prints on Paige's toothbrush matched the ones on the phone. *Come on, guys! Hurry up!*

Finally, a buzz came from my phone.

It was the much-anticipated text from *Aunt Jackie.*

And it read *Not a match.*

Not a match? How can that be? How could the evidence confirm that Paige was not the person whose

prints appeared on both the cell phone and her cup from
Club Bassline? I closed my eyes and pressed my finger-
tips to the lids, trying to make sense of things. The only
explanation was that the dealer had been at Club Bassline
last night, had touched Paige's cup, and I'd missed him.
He'd been right under my nose and I'd been too busy
dancing with a sexy poodle to even notice. Some undercover cop I was, some aspiring detective. Maybe I wasn't
cut out to be an investigator. Maybe I should just focus
on writing parking tickets.

Defeated, I glanced over at Paige and Chao. While
her face and gestures were animated, belying her excitement at seeing him, his face and posture were relaxed.
He stood with one arm draped over the fence, the thumb
of the other hand hooked casually through a belt loop.

*Wait a second. Something about his stance seems
familiar . . .*

The thumb hooked through the belt loop. The guy
from the dash cam footage taken at Tio's Taco Stand,
the one who'd seemed vaguely familiar, he'd walked
with his thumb hooked through a belt loop, too.

"Oh, my God," I said softly on a breath, talking to
myself. *Could Chao be the dealer?*

"What?" Alexa asked, her cheek bulging with pizza.

"Oh, nothing," I said. "Just talking to myself."

My brain quickly took inventory of the evidence. The
prints on the cell phone that we knew for certain belonged to the dealer matched prints lifted from Paige's
cup from Club Bassline. I'd assumed the prints were
Paige's, but could they be Chaoxiang's instead?

They could!

He'd taken a drink from her cup last night at Club

Bassline. I'd forgotten about it until now. Also, he was from China, where the chemicals needed to make MDMA were less regulated and thus easier to obtain. It was possible he had connections there.

Still, none of this evidence was a hundred percent sure, irrefutable. But you know what would be? *An alert from Brigit.*

I roused my partner from her spot at my feet and attached her leash. I led her over to Paige and Chaoxiang, walking slowly and even stopping a couple times along the way to let Brigit sniff the shoes and towels and clothing strewn about, as any dog, professional K-9 or otherwise, would do. As we approached our quarry, I bent down and whispered the order in Brigit's ear to scent for drugs. Her intelligent eyes met mine, letting me know she understood. *Gotcha, partner. I'm on the case.*

I led my partner up to Paige and Chaoxiang, offering a welcoming smile, a "Hey!", and a flirtatious head toss that I hoped would distract them both from Brigit sniffing Chao's legs down below our line of vision.

Paige hadn't introduced me to Chao at the rally or the nightclub. It was an implicit compliment, I supposed, as if she wanted to keep him away from other girls he might find attractive. Of course she had no choice now. She couldn't very well ignore me when I was standing right in front of her. Or at least I'd thought so. Instead of introducing us, she stared at me with her laser-beam eyes again. I could almost feel them cutting through my skin, searing all the way to the bone, etching a message. *Back off.*

Given that Paige had forgotten her manners, I turned to Chaoxiang. "Hi. My name's Morgan. I'm Paige's new suitemate."

Chao dipped his head. "I'm Chao."

Down at my knees, Brigit issued her passive alert which, to anyone else would simply look like she'd decided to sit. But I knew better. *Chao has drugs on him.* It was clear he was the dealer. Paige's incessant glare told me something, too. Her motive for helping him distribute his dirty wares, for writing the ads on the bathroom walls in the dorms, for picking up his cash drop at the gas station. She was a woman in love, desperately trying to please her man, willing to do whatever it took to keep him from walking away completely. Love made people do heroic, wonderful, selfless things. But love also made people do stupid, dangerous, even criminal things. Women's prisons were full of lovelorn women who'd been led astray or even taken a rap for their man. *The things we do for love.*

Chao eyed me closely as he took a sip of his beer. I wondered if he had any inkling I was the "bluebonnet" who'd ordered Molly from him.

"That beer looks good," I said. "Think I'll get one myself." I led Brigit over to a cooler nearby and fished a beer out of the ice and near-freezing water. *Brrr!*

I glanced around for somewhere private I could make a phone call. *The clubhouse.* I carried the beer into the small building on the patio, Brigit padding along beside me. Alexa was sitting at a table inside now, eating pizza and playing quarters with two boys and another girl and losing miserably judging from the way she tilted to one side. I set my beer on the table next to her. "I'll be right back to get this." I slipped into the bathroom, bringing Brigit with me and locking the door behind us.

Inside, I dialed Detective Jackson, speaking in a

whisper. "There's a guy at this party who drank out of Paige's cup last night. I'd forgotten about it until I saw him here. Brigit just alerted on him. His first name is Chaoxiang. I don't have a last name."

"I'll get officers over there right away. What's the address?"

I gave her the number and street and ended the call. Before exiting the bathroom, I took a deep breath to calm myself. I didn't want my behavior to somehow put anyone on notice that something big was about to go down.

I rounded up my beer from the table and headed back outside to the pool. Paige and Chao were sitting sideways on the lounge chair now, Paige's beach bag under the chaise behind their feet. Paige had her arm draped over Chao's back, a possessive hand curved over his shoulder. *Poor, poor girl.*

I took a seat on the edge of the pool, dangling my legs in the water as I sipped the beer. The faint smell of burning marijuana wafted over from a group huddled around a built-in grill outside the fenced pool area. A group of young men who'd been shotgunning Budweisers decided now was a good time for a cannonball contest.

"Boo-ya!" yelled the first as he took a running leap into the air. The bulky guy impacted the water's surface with a huge *KERSPLASH* that sent a tsunami out in every direction, including mine and Brigit's. The water lapped over the side of the pool, dousing me and my dog. Brigit jumped to her feet.

Not to be outdone, the next guy ran, hopped into the air, and performed a flip before cannonballing into the water. *Splash!* Water rained down on everyone around the pool, causing a few of the girls to shriek and the boys to laugh.

While the boys' antics might be a bit annoying to someone just trying to relax poolside, the show provided a great distraction that would come in handy when my fellow officers arrived. Officers would have a much easier time sneaking up on the group if everyone was focused on the guys in the pool rather than the cruisers pulling up in the parking lot.

To that end, when the boys had completed their turns and things threatened to settle down, I raised my beer and hollered, "Girls' turn!"

I set my beer on a nearby table and took a running leap at the deep end of the pool, jumping into the air and performing what cheerleaders and baton twirlers called a Texas T, both legs spread wide, hands reached for toes.

I surfaced to applause, whistles, and catcalls. Also Chao watching me with a smile tugging at his lip and Paige watching him with hurt, angry eyes.

She stood from the lounge. "I'm next!" she cried. She ran at the pool and jumped, attempting a flip but not quite rotating far enough and landing flat on her back, a reverse bellyflop. *SMACK!*

"Ho-lee shit!" called one of the boys, cackling with laughter. "That had to hurt!"

Paige surfaced, her face as red as her back.

In my peripheral vision, I saw two black-and-white cruisers pull up in the parking lot to my right. Nobody else seemed to have noticed yet. *Good.*

A boy pushed a girl in the direction of the pool. "Show us what you got!"

The girl giggled, ran at the pool, and jumped in, arms and legs flailing in the air.

"What the hell was that?" the boy called when she surfaced.

"Police!" came Derek Mackey's voice over a bull-horn. "Nobody move."

I turned to see the Big Dick approaching, along with Officer Spalding, Officer Hinojosa, and another K-9 team comprised of Officer Eklund and his Belgian Malinois, Brutus. The officers had their flashlights out, ready to shine a spotlight on anyone who might try to run off. There was a chorus of tinny thuds as every underage drinker let their beer slide from their hand to the ground and took a giant step back as if playing a solitary game of Mother May I? *Drinking? Who me? You're quite mistaken, Officer.*

I did the same, slipping my beer between my legs and letting it fall into the pool. It bobbed for a moment, then turned sideways, filled with water, and sank to the bottom, leaving a yellowish trail in its wake.

A beam of light found my face, blinding me.

"I saw that!" Mackey shouted. "Stay right there!"

Is Derek really going to take advantage of this situation to harass me? I suppose I should've expected as much.

A couple of the boys and one girl tried to run, but Hinojosa headed them off at the pass and corralled them back toward the enclosed patio.

Brigit stood next to me, her tail wagging as she watched her canine coworker sniff his way around the area. Brutus alerted on a towel near the crowd at the grill.

When Eklund picked up the towel, a bag containing several rolled-up joints fell out.

"Who does this belong to?" Eklund demanded.

Nobody spoke, presumably thinking there was strength in solidarity.

"All right," Eklund said. "You're all going in."

Two boys in the group caved and pointed at a third, who responded by throwing up his hands and crying, "You assholes!"

I cut a glance at Paige. She sat still on the lounge, her arms crossed over her chest, a scowl on her face. But she sat alone.

Where the hell is Chaoxiang?

My eyes frantically scanned the complex. He was nowhere to be seen.

DAMMIT! Had he slipped away? I had to alert the officers somehow. To get one of them on his track.

I stood up next to the pool.

Mackey was in my face in an instant, his breath reeking of the extra onions he always requested on his burgers. "I told you not to move! What part of 'stay right there' do you not understand?"

"Chao's gone," I snapped as quietly as possible. "He was sitting next to the girl on that lounge chair last I saw him. Get Brutus on his trail. Now!"

It took Derek a moment to realize what I was saying. But when it registered, he stalked over to Eklund and leaned down to whisper in his ear. Eklund glanced my way, led Brutus over to Paige, and issued him the order to track. Brutus put his nose to the ground and took off toward the gate.

Standing there, doing nothing, was hard. I wanted to

get Brigit on Chao's trail, too, not because Brutus wasn't up to the task—he was—but because I wanted this bust. I was the one who'd gone undercover, lived in a tiny dorm room, held a girl's hair back while she puked. And, dammit, I wanted to take Chao down. Making an arrest, taking a bad guy off the streets, was the ultimate in job satisfaction for a cop, and I was being denied that satisfaction.

Still, once Brutus had nabbed Chao and brought him back here, I could toss my cover and at least celebrate with my fellow officers, right?

Unfortunately, that's not what happened. Officer Eklund and Brutus returned a few minutes later, alone, Chaoxiang's trail apparently running cold. No doubt Chao had hopped into his car and hightailed it away from the complex.

I screamed in frustration on the inside. *ARRRGH!* This wasn't the end of things, of course. There was more than enough evidence for Paige to be taken in for questioning now. After all, the dealer's prints were on her cup from the bar and she appeared in the dash cam footage at the gas station.

Derek had been making his way around the gated pool area, checking IDs for those who were drinking, issuing citations for minor-in-possession to those who were underage and smelled of alcohol. When he reached Paige, she reluctantly offered her driver's license. He took a look at it and said, "Let me smell your breath."

She shook her head, refusing.

Derek expanded like a puffer fish. The guy didn't like being challenged by anyone, but having a young woman like Paige stand up to him, especially when she stood an entire foot shorter, had clearly pissed him off in an epic way.

As I watched, Derek reached down and grabbed the bag from under Paige's chair. "Is this yours?"

She said nothing, again refusing to cooperate.

Derek plunked the bag down on the chair and bent over to rummage through it. It was then I spotted Alexa standing at the fence, her cell phone out, videotaping the search. She wasn't the only one recording the events. All around the place kids had their phones aimed at the officers.

"Well, lookee here!" Derek cried, raising a victorious hand. A clear bag was clutched in his fist. It was filled with what appeared to be a dozen or so white capsules. *Molly.*

Paige's mouth dropped and her eyes went wide. "That's not mine!" she cried. She looked sincerely surprised. Shocked, even.

Derek raised the beach bag. "This is your bag, isn't it?"

"Yes, but—"

"Eklund!" Derek shouted. "Get Brutus over here."

Eklund led the Malinois over to the chair.

Derek held the bag in front of the dog's face. "What do you say, Brutus? Is this shit illegal?"

Brutus sniffed at the bag and sat, issuing a passive alert.

Derek cackled that nasty cackle that was like sandpaper on my nerves. He dropped the pills back into Paige's beach bag. "Cuff her, Eklund. I'll get the darkhaired one with the mutt."

Derek stormed my way and got in my face once again. "Give me your wrists!" he barked.

Hey, if he was going to take me in, I might as well have some fun with this, right? I raised both of my hands in front of me in a zombie pose. Derek reached for my forearm, using more force than necessary, clearly taking advantage of the situation to give me some crap. But he'd seemed to have forgotten that I could give as good as I could get. Rather than letting him cuff my wrist, I jerked my arm out of his hold, put my hands to his chest, and shoved him with all the force I could muster. His arms windmilled as he fell backward, a look of utter shock on his face as he plummeted ass first into the water. Nothing had ever sounded as satisfying to me as the ensuing *splash!*

FORTY-EIGHT
MUTT IN A MUG SHOT

Brigit

Brutus was on duty tonight. He was an okay coworker. He gave her a friendly tail wag when they crossed paths and he'd never tried to mount her. She would've had him on his back and her fangs at his throat if he had. He had a good nose, too, though not as skilled as Brigit's, of course.

They stood near the squad cars, engaged in a silent K-9 exchange.

Having a good shift? Brigit asked.

Not bad, he replied. *Would've been better if I could've had a slice of that pepperoni and sausage pizza I smell on your breath. My human wouldn't let me take one.*

Don't ask next time, she advised. *It's easier to get forgiveness than permission.*

The next thing she knew, Megan was directing her into the back of Mackey's squad car. Brigit could tell it was his by the smell. One part feet, one part onions, one part dumbass.

Unlike the specially equipped K-9 cruiser she and

Megan used on the job, this cruiser was outfitted for human transport. She climbed onto the seat, squeezing in between Megan and Paige. There was barely enough room for her to fit her fluffy rear between theirs. She looked out the window and saw Brutus being loaded into his enclosure. Too bad she couldn't ride with him and catch up on the office gossip.

FORTY-NINE
A MONUMENTAL FAILURE

The Dealer

What a way to spend a Saturday night. Stuck at work, reviewing a three-hundred-page bill on agriculture subsidies. Is this what his life had come to? Why he'd run for office? To spend his weekend considering corn, cotton, and kale?

Tossing the behemoth tome aside, he stared out his office window, looking out into the dark at the enormous, well-lit phallic symbol that was the Washington Monument.

His desk phone rang. He checked the readout. It was the assistant chief of staff from his Fort Worth office. He picked up the phone and put the receiver to his ear, summoning the grandfatherly persona that had served him so well all these years. "Hello, there. What might you be calling about on a fine Saturday night such as this?"

What he heard next made him want to throw the phone against the wall. "She *what*?" he cried, his throat so tight he could barely get the words out.

His chief repeated the message. *This couldn't have come at a worse time.*

"Book me on the next flight out of Dulles."

He slammed the phone down and turned to look out the window again. The Washington Monument no longer looked like a phallic symbol. Nope, it was the world, giving him the finger.

FIFTY
GIRLS GONE WILD

Megan

"Stand on the line," said the booking officer behind the desk.

I looked down, putting my toes up to the black tape on the floor. I was still wearing my bikini. My mug shot would make a good cover for the next Girls Gone Wild video.

There was a flash as the camera captured my image for my mug shot. Shoving Derek into the pool had provided me no end of satisfaction, but it had also gotten me handcuffed and hauled off on charges of resisting arrest and assaulting a police officer. No civilian could have done what I did and avoid arrest, so he'd had to take me in, too, to keep up appearances. Of course, under the circumstances, nothing would come of the charges. Still, for Paige's sake, I had to pretend to be worried. I chewed my lip and blinked my eyes a lot, as if fighting back tears.

"Turn to your left," the officer said now.

I did as I'd been told, and he snapped a profile shot,

another flash lighting up the room. It really was a good thing I didn't have epilepsy or I'd be in full grand mal by now.

When he finished with me, he repeated the process with Paige. Her cheeks were tearstained and her gaze drifted down.

"Look up," he said without feeling. "I need to see your eyes."

She looked up at the camera. I noticed she was shaking. She probably felt terrified and angry and forsaken. Chaoxiang had done the girl no favors.

After the booking officer had taken her picture in profile, too, he led us down the hall to the holding cell. The area was dimly lit, quiet, and smelled of bleach and regret. He slid the door open and we stepped inside, joining two other women. One was a fiftyish dishwater blonde with gray roots. She leaned against the wall, asleep with her mouth open. The other appeared to be in her early twenties. She had her knees drawn up to her chest and was slowly rocking herself.

We took seats on the hard metal benches that were bolted to the wall on the left. Brigit hopped up and lay down next to me, draping her head over my thigh.

Now that Paige and I were alone, I could ask her some questions, see what information she might reveal.

I turned to her and whispered, "Where'd you get all that Molly?"

"It wasn't mine!" she whispered back, her voice cracking with emotion. "I don't know how it got into my bag!"

Sheesh, wasn't it obvious? "Could Chaoxiang have put it there?"

"No!" she cried, so loud the sleeping woman opened one bloodshot eye to peep at us. "He wouldn't do that to me!"

Don't be so sure, I wanted to tell her. In my line of work, I'd seen men not only frame the women they supposedly loved, but beat them within an inch of their lives. Thinking over her words, I realized they implied that Chao had access to drugs. Otherwise, she would have responded with something like *Chao doesn't use Molly* or *Chao didn't have anything on him tonight.*

I leaned a little closer. "So Chao uses the stuff, though? Or sells it? There was an awful lot in that bag."

Paige cut me a confused look, as if unsure whether she should open up to me, whether the cat was already out of the bag or not. Apparently, she decided to shove the cat back in. "I think that cop planted the drugs on me. That red-haired jerk who searched my bag. Did you see how he bent over it so nobody could tell what he was doing?"

"Why would he plant drugs on you?" As I asked her the question, I also asked it of myself. While Paige could only shrug in response, some quick answers came to me. Derek might have planted the drugs to look like a hero, get some attention. Derek might have planted the drugs to increase his arrest statistics. Derek might have planted the drugs to try to restore his reputation after losing the evidence in the earlier bust. Of course this last answer told me both why Derek might plant drugs and where he would have gotten them in the first place.

Uh-oh . . .

Despite these thoughts, none of these reasons seemed good enough for Derek to risk his career and his status as the chief's golden boy. I knew, without a doubt, that Derek hadn't planted those drugs on Paige.

Didn't I?

I scrubbed a hand down my face as if to wipe away that horrible thought. *No.* Derek had not planted those drugs. Chao had put the drugs there, ditched what had been in his pocket in case the cops caught up with him.

We'd been able to make a phone call when we'd arrived at booking. Paige had called her parents, who in turn had called the law office of Anthony Giacomo, a notorious and notoriously successful criminal defense attorney in Dallas. He'd successfully defended the accused in a number of high-profile cases in the metroplex, and his name was synonymous with a get-out-of-jail-free card. Not that his representation came free, of course. With his track record and reputation, he was able to charge top dollar for his services. Fortunately for Paige, Giacomo's high rates were no problem for her parents and the attorney's assistant had promptly arranged bail. I'd been forced to call my fictional uncle Buster. Paige was sprung first. Looked like her parents were getting their money's worth.

"McQuaid," called the booking officer as he stepped to the cell door. "You're out."

"Thank God!" she cried, rushing to the door and exiting without so much as a glance in my direction.

Gee, I'll miss you, too, I thought.

Uncle Buster arrived a half hour later, standing next to the officer at the door. He glanced over at the girl rocking herself before returning his gaze to me. "I hope you're proud of yourself, young lady!" he shouted.

"You can drop the act," I said cordially as I led

Brigit from the cell. "That's not Paige. She was already released."

"In that case," he said, his tone now friendly and sarcasm-free as he gave me a smile and a pat on the shoulder, "I hope you're proud of yourself, young lady."

"I'd be more proud if we'd caught Chaoxiang."

"We got a search warrant," Bustamente told me. "Officers are on their way to his apartment."

"Yesss!" I clenched victorious fists at my chin. "One more dealer off the streets."

Bustamente reached down and ruffled Brigit's ears. "You two need a ride home?"

"I'd appreciate that."

I woke in my own bed late the next morning, with Seth lying next to me, facedown with his arms arched over his head, the army eagle on his back staring up at me as if to say *I know what you did last night. Good work, soldier.*

I rolled out of bed, both Brigit and Blast climbing off the foot to follow me. I padded into the kitchen and let them out back. Brigit immediately took off after a squirrel, chasing it up a tree and leaping up onto the trunk. As if she had any hope of catching the quick rodent. But I had to admire her eternal optimism. She must really think she'd catch one someday.

I found a note from Frankie on the counter. *At derby practice.* Looked like Seth and I would have the place to ourselves for a while.

I went to the bathroom and took a shower, letting the hot water flow over me, feeling no pressure to rush so the next girl could use it before having to get to class. It felt so good to be back in my own place. Of course I'd need to swing by the dorm later to grab my things. I figured I'd tell Emily, Paige, and Alexa that after my uncle Buster had bailed me out, he'd insisted I live with him and my aunt until I could show sufficient maturity for them to trust me again. *That sounds plausible, right?* They might wonder why they didn't run into me on campus but, then again, it was a big campus. And it's not like we'd been close. They'd probably forget about me fairly quickly.

When I returned to the bedroom, Seth was stirring.

"Wake up, lazybones," I said.

He rolled over, the eagle disappearing underneath him. "Don't ever go undercover again," he said.

"Why not?"

He sat up, plumping a pillow behind him. "Because life is boring when you're not around."

His sweet words warmed my heart. Unfortunately, my heart didn't stay warm for long. My cell phone bleeped from the nightstand. I stepped over, saw that it was Detective Jackson calling, and took the call. "Hi, Detective."

"I've got bad news," she said. "The address we had for Chao was out-of-date. Nobody seems to have a current one for him. He must have sublet a place, or be renting a room from someone."

"Paige would probably know where he lives."

"She's lawyered up. She's not talking."

Ugh. "So you couldn't get any evidence on him?"

"No evidence. No fingerprints. Nothing. The same prints that were on the library cell phone and Paige's cup are on the bag from last night. Paige's prints aren't on the bag. She never touched it. The only other prints on the bag are Officer Mackey's."

Another *ugh*.

"We need you back at that dorm," Jackson said. "Work on Paige. See if you can get her to admit something."

"But I just got back home!"

Jackson scoffed. "You're the one who asked for this undercover gig, remember?"

She had me there. "All right. I'll go back to the dorm."

From his place against the pillow, Seth frowned. I raised a palm. What could I do? The investigation had to come first.

I ended the call with Detective Jackson. "I'm a college kid again."

"So I was just a one-night stand? A booty call?" Seth's grin said he didn't mind being either of those things, at least not for me. He climbed out of bed. "How much longer do you think till it's over?"

"Not too much longer," I said. "I'm going to work on Paige, see if I can get her to tell me where Chao lives or admit she was working with him to sell Molly."

He reached out and grabbed a tendril of my hair, twisting it around his finger. "If anyone can get this case resolved, it's you and Brigit."

FIFTY-ONE
TWO DOG NIGHT

Brigit

She hadn't liked being in the jail cell. While it was much bigger than the cage she'd been forced to live in at the animal shelter after her original owner failed to come bail her out, it was too similar for her comfort. Luckily, Megan had petted her and reassured her that everything was going to be okay.

When they'd been released, they'd come back home. Seth and Blast had come over, too. Brigit and Blast had wrestled on the rug, chewed each other's necks until they were wet with slobber, and then slept side by side at the foot of Megan's bed.

But now, Megan was taking her back to the dorm. *Yuck.* At least the nice boy was there to greet them in the lobby. He bent down and gave Brigit an all-over scratch. She thanked him with a lick across the chin.

FIFTY-TWO
DELETE, DELETE, DELETE

Senator Sutton, the Dealer

It took everything in him not to backhand the little bitch across the face. "How many times were you told not to use the office computer for any personal purpose? Huh? How many?"

There were tears in the girl's eyes, but he didn't give a shit. He'd spent years carefully and expertly forming alliances, negotiating and making trades, maneuvering through the complex political machinery that formed Washington, D.C., all the while doing so in a manner that would ensure his reputation was above reproach. And now, this stupid, stupid girl could undo everything he'd worked so hard for.

"I don't know," she mumbled. "Once or twice."

"Bullshit!" he barked, his vehemence surprising not just her but himself, as well. He grabbed the stapler off his desk and flung it across the room. It hit the wall and exploded into a barrage of plastic and metal confetti.

Everything was spinning out of control, himself in-cluded. He'd never felt so powerless. The latest reports showed that Essie Espinoza had edged him out in the polls. He was doing his damnedest to reverse that trend, but with China adamantly refusing to consider adopting the China–U.S. Partnership he'd proposed, he looked weak and ineffectual, the hundreds of earlier deals he'd managed to broker forgotten or ignored. He couldn't afford a scandal, especially not right now. If the media discovered an intern had been dealing Molly out of his office it would push his campaign over the edge and that money he'd taken and spent would be for naught.

He wondered how this little twit even knew how to run a drug business, where she got the products. After all, there weren't exactly want ads for this type of work. *Sales help needed in illegal pharmaceutical industry. Sparkling personalities only, please.*

He needed details, had to know how far his liability might extend. "How'd you get into this?" he demanded. "Who are you working for?" When she looked away he grabbed her by the chin and turned her head to face him. "I asked you a question," he hissed. "And you're going to give me an answer."

Though her face was aimed in his direction, her eyes looked down. "Chaoxiang Wu," she said, her voice barely louder than a whisper.

"Wu? The minister of commerce's son?"

She nodded.

He let go of her chin. *Fuck!* He should've known that boy was bad news. The kid was too smooth, a charmer, a worldly boy with an exotic attractiveness. Chaoxiang had come to Sutton's offices with his father several times, both in Washington and here in Fort Worth. Hell, it was Sutton himself who'd suggested the kid apply to

TCU! The senator remembered coming out of his office here in Fort Worth after a private meeting with Chao's father and finding the kid flirting with his intern. She'd been looking up at the boy with puppy-dog eyes, totally smitten.

The kid had probably obtained the drugs from China, where chemical regulation was more lax. It made little sense, he realized, but he was especially enraged that the drugs the kid was selling were from China rather than being made domestically. More dollars in the two countries' trade gap.

But, being the expert dealer he was, Sutton also realized the situation gave him leverage, a big bargaining chip. Surely the minister of commerce would want to avoid the negative publicity the arrest of his son would cause, to minimize the effects on his son's otherwise bright future, for his son to be able to finish college without the threat of criminal prosecution. Others in the Chinese government would want to avoid the embarrassment as well, sweep the matter under the rug, pretend it never happened, just as they did with the bloody massacre at Tiananmen Square in 1989.

If the senator could finagle things just right, he might be able to strong-arm the minister into supporting the CUSP legislation and lure voters back into his camp. He'd give this some thought . . .

But for now, he had to deal with the matter at hand. And the matter at hand was Paige McQuaid and the trail of electronic bread crumbs she'd left, bread crumbs that could lead the police—*and a career-ending scandal*—straight to his door.

Sutton leaned over Paige as she sat hunched before

the desktop computer. "My chief of staff says he told everyone in the office multiple times not to engage in personal activity on the office computers. Any of your e-mails could be subpoenaed. Why didn't you just use your goddamn phone?"

"My battery died," she said, a tear escaping to slide down her cheek. She hiccupped, trying not to cry. "I didn't have the charger with me."

He waved his hand and she flinched, as if she thought he'd hit her. *God, how he'd love to.* "Delete it all!" he demanded. "Delete all of those e-mails from your account and delete your browser history, too. Delete! Delete! Delete!"

He stood over her while she frantically worked the keyboard and mouse. When she'd erased all of the e-mails in the *funtimemolly* account, as well as her browser history, he put his face right in hers, so close he could see the pimple beginning to form on her forehead. "If anyone ever asks why this information was deleted, you did it on your own. To cover your ass and that boy's. Understand?"

"Yes, sir," she said meekly.

"Now," he demanded, standing back up. "Are there any other loose ends we need to worry about?"

FIFTY-THREE
PREEMPTED

Megan

Detective Jackson texted me during the last twenty minutes of my Monday-morning political science class. Once again I headed to the back door, the professor casting me a look of disdain. "Are we boring you?" he called across the room.

I couldn't blame him for being annoyed. "Sorry!" I called. "My grandfather's been in the hospital and I just got a text to call my mom."

When he blanched, a frisson of guilt went through me for lying to him and making him look like an ass. "All right," he said. "That's understandable. Go make your call."

Brigit and I slunk out of the room and hurried outside, looking for a private place where I could speak with the detective. Given that the students tended to stick to the sidewalks, I scurried to the center of an open greenbelt and dialed her.

"We've got problems," she said without preamble.

"What kind of problems?"

"You know how people say 'don't make a federal case out of it'?"

"Yeah?"

"Well, Senator Sutton's made a federal case out of it. He's pulled rank. He says that since it appears Derek planted the drugs, it's inappropriate for the Fort Worth Police Department to investigate Paige. He says there's a conflict of interest."

The feds were getting *my* case? *Nooo!*

"But Sutton works for the federal government!" I cried. "And Paige is his intern. He's got a conflict of interest, too."

"But he doesn't work for the Drug Enforcement Agency," she said. "There's at least a little distance between them. Plus, Sutton claims that the evidence planted on Paige could be the lost drugs from the Hahn arrest."

"How would he even know about that?"

"Good question. My guess is someone leaked the information about Derek losing the drug evidence to the DEA."

"Who?"

"Wish I knew," she said. "Lots of our officers know people in the federal government, particularly those who work in law enforcement. Some have worked on joint task forces. It would be virtually impossible to figure out who's responsible for the leak."

What she said was true. I'd worked loosely with the feds before. A criminal investigator for the IRS had been working a case at a jewelry store in Chisholm Trail Mall over the Christmas holidays. She and I had gotten to know each other. We'd even played matchmakers for the shopping mall Santa.

"Officer Mackey has been put on administrative leave. Internal Affairs will run an investigation. Heck, you might be summoned to provide evidence. You were at the pool party where he allegedly planted the drugs. You also saw him twice at Flynn Blythe's apartment. If you spotted him there two times, he'd probably been there many more. And why?"

It was a good question. One I'd asked myself several times.

Jackson continued. "Paige McQuaid's attorney filed a formal grievance against Officer Mackey this morning, too."

I pinched the bridge of my nose in frustration. "What's Chief Garelik have to say about all of this?" To have the case usurped by the federal government after the time, effort, and expense his department had put into the investigation was insulting, and surely he was beyond pissed that his golden boy had been accused of being a dirty cop.

"When I went by his office this morning to tell him, he nearly exploded."

"Is the DEA going to prioritize this case? Move in on Chaoxiang?"

"It's too late," she said. "We got word he boarded a flight to Beijing yesterday. He's probably playing it safe, waiting to see if he's implicated before deciding whether to return."

"He's gone? What does that mean for the investigation?"

"Honestly? I'd say it's dead in the water. Any competent defense attorney would be able to get Paige McQuaid off scot-free. Her prints weren't on the phone or the bag of Molly, and her appearance at the gas station could easily be explained away by its proximity to the campus. Besides, the DEA has bigger fish to fry, Mexican cartels and whatnot. Without prints to link Chaoxiang Wu's to the crime, they're back to square one. This case won't go anywhere in their hands."

"So I did all of this work for nothing?"

"Looks that way."

I exhaled a long, slow breath. "I g-guess I'm done here, huh?"

"Yeah," she said. "You can pack up your things and go home."

We ended the call and I slid the phone into my pocket, taking a moment to breathe and process my thoughts and emotions. They were all over the place. I was angry that Senator Sutton had taken the case away from the Fort Worth Police Department. I was frustrated that all of the work I'd put in on this investigation was for naught. I was concerned that Derek had been wrongfully accused. I was equally concerned that he hadn't.

But I'd known when I went into police work that there was no end game to crime. It would never be over for good. Not all crimes would be solved. Not all lawbreakers would be caught. Not all victims would receive justice. Crime was a deep, self-inflicted wound on society, and all I could hope to do was staunch the flow of blood.

Wow. That's enough philosophical pondering for one day, isn't it?

"C'mon, girl," I said to my partner. "Let's go pack."

I led Brigit back to the dorm. Hunter's curly head was bent over a book in the study lounge off the lobby. After I rounded up my things, I'd stop in and tell him good-bye, thank him for keeping my secrets. Wish him luck with the girls.

Brigit and I took the stairs to the second floor. I slid my student ID through the skimmer, realizing it was the last time I'd be acting as Morgan Lewis. *Good-bye, Morgan,* I told myself. *It's been nice knowing you.*

The room was quiet. Emily was at her morning class. Looked like I wouldn't get a chance to say good-bye to her. I hoped she'd get her stress under control, go speak to a counselor like I'd suggested.

I rounded up a sticky note from my desk and wrote *My parents are making me move in with my aunt and uncle. Good-bye and good luck. Fondly, Morgan.*

I retrieved my suitcases from the closet and filled them with the clothes and shoes I'd brought. I pulled the comforter and sheets off the bed, stuffing them into the suitcase along with the clothes, having to unzip the extender so everything would fit. I grabbed my other textbook and slid it into my backpack along with my other book and laptop. I could sell the books back to the bookstore later. I'd get only pennies on the dollar, of course, but it was better than nothing.

Having packed everything in the room, I opened the door to the bathroom and stepped inside to get my makeup and toiletries. Loud voices coming from Paige and Alexa's room caught my attention. The two were clearly arguing. Looked like Alexa had finally had enough and was sticking up for herself. *Good for her.*

"You can't just delete stuff from another person's phone!" Alexa cried.

"I'm the one in the video," Paige snapped. "Not you. I had every right to delete it."

Video? What video?

"Besides," Paige continued. "Senator Sut—"

She stopped speaking.

"What does Senator Sutton have to do with this?" Alexa asked.

Paige hesitated a moment before saying, "Let's just say he wouldn't be happy if that video had gotten out. It's better if everyone's looking at that cop instead of me."

"It's not better for the cop!" Alexa shot back.

"Why are you on his side?" Paige said, her tone more conciliatory now. "He gave you a ticket for minor-in-possession, and you saw how he treated Morgan. He basically assaulted her. I'm telling you. Those drugs weren't mine. My prints weren't on the bag. Besides, you think they're going to prosecute a cop?" She scoffed. "Not likely. The police have been shooting unarmed people left and right and nobody does anything."

Paige was way overstating the case. Unfortunately, Alexa found it convincing. Or at least convincing enough. She offered no further protest.

I realized now that they were talking about the video Alexa had taken with her phone Saturday night. She'd been in the perfect position to record Derek searching Paige's bag. I gathered that the recording proved Derek's innocence. It was both a relief to know for certain that he hadn't planted the drugs on Paige, but also a frustration to realize that evidence that could have proved him innocent was gone now. And that comment about

Senator Sutton. What exactly had Paige meant by that? Did Sutton know about the video?

I rapped on the door to their room. "Can I come in?"

"It's open!" Alexa called.

I stepped through the door. "I came to say good-bye," I told them. "I have to move in with my aunt and uncle for a while until I'm"—I formed air quotes with my fingers—" 'mature' enough to move back out on my own." I rolled my eyes.

"That's so stupid," Paige said. "You hardly did anything wrong."

"I know, right? Anyway, did I hear you two talking about the video Alexa took at the pool party? When the cops were there?"

The two exchanged a glance.

"Yeah," Paige said tentatively, her head tilting. "What about it? What did you hear?"

I forced a nonchalant shrug. "Not much. You were smart to delete it. I mean, I know those drugs weren't yours, but that video could make you look guiltier. Like maybe you were holding the stash for someone."

Paige didn't deny anything I said, didn't refute my implied accusation that she'd tampered with evidence. Instead, she came over and gave me a hug. "We'll miss you. Stop by and see us sometime, okay?"

"I will." *When hell freezes over.*

On my way through the lobby, I turned into the study lounge and rolled my suitcases over to Hunter, Brigit trailing along, keeping a wary distance from the wheels of my luggage.

Hunter looked up from his history textbook, his gaze moving down to my bags. "You moving out?"

"Yeah." For the benefit of any of the other students in the room who might be listening, I gave him the same story I'd given my suitemates. "My parents don't trust me anymore. They're making me move in with my aunt and uncle." I gave Hunter a discreet wink.

He winked back to let me know he got the implied message and that my secrets were safe with him. He stood and opened his arms. "It won't the same around here without you and Britney."

We exchanged a warm hug.

"Good luck with your classes," I told him as I released him and stepped back. "And the girls," I added in a whisper. I had no doubt he'd do well on both fronts.

He offered a roguish grin. "If you decide a younger guy might be your thing after all, you know where to find me."

Not wanting to be left out, Brigit woofed up at Hunter and wagged her tail, offering her own good-bye.

He knelt down and rubbed her back and scratched her behind both ears. "Bye, girl. Be good."

She gave his cheek a wet, warm lick, and he responded by hugging her around the neck and burying his face in her fur. I felt a little tug at my heart. Hunter would make some girl really happy someday.

I grabbed the handle of my suitcase and said, "C'mon, girl."

With one last glance back at Hunter, Brigit and I left the lounge and walked through the foyer to the front doors. On our way down the ramp, we spotted Emily coming up the sidewalk.

She spotted us at the same time, her face clouding in

concern as we met on the concrete. "What's with the suitcase?"

"My parents are making me move in with my aunt and uncle for a while. I left you a note."

She exhaled sharply. "I'm losing another roommate? That side of the room must be cursed." She shook her head in disgust, though her face softened a moment later. "I hope my next one is half as nice as you, Morgan. You were . . ." She seemed to be searching for the exact words, but gave up quickly, probably not wanting to sound sappy. She left it at, "You were a good roomie."

"So were you," I said.

"No I wasn't," she replied without malice.

"Well . . ." Now it was my turn to search for words. "At least you kept things interesting."

She snorted but smiled, giving me a quick and awkward one-armed hug before scurrying into the dorm.

As I led Brigit across the campus to the car, I found myself worrying about the naïve and vulnerable kids I was leaving behind. If the case were abandoned, would Chao continue to sell Molly to his fellow students? Would more young people succumb to the harmful effects of the drugs and suffer permanent health problems, or worse? Was there nothing I could do to stop the flow of drugs? To hold the dealers accountable for their crimes?

Were some criminals simply above the law?

FIFTY-FOUR
DOGGONE IT

Brigit

As they left the dorm, Megan stopped and talked to the nice boy. He gave Brigit extra scratches and rubs today, even a hug.

She hoped he'd get a dog of his own one day. He'd make one a really good friend.

FIFTY-FIVE
LEVERAGE

Senator Sutton

He stared across his desk at Wu. The minister of commerce had lost the cockiness he'd had when Sutton had attempted to negotiate before. God, it felt good to finally have some leverage.

"All I have to do is point the finger at your son," he told Wu, "and he'll be ruined. He'll be put on a watch list and arrested the instant he tries to reenter the United States. Any dreams he has, any dreams you and your wife have for him, will be over."

He almost felt bad to see the anxiety in the man's eyes. *Almost.* It felt good to have some power back, for someone to be listening to him again. He'd been ignored far too often lately. By the press. By voters. By his fellow politicians.

He arched a brow and twisted the metaphorical knife. "The news that your son has been selling drugs made from ingredients he obtained in China won't be good for your career, either."

Wu's eyes narrowed. "Nor would it be good for your

campaign for the press and voters to know your intern was helping my son sell those drugs."

Wu had a point, of course, which was precisely how this had all come about. But Wu had much more to lose than Sutton. Sutton's connection to his intern was much more tenuous than the connection between father and son. Besides, Wu was younger by two decades and had many more years left in public service—assuming his career wasn't ended early by the shame of a family drug scandal. The senator told him as much. "I'm only planning to serve one more term. This will be my last campaign. If I'm not reelected, I'll just ease into an early retirement."

It was a bald-faced lie. His aspirations ran much higher. He had his sights set on the presidency, moving into that nice little residence at 1600 Pennsylvania Avenue in D.C. He'd rather not deal with a scandal at all, but if he could at least stave it off until after the election in November he'd be in much better shape. It was extremely difficult to recall a sitting senator. But right now was a critical time in the campaign season. People were making up their minds, making firm decisions on who they would back. If the scandal hit now, it could be the final nail in the coffin of his campaign.

Wu seethed. "What do you want from me?"

Senator Sutton leaned back in his chair. "I want you to come out publicly in favor of my CUSP bill. *Immediately*. Then I want you to convince whoever needs convincing in China to get on board." If he could get positive media attention on the progress he'd made, surely the tide would turn in his favor.

Wu threw up his hands. "How can this CUSP agreement be good for China?"

"It's simple, really," Sutton said. "Your people will be able to buy American products more cheaply than they can now. The CUSP will help China overcome some of the bad press it's gotten for labor abuses, like the iPhone scandal. Workers in your country will be paid fair wages and have more money to spend, which will in turn increase demand for all products and stimulate the Chinese economy. Everyone will win."

Wu didn't look convinced, but he really didn't have much choice in the matter. Not if he loved his son. "I will do as you ask," he said finally on a sigh.

"Great! It's a deal, then." Sutton stood and walked around his desk to shake Wu's hand. "I'll see you out."

He led the minister out of his office, down the hall, and through the foyer, stepping with him out into the hallway.

Ding! The elevator doors slid open and Paige stepped out. Part of him still wanted to backhand her, but part of him wanted to grab her and plant a big kiss on her cheek. Her stupid little criminal enterprise with Wu's son had put the senator at risk, but it had also provided him just the clout he needed to back Wu into a corner, to make progress on the CUSP, and to get the prick and his ilk back on his side, to throw their full support behind him.

"Hello, Senator," she said, looking both contrite and surprised at the same time. It seemed she hadn't expected to see Minister Wu standing there with him. Her gaze went past the minster, obviously seeking his son. Good luck with that. The kid was knocking back *moo goo gai pan* in Beijing by now.

"Hello, Miss McQuaid," Sutton said, reaching out a hand to hold the door for Wu. "I trust you were able to finish your homework?"

He was speaking in code, but he knew she'd understand. She was a smart girl according to his chief of staff, who'd hired her. Had a 3.8 GPA and made the dean's list each semester. Her parents were very wealthy and well connected. They'd contributed thousands to his campaigns over the years, encouraged their friends to do likewise, even hosted informal fund-raising receptions for him at their lovely home in Southlake, which sat just one neighborhood over from the one the senator and his wife owned.

Paige nodded, but bit her lip.

"Something wrong?" he asked. "Did you have trouble with the homework?"

Her gaze went from Sutton to Wu.

"He knows what's going on," Sutton said softly. While his voice was still low, he spoke more emphatically now. "Was there a problem?"

"Nothing major," she said. "At least I don't think so. It's just that a girl who lives in the other side of our suite overheard me and my roommate talking. My roommate got mad when I deleted the video from her phone without asking her first. I'd never said that you . . ." She let the two men mentally complete the sentence. "Anyway, Morgan seemed to have figured out why I was deleting it."

Sutton's heart skittered in his chest. "That someone had asked you to do so, you mean?"

"Yeah."

He felt panic rising up, gripping his guts like a claw.

"And did Morgan figure out exactly who that someone might have been?" That it was *him*?

Once again the little twit said, "Yeah."

Fuck! This was no longer simply a drug scandal. He could face felony charges for tampering with evidence. While he might have been able to survive bad press relating to a rogue intern, even if it came out that she'd met her accomplice in Sutton's local office and used official computers to set up cash drops, there was no way in hell he could survive the accusation that he himself had tampered with evidence to cover it up. It would be a modern-day Watergate, with himself playing the role of Richard Nixon. *Mollygate.* The press would have a field day with it. He could see Trish LeGrande now, demanding answers and making accusatory retorts when he provided none. The media who'd been a politician's biggest backers were the first to turn on him or her when they discovered their favorite lawmaker was actually a lawbreaker.

But would people believe a couple of college girls? Paige they'd surely dismiss out of hand. Who'd believe a drug dealer? But her friend Morgan could be another matter. If she stepped up to share her suspicions, he wasn't sure whether people would believe her or not. He could be panicking for no reason. There was a good chance it would go no further.

Then again, if anyone started digging, they might discover that Paige's incriminatory e-mails and browser history had been deleted from his computer at his local office. Of course, he could claim Paige had done so on her own, without his knowledge. After all, it wasn't like he knew the girl well or spent much time in Fort Worth, at least not until recently.

He felt only a momentary sense of relief before a ter-
rifying thought tiptoed into his mind. He'd had her sign
in with her own user ID and password, but she'd used *his*
computer, at *his* desk. *Dammit!* How could he have been
so stupid! Would someone be able to tell which computer had been used to delete the information? And
would they be able to tell when the e-mails and history
had been removed? That it had occurred on Sunday,
when the office was closed? Interns were not given keys
to the office. Law enforcement would realize someone
had let Paige in. While it wasn't unusual for the senator
or his chief of staff to to be in the office on a Saturday or
Sunday, interns rarely worked weekends, and even then
came in only if there was a special project under way.

Paige chewed her lip again. "Morgan was arrested
with me on Saturday, at the pool party. She was drinking underage and pushed a cop into the pool. She moved
out of the dorm this morning, and she'd only just moved
in last week. She's been asking everyone a bunch of
questions, you know, about the kids at the dorm who got
sick. I just thought she was getting to know everyone
and trying to be friendly, and maybe I'm being paranoid,
but . . ."

Senator Sutton didn't like that *but*. Not at all.

"Any chance you have a picture of this girl?" the senator asked.

Paige whipped her phone out of her pocket and pulled
up a photo of herself flanked by two girls. One was a
pretty girl with dark skin and bronze hair. The other
had skin like light toast and long black hair, a few freck-
les scattered across her face. Something about her
looked slightly familiar, though he couldn't place her.

Until he saw the dog.

The enormous shepherd mix looked eerily similar to the one he'd petted at the Fourth of July celebration at Panther Pavilion after he'd given his speech.

He returned his focus to the dark-haired girl, trying to picture her in a police uniform with her hair pulled back into a bun. While he might not have recognized the young woman alone, the fact that she resembled the handler he'd spoken with and her dog resembled the K-9 was too much to be mere coincidence.

It's them.

Holy hell!

Any hope he'd had that things would go no further was gone now. He handed the phone back to Paige, fighting the urge to cram it down her throat and choke her to death. "That girl's a local police officer. I met her on the Fourth of July."

Paige's eyes popped wide.

Though panic gripped Sutton's heart and threatened to squeeze it to death, he forced himself to remain calm. "The drug investigation is in the DEA's hands now. They've told me that without a match for the second set of prints they can't proceed." He bent down and looked Paige right in the eye. "I trust your attorney has instructed you not to speak with law enforcement?"

She nodded.

Thank God she'd hired Anthony Giacomo. The guy was known as a legal wizard, a one-man army when it came to criminal defense. He'd even managed to successfully defend an IRS investigator after she'd shot a target four times in the leg. Sutton's office had received more than one complaint about how that matter had

turned out, constituents questioning if shooting tax-
payers was going to become a new way of doing business
at the IRS, an aggressive collection method, if they'd
become no better than loan sharks who sent their goons
after those who couldn't pay up. Of course the media
had sensationalized the event, glossing over the fact that
the victim had taken a shot at the agent before she'd
opened fire. Self-defense wasn't as sexy as scandal.

He put a hand on Paige's shoulder. "It's more important than ever that you follow Mr. Giacomo's advice and
say nothing. About the drugs and deleting the video.
Otherwise, you could be brought up on charges of tampering with evidence, too. You understand that, right?"

She nodded, her eyes bright with anxiety.

Though he'd just as soon rip her arm off, he gave her
shoulder a reassuring squeeze. "It'll all be okay, hon.
Just keep your mouth shut tight. Now get on into the office and get to work."

She turned and hurried off.

Once she'd gone, the senator's eyes met Wu's. "Paige
is the only one who knows whose prints those are. She
can bring us both down. And that cop's catching on. If
she does any more snooping, you and I are screwed."
He paused a moment to let that sink in before adding,
"We can't let that happen, can we?"

"No," Wu agreed. "You'll take care of them?"

"We'll do it together." Sutton offered a smile that was
anything but congenial. "You'll supply the cheap Chinese labor, and I'll supply an American-made car, gun,
bullets."

FIFTY-SIX
FAST AND FURRY-OUS

Megan

Detective Jackson hadn't been in the station when I'd gone by to return the Jeep. I wanted to tell her what I'd overhead, that Paige had deleted the video from Alexa's phone and that it appeared she might have done so on orders from Senator Sutton, but the detective was out for the afternoon working other cases and had left orders with Melinda that she wasn't to be interrupted unless it was an emergency. My news could wait. After all, the video from the pool party had already been deleted from Alexa's phone. It was too late to do anything about it now.

Monday evening, I packed Brigit into my tiny blue Smart Car and drove up to the skating rink in Lewisville to cheer on Frankie and the rest of the Fort Worth Whoop Ass in their bout against the Fredericksburg Femme Fatales. I might have lost my drug case to the feds, but I'd sure as hell root for my roommate to skate her way to victory.

I sat on the sidelines with the mostly male crowd who'd come to watch their girlfriends play. The skaters went round and round and round, skating and scoring and occasionally wiping out and sliding across the well-polished track. The guys seemed to find the female aggression titillating, jumping to their feet and shouting in glee whenever things got particularly rough on the track. *Sheesh.*

When the guy next to me sat down after shouting encouragement to the skaters, I turned to him, "This turns you on, doesn't it?"

"Like nothing else!" he admitted with a shameless smile.

Despite being in firefighter training, Frankie was on fire herself tonight, skating harder and faster than I'd ever seen her, a blue-haired blur as she sped past, maneuvering like a pro.

I cupped my hands around my mouth and shouted. "Go, Frankie!"

The guy nudged me. "It turns you on, too, doesn't it?"

Double sheesh. "I'm only here to support my roommate."

"Roommate," he repeated with an exaggerated wink. "Sure."

When the bout wound up, the Whoop Ass had lived up to its name, thoroughly trouncing the Femme Fatales with a final score of 343 to 81.

After Frankie exchanged ass pats with her teammates and congenial nods and hand slaps with the opposing team, she rolled off the track and in my direction, raising her palms for a double high five.

"Great bout!" I said.

Brigit raised one paw for a single high five.

Frankie grinned. "Hauling around all that heavy

equipment in the fire academy has made me so much stronger. My stamina is better, too."

"It shows. You looked great out there."

She beamed with pride. "Thanks!"

We parted ways a few minutes later. She planned to go out with the other girls on the team to celebrate, and I didn't want to horn in. Besides, after living in a dorm the last week and being constantly around people, I was looking forward to some quiet time alone.

Brigit and I headed south down State Highway 121, traveling in the rightmost lane. It was after nine o'clock by then, and given that it was a weeknight, traffic was relatively light, much lighter than it had been when I'd driven up this way earlier and caught the tail end of rush-hour traffic.

The roads up this way seemed to be under constant construction. Orange barrels were visible up ahead, cordoning off a zone where large equipment was parked. As we approached the work zone, a vehicle zoomed up behind me. Judging from the height of its headlights, it had to be a pickup truck or SUV. The car pulled up to within inches of my back bumper and turned on its bright lights, blinding me. *Jackass.* Why didn't the driver just move into the adjacent lane?

Bump!

My car lurched forward, my head whipping as the vehicle collided with my back bumper.

Holy shit, the driver must be drunk! My heart hammered in my chest and my body temperature spiked as adrenaline surged through it. Too bad I wasn't in my cruiser. Brigit and I would be better protected, and I could arrest the bastard for driving under the influence and write him a whole slew of tickets. Reckless driving. Following too closely. Vehicular assault.

Knowing the driver would plow into me if I braked, I punched the gas and changed lanes, hoping to get out of his way. As soon as I could safely do so, I'd call 911 so officers could pull him over and get him off the highway. The way he was driving he was likely to kill somebody.

A split second after I changed lanes, the vehicle did, too, bumping me again, much harder this time.

BUMP!

While my seat belt held me back against my seat, Brigit's doggie seat belt wasn't quite up to the task. Her nose hit the front windshield and she cried out in pain. *Yelp!*

Now I wasn't just scared. I was furious! *Nobody hurts my Briggie Boo without answering to me.*

I zipped back into the right lane. The car zipped right along with me.

What the hell is going on here? I was beginning to think this was more than merely a drunk driver having a hard time controlling his car.

When he bumped me again, this time twice in quick succession—*BUMP! BUMP!*—I realized the driver wasn't just *likely* to kill somebody, he was actually *trying* to kill somebody.

And that somebody was *me*.

But who was trying to end my life?

And why?

I zipped across two lanes to the far left lane, but my pursuer was in a faster, more powerful vehicle and there was no way I could outrun or outmaneuver him. I was screwed. The only thing I could hope for was that my and Brigit's deaths would be quick and painless, and that it was really true that all dogs go to heaven. I couldn't imagine a happy afterlife without her.

Racking my brain for ideas, I decided to try a fake. I zipped right half a lane, then zipped left again. *Shit!* The car was behind me before I could brake and try to force him past.

I whipped over to the right. The car was on me again. This time when the driver bumped me, he tapped my back fender, sending my car spinning like a Tilt-A-Whirl. Flashes of orange flew by my windshield as my car spun out. *Poom!* My car hit an orange barrel, the impact rocking the chassis. *Poom!* Another barrel.

I took my foot off the pedal and tried to steer into the skid like I'd learned in driver's ed all those years ago. We gained traction just in time for me to spot something in our path that was big and yellow and made of bone-crushing metal. *Holy shit, we're headed for a bulldozer!*

On instinct, I jerked the wheel and my car hurtled into a small space between the bulldozer and the concrete barrier on the opposite side. *Crrrrrk!* The outside of my doors scraped along the barrier and the bulldozer until the space narrowed too much for the car to move forward. We were jerked to a neck-snapping stop, trapped between the equipment and the wall.

My breaths came fast and flashing lights danced around my vision, as if I were back at Club Bassline. Brigit cowered on her seat, whimpering. It took a full thirty seconds for me to get my breathing under control. When I did, I grabbed my purse from the passenger floorboard and fished out my phone. My hand was shak-

ing so bad, I had a hard time calling 911, first hitting
9–4–4, then 9–2–2.

"Dammit!"

Finally, I got the numbers right.

"Nine-one-one," came a man's voice. "What's your
emergency?"

"Someone just ran me off the road!" I shrieked.

"Where are you?"

I gave the dispatcher my approximate location, my
voice and chest hitching as I fought to catch my breath.

"Any injuries?"

I looked over at Brigit. She looked okay. I'm sure her
nose was sore, but at least her long snout had prevented
her head from impacting the windshield and giving her
a canine concussion.

"We're shaken up," I told the man, "but we're okay.
We're trapped in the car. It's in the construction zone,
wedged between a bulldozer and the cement barrier."

"I'll get an officer out there right away. Did the other
driver stop to help you?"

"Help me?" I snorted. "He was trying to kill me!"

"Is this a domestic violence situation, ma'am?"

"No. I have no idea what kind of situation this is!"

"Is the other driver still around?"

"I don't think so. I hope not!"

I assumed the driver had continued on after forcing
me to spin out, but I couldn't be certain. I couldn't open
the doors to get out and run. If he was still around, Brigit and I were sitting ducks. *Please, God!* I mentally
screamed in prayer. *Let us live!*

Evidently, God was on a coffee break.

I couldn't see to my left because the bulldozer was

in the way. More construction equipment was parked ahead, blocking much of my view to the front.

Wait. Is something moving up there?

I sucked in a terrified breath as a person eased around a steamroller twenty yards ahead. As if the night weren't enough to hide his identity, he was dressed head to toe in dark clothing and wore a ball cap that cast his face in shadow, the closest streetlight insufficient to battle the darkness. He stalked toward my car in wide, purposeful strides.

"Oh, God! Oh, God! Oh, God!" I rammed my elbow against the back window, hoping I could break it so that Brigit and I could escape. *Bam!* No such luck. Smart Cars might be small, but the construction is solid. The only thing I'd managed to do was ensure myself a huge bruise come morning . . . *if* I lived to see another morning. Things were looking doubtful.

When he was sufficiently hidden from the passing traffic by the steamroller, he raised his arm.

Holy shit! He's got a gun!

I grabbed Brigit around the neck and pulled her down, throwing myself on top of her to shield her the best that I could. My head stuck up a few inches over the dash and I watched in helpless horror as the man took aim.

Pop! Pop-pop-pop!

The gun's muzzle flashed ahead of me just as the lights of an approaching police car flashed behind me. My front windshield and back window burst into a million pieces raining down on me and my partner. A shriek tore from my throat, searing my vocal chords.

The cruiser's flashing lights grew brighter as it pulled

up behind the bulldozer that had me trapped. A moment later an officer peered down at me and Brigit through my back window. "You okay in there?"

I looked up at him, opened my mouth, and burst into tears.

An hour later, I sat on an exam table in a minor emergency clinic, an older female doctor using tweezers and a magnifying glass to remove shards of windshield debris from my face and arms.

"You're lucky," she said. "None of these cuts were deep enough to need stitches. How did this car accident happen, exactly?"

"Someone bashed the back of my car with theirs, ran me off the road, and then fired a gun at me."

Her mouth dropped. "Goodness gracious! All it said in your chart was that you were in an automobile accident. Why was somebody shooting at you?"

"That's a good question." And one I'd been mulling over as she'd worked on me. Unfortunately, given that the bulldozer had obscured the shooter who was firing at me, the officer who'd stopped to help me hadn't seen the muzzle flashes. By the time I'd recovered my wits enough to speak, the shooter had made off and the officer wasn't able to catch him.

As a cop, I'd made quite a few enemies. Shoplifters. Drunk drivers. Wife beaters. No doubt many of them wished me dead. Still, I couldn't point to any particular one who'd go so far as to actually *make* me dead.

She reached into a drawer and pulled out a tube of ointment, dabbing it on my wounds. "This will help stave off infection."

"Great." It was bad enough that my face looked like it had been used for practice in a beginners' class at an acupuncture school. I didn't need my wounds becoming red and infected, too.

A few more dabs and she pronounced me, "Good to go."

"Thanks so much."

I returned to the waiting room, where Seth and Brigit waited for me. Both stood when I came through the door. While Brigit wagged her tail, her furry brow was furrowed in concern. Seth's fur-free brow was furrowed, too.

"My God!" he said. "Is that the best they could do?"

"Gee," I retorted. "Way to make a girl feel attractive."

"You know what I mean." He put a reassuring arm around my shoulders and walked me outside to his car. "You think it's safe for you to go home?"

He had a good point. Obviously, whoever had tried to run me off the road and shot at me had followed me to the skating rink. There was a very good chance the shooter knew where I lived and had followed me from my house. Fortunately, when I'd called the captain earlier to tell him what happened, he'd insisting on assigning an officer to serve as my protection detail.

"The captain's got a unit watching my house," I told Seth, "and other officers will be shadowing me for a while."

"How long?" he asked.

"Until the captain feels sure I'm safe," I said, "or until this plays out."

Seth frowned. " *'Plays out?'* I don't like the sound of that."

I let out a long breath. "Neither do I."

"I'm staying with you tonight, too," he said as he opened my door.

"You'll get no argument from me." I could use his comfort, would sleep better with him there. I slid into the passenger seat while he situated Brigit in the back.

We drove back to my house to find Summer parked in a cruiser out front. She climbed out of her car as Seth turned into the driveway.

"She's your protection?" Seth asked, clearly not impressed.

"What's the problem?" I said. "Is it because she's a woman?"

He gave me a wry look. "I know better than to go there, Megan. It's not that. It's just that I'd prefer she were seven feet tall and built like a defensive lineman. In fact, I wish they'd assigned the entire SWAT team to keep you surrounded until whoever tried to kill you is brought in or dead."

His concern was touching. I reached out and put my finger in his chin dimple, my odd and special little sign of affection for him. "Thanks for worrying about me."

Honestly, I shared his concerns about my safety. Ironically, I'd wished Derek hadn't been put on leave so he could be assigned to be my bodyguard. Not that he'd be excited by the chance to take a bullet for me, per se, but he loved getting to flex his muscle and this would have been the perfect opportunity. Plus, he was crazy brave and would enjoy the confrontation. If anyone attempted to shoot me again tonight, he'd tackle them, rip off their trigger finger with his teeth, then shove that finger where the sun doesn't shine.

I climbed out of the car. "Hey, Summer."

She gasped when she drew close enough to see my face, reflexively slapping her hand over her mouth. "Oh, my God!"

Her reaction wasn't exactly reassuring. "I take it you don't approve of my ambush makeover?"

She shook her head and grabbed me in a tight hug. "I could hardly believe the news when I heard! I'm glad you're okay!"

"Thanks," I replied. "And thanks for doing guard duty. I realize this puts you at risk, too."

She lifted a shoulder in a half shrug. "What are friends for?"

"You have coffee?" I asked. She'd need it, sitting out here all night. When she replied in the negative, I said, "I'll make a pot and bring some out to you."

"That sounds great."

Seth and I went inside. Zoe padded up, greeting us with a *meow?* as if to ask *what's up?* I scratched under her chin and proceeded to the kitchen to start the coffee-maker. Once it was gurgling, I ventured into the bathroom to take a look at myself. *Dear Lord!* My face looked like raw meat. I only hoped the cuts wouldn't leave any scars.

When the coffee was ready, I filled a travel mug and added some organic soymilk and sugar to it. I also rounded up a spare key so Summer could come inside during the night to get more coffee or use the facilities when needed.

Seth reached out a hand. "I'll take the coffee and key out to her."

"Thanks."

As he stepped out, Frankie stepped in. "Holy shit, Megan! I just talked to Summer out there and she said someone ran you off the road and shot at you?"

"Yeah. It's b-been a really fun night."

She came over and gave me a hug, too. "Who the hell would try to kill you like that?"

"Good question," I said.

As far as I knew, none of the TCU students, other than Hunter, knew I was a cop. And even if Paige had figured out her short-term suitemate had actually been a police officer working undercover, I sincerely doubted she'd send someone after me. There was no need. Anthony Giacomo would surely get her off on any potential charges. The shooter was likely someone from an earlier investigation, maybe someone I'd helped to convict who had since been released from prison. But given that I hadn't been on the job long, only a year and a half, it would have to be someone who hadn't been sentenced to much time. There were several possible suspects who met that criteria. Still, none were particularly violent.

"I'm exhausted," I told her. "I'm going to bed."

"Okay," she said. "Sleep tight."

Oh, I'd sleep tight all right. Every muscle in my body had been clenched since the first time the car had bumped me, and they had yet to relax. It was a wonder some of my bones hadn't snapped.

An hour later, I was lying in bed with Seth pressed up against my back, spooning me. I, in turn, was spooning Brigit, who was curled up in front of me. As hard as I was trying to go to sleep, the adrenaline had not quite worn off yet and my mind wouldn't quiet. *Ugh*.

My cell phone rang from the nightstand. I grabbed it

and checked the readout. *Detective Jackson.* I'd spoken with her earlier, after the incident. Could she be calling to tell me they'd made an arrest?

I sat up, disturbing Brigit and Seth, but it couldn't be helped. "Hi, Detective. Any news? D-did you figure out who tried to kill me?"

"Not yet," she said. "One eyewitness called the Grapevine Police Department and said she'd seen you spin out. She saw a black Chevy Suburban pull over and assumed the driver was going to help you so she didn't stop herself. She'd been too far back to be able to tell exactly what was going on. She thought you were the one driving erratically and that the Chevy had been swerving to avoid you. She called 911, but she didn't get the Suburban's license plate number."

We might not have the plate, but at least we knew what kind of car it was. The department would issue a be-on-the-lookout alert to car repair shops in the area. If someone brought a black Suburban in to have front end damage repaired, they'd have some explaining to do.

Jackson continued. "I'm actually calling with some other news. I just got word that there was a shooting on campus at TCU. Paige McQuaid was shot in the back as she returned to the dorm."

Forget those other possible suspects. The fact that Paige had been shot on the same night someone opened fire on me was too much to be coincidence. There was no doubt in my mind now that whoever had run me off the road and shot up my car was related to my under-cover Molly investigation.

I was almost afraid to ask the next question. I mean,

Paige was no saint. I knew that. She had been helping Chao deal drugs to her fellow students, and several had suffered as a result. But she wasn't a hardened, violent criminal. She'd done some very stupid things, for very stupid reasons. Love turned people into idiots sometimes. She deserved to be punished, sure, but she deserved a chance to set herself straight, too. She didn't deserve to die. "How's Paige doing?" I asked, my voice sounding as tentative as I felt. "Did she survive?"

"She's in surgery at JPS as we speak. That's all I know right now."

JPS stood for John Peter Smith Hospital, the only facility in the city with a Level 1 trauma center. While part of me was relieved to hear she'd made it through the incident itself, I knew gunshot victims could die on the operating table. She wasn't out of the woods yet.

"Did they catch the person who shot her?"

"No," Jackson replied. "Witnesses only saw a person dressed in black shooting from behind a tree. He ran off after firing the shots."

I mulled all of this over for a moment. "What does this all mean?"

"It means you and I are meeting with Chief Garelik first thing in the morning. Be there at eight."

"All right. See you then." When I ended the call, Seth asked what was going on. I told him about Paige getting shot, that the two incidents were too coincidental to be unrelated.

"That narrows down the list of potential suspects, doesn't it?" he asked. "It would have to be someone with something to lose if the drug case moved forward."

That person would be Chaoxiang. But he was safely back in China, beyond the reach of American law enforcement.

My mind toyed with the thought. *Who else has something to lose?*

FIFTY-SEVEN
PACK ATTACK

Brigit

The dog lay in bed, snuggled back against her partner and fellow pack member. While it might appear she was dozing, she was unable to sleep. Her nose hurt from where she'd banged it against the inside of the windshield, and she felt too agitated to relax. Megan's phone ringing out of the blue hadn't helped, either.

She settled her head on her paws and heaved a heavy sigh. Zoe seemed to sense something was wrong. Cats were dumb creatures, so inferior to dogs, but every once in a while Zoe showed some signs of intelligence. The cat stood next to the bed, rose up to put her paws on the side of the mattress, and extended her nose to sniff Brigit's face.

A second later, she hopped up onto the bed and began to lick Brigit's forehead with her raspy tongue. *Slick, slick, slick.* Brigit didn't like that her head would smell like fish bits, but she appreciated Zoe's concern. She gave the cat's face a lick in return.

Oddly, Zoe's salmon-scented licks were just the comfort Brigit needed. *Slick, slick, slick.* She felt her mind finally drifting off . . .

FIFTY-EIGHT
THE UPSHOT

Senator Sutton

She was out like a light. He slipped out of bed and tiptoed out of the room, quietly closing the door behind him. He made his way across the living room and through the open French doors of his study, shutting those behind him, too.

He dialed the hotel number on his landline. Thankfully, local calls didn't show up in phone records.

Wu answered on the first ring, sounding shaken. "It's done."

Sutton didn't bother replying. He simply returned the receiver to the cradle, poured himself three fingers of whiskey from the bottle on his desk, and tossed it back, the burn like a cleansing fire.

FIFTY-NINE

EVIDENCE AND THE LACK THEREOF

Megan

With my personal vehicle at the repair shop, Frankie gave me a ride to the station bright and early the next morning. Detective Jackson, my partner, and I took my squad car to the police headquarters downtown, where we headed directly to Chief Garelik's office. The bulk under the detective's blazer told me she'd worn her Kevlar vest today. Better safe than sorry, given what happened to me last night.

With the wood paneling, a gun rack, and a number of animal heads adorning the walls, the chief's office looked more like a hunting lodge than a business space. Brigit looked up at the mounted head of a javelina, a tuft of coarse hair on top of its head, its mouth open to show its pointy teeth, make it look fierce. She issued a soft, rumbling growl. *Grrrrr.*

The broad, bulky chief filled his high-backed chair, looking more enraged than I'd ever seen him. Every capillary in his face appeared ready to burst, his silver hair like molten metal on his hot head.

Derek was already seated on one of the chief's imitation leather wing chairs, which he'd pulled up to the side of the chief's desk, facing us, making it clear he and the chief were on the same side. Given his competitive nature, he seemed to forget that we were *all* on the same side. The side of truth and justice.

While the detective sat in the other wing chair, I rounded up a plastic chair from the small foyer outside and carried it in for myself, directing Brigit to lie at my feet.

"This can't stand!" the chief barked without preamble once I'd closed the door behind me. "Something's got to be done."

"I've been doing some thinking," the detective said. "Whoever shot at Megan and Paige McQuaid has to be involved in the Molly ring. That's the only connection between the two of them. The person who's most likely to be able to identify a suspect is Paige. She wasn't willing to talk before, but now that she's become a target herself things could be different. I'm more concerned about catching the shooter who played target practice with our K-9 team than I am in putting a coed behind bars. If we offer her immunity on the drug case, maybe she can tell us who the gunman is, or at least lead us in his direction."

The chief leaned forward, putting two fists on his desk. "I want Officer Mackey cleared. Completely. You understand me? Any deal has to include a provision requiring that little lying bitch to testify before Internal Affairs about the video she deleted from her roommate's phone, that it showed Derek didn't plant the drugs."

"Agreed," Jackson said.

The chief sat back in his chair now. "I'd love to put Senator Sutton in his place, too." He jabbed his index finger in the air. "How dare he insinuate my department is incompetent and unethical! Who the hell does he think he is?"

"We could pursue the evidence-tampering angle," Jackson suggested. "If Paige says Sutton told her to delete the video, it could be enough to convince the DA to charge him. It would be Paige's word against Sutton's, and it wouldn't be a strong case, but it would be something."

Chief Garelik frowned. "There's no way in hell the DA is going to risk his reputation by filing charges against a U.S. senator unless he's sure they'll fly. There would have to be more evidence."

"We'll see if we can get any," the detective said. She stood from her chair. "I'll call the DA's office right away and get a prosecutor assigned to work out an immunity deal. The Feds will have to agree, but given this violent turn of events it shouldn't be a problem. I'll be in touch once we know more."

The chief merely nodded in acknowledgment.

I followed Jackson out of the chief's office. She was already on her cell phone as we climbed onto the elevator. Derek caught up to us and climbed on, too.

While Jackson talked on her phone, her index finger against her free ear to block out stray noise, I softly spoke to Derek. "Why have you been at Flynn Blythe's place so often?"

He cut a glance my way, one that appeared both annoyed and slightly embarrassed. He let out a resigned huff before speaking. "That asshole's been in and out of jail so many times I thought it would be easy to catch him red-handed if I popped in on him often enough."

That was all he said, but I could fill in the blanks. He'd been looking for an easy arrest to better his stats, a chance at redemption for losing the drugs at Panther Pavilion. I suppose I couldn't fault him too much for that.

By the time we'd made it out to my cruiser, a prosecutor had agreed to contact Paige's attorney to work on an immunity deal. Soon thereafter, Anthony Giacomo had agreed to meet all of us at Paige's hospital room at John Peter Smith Hospital.

Officer Spalding was on my bodyguard detail this morning, and he trailed my cruiser in his own as we made our way to the hospital. We took spots side by side in the parking garage, and he silently followed me, Brigit, and the detective inside. All of us kept an eagle eye out for anyone who might have trailed us with the intent to do us bodily harm. If such was the case, at least we'd be in proximity to medical care.

Jackson and I took seats in a small lobby near the intensive care unit to wait. Brigit plopped down at my feet, while Spalding stood near the doorway where he could keep an eye on the hall and those coming out of the elevator and stairwells. If someone showed up with the intent of trying to finish the job they'd started last night, Spalding would ensure they didn't get the chance.

The prosecutor was the first to arrive. She was a tall, middle-aged woman with brown hair shot through with a gray that matched the color of her pantsuit. The detective and I stood to greet her. Brigit rose from the floor, as well.

"Good morning, Detective Jackson," the prosecutor said, extending her hand.

After they greeted each other, Jackson turned to me. "This is Officer Megan Luz and her K-9 Brigit."

The woman shook my hand now. "I understand you two went undercover at the university and busted up the Molly ring."

I nodded in agreement, feeling a little bit like a fraud. We might have busted up the ring, but we hadn't been able to actually bust anyone. It was unsatisfying. Like going to a party and having a good time but coming home without a goody bag.

We resumed our seats and the two women chatted about other pending trials as we waited for Anthony Giacomo to make the thirty-mile drive over from Dallas. A half hour later, he swept into the room.

Giacomo was a small man with dark hair and dark eyes that were simultaneously bright with intelligence. He had a flashy fashion sense, today wearing a teal-colored shirt under a black suit and a black-and-teal diamond-print tie. A small gold hoop hung from one earlobe. He was like a stylish pirate of jurisprudence. I bet he made good legal *arr*guments.

"Hello, lovely ladies of the law." He shook hands all around and we exchanged introductions. When we were done, he held out a hand to indicate the way to Paige's room. "Let's go make sure my client's ass is covered," he said, "metaphorically speaking, of course. Those hospital gowns leave nothing to the imagination."

We followed Giacomo to Paige's room, where Spalding posted himself just outside the door.

While only one or two people at a time were normally

allowed into the rooms in ICU, the doctors had granted an exception under the circumstances. Paige's mother and father, both red-eyed, sat next to the bed. She lay propped on one side on the mattress, the white sheets bunched up around her. Without her makeup and attitude, she seemed smaller and younger, a child even.

As we stepped in, her eyes sought mine. While I would have expected them to hold anger and resentment, maybe even some betrayal, they only held regret and shame and loss. "Hi, Morgan."

"It's Megan, actually," I said. I held up my partner's leash. "This is Brigit."

She offered a wan smile at that.

I eyed her closely. "You look better than I'd expected after taking three bullets."

"I had two textbooks in my backpack. They slowed the bullets down."

She'd gotten lucky. Good thing she hadn't opted to access the books online instead of buying print copies.

Giacomo held out a hand to the prosecutor. "The immunity agreement, my dear?"

She pulled a thin document out of her briefcase and handed it to him. He sat down at the foot of Paige's bed and spent a moment perusing it. "Looks good." He signed in his designated spot with a fancy flourish and set the paper on the rolling table for Paige, next to the remnants of her early lunch, handing her the pen to sign. "Here you go, hon. Last page."

Paige signed the document, too.

Giacomo picked it back up and handed it to the assistant district attorney before turning back to Paige. "You going to eat that blue Jell-O?" When she shook her head, he picked up the bowl and spoon and nodded to me and the detective. "Okay, ladies," he said. "Have at my client."

While Giacomo poked at the jiggling dessert, Paige's father stood to give Jackson his chair at the head of Paige's bed.

Once the detective was seated, she whipped out a notepad. "Who shot you, Paige?"

Paige shook her head, tears welling up in her eyes. "I have no idea. I didn't see the person. I didn't even know what was happening at first. I heard a popping noise and thought someone was setting off fireworks. It wasn't until I was hit that I realized someone was shooting."

"Could it be someone Chaoxiang knew?" Jackson asked. "Maybe a friend or acquaintance of his?"

Paige looked sick at the thought, her already pale face growing even more pale. When she replied, she spoke softly, sounding even less sure. "I don't know. Chao didn't introduce me to any of his friends."

She'd been his dirty little secret, a thing he kept on the side. Someone he'd used for his own selfish purposes, going so far as to ditch his stash in her bag at the pool party, leaving her to suffer the consequences in order to save his own skin. Poor girl.

"How often did you use Molly yourself?" Jackson asked.

Paige looked down. "Not very often," she said softly. "Usually only when I was with Chao."

Or when Chao tossed her aside for another girl, like he'd done that night at Club Bassline. I interrupted, curious. "What about Alexa? Did she use Molly, too? Did she know you were helping Chao sell it to other students?"

Paige shook her head. "No. Alexa had no idea what I was doing. She drinks sometimes but she'd never take drugs." Her voice quavered with emotion as she finished the thought. "I'm not sure she would have wanted to be my friend if she knew."

I suspected Alexa had put the clues together and knew more than Paige realized, but there was no point in correcting her. Paige had been lucky to have a friend like Alexa looking out for her and sticking by her.

"What about Miranda Hernandez?" the detective asked. "Did Chao sell Molly to her?"

Paige nodded.

"Colby Tibbs and Ashleigh White, too?"

She nodded again.

Good. The fact that Chao had sold to all of these students told us that there may not be as many dealers out there as we'd feared.

"How did you first meet Chaoxing Wu?" Jackson asked.

"At Senator Sutton's office," Paige said. "He came in one time with his father. His dad's some kind of government official over in China."

"Why didn't Chao just sell the drugs directly to the other students? Why use the e-mail and post office boxes?"

"He didn't want anyone to know who they were buying from," she said. "He thought there was less chance of getting caught if nobody saw him face-to-face. He knew if he got arrested he'd be sent back to China and it could make things bad for his father."

Over the next few minutes, Detective Jackson peppered Paige with more questions. *Was anyone else helping Chao sell, maybe a guy named Graham Hahn?* Paige didn't know, and she didn't recognize the name. Chao had never mentioned anyone else, but it was possible. *How long had he been selling Molly at TCU?* She wasn't sure. *Why and how did she get involved in his nefarious scheme?*

"Why?" Tears formed in her eyes. "Because I was stupid. I thought he really cared about me."

That comment caused her father to yank the door open and storm out of the room in rage. Clearly it wasn't easy for a man to see his daughter taken advantage of and manipulated by a boy, especially when that manipulation put her at risk of serving jail time and ending up with a criminal record that would haunt her for life.

Paige grimaced as the door swung shut. Clearly it wasn't easy to know you'd majorly disappointed your parents, either. She turned back to the detective. "Chao and I went out a few times before he mentioned Molly. He asked if I'd ever used it. I hadn't, but he said it was an incredible experience and that I should try it and find out for myself."

I wasn't this girl's parent, but it took everything in me not to ask the quintessential parent-of-a-kid-who-did-something-dumb question. *If he'd suggested you jump off a bridge, would you have done that, too?*

Jackson jotted some notes on a pad. "What was the extent of your involvement in the drug sales?"

"I wrote the phone number for the cell phone in the girls' bathrooms in all of the dorms," she said. "Occasionally I'd pick up money for him. I answered a few of the e-mails, too."

Jackson nodded. "We traced the IP address for the e-mail response sent to Officer Luz to the campus library. Did you always respond to the *funtimemolly* e-mails from there?"

"Not always," she said. "A couple of times I responded from my computer at work."

"At work?" I repeated, reflexively taking a step closer to her bed. "You mean at Senator Sutton's office?"

"Yes."

Jackson and I exchanged glances. She lifted her brows in a subtle signal that I could ask the question that was in both of our minds now.

"As you know, Paige, I overheard you and Alexa arguing after you deleted the video from Alexa's phone. It's my understanding that Senator Sutton knew of the video and told you to see about having it deleted. What about the e-mails you sent from his office? Was he aware of those?"

She hesitated a moment, probably realizing the deep doo-doo her response would put her former boss in. She looked to her attorney for guidance. Having secured her immunity, however, he was much more interested in his client's dessert than his client herself. He continued to spoon blue gelatin into his mouth and didn't even look her way.

"You've made a deal, Miss McQuaid," Detective Jackson reminded Paige. "If you don't answer the questions we ask you, you're back to square one and you lose your immunity."

Giacomo finally looked up from the Jell-O and motioned with the spoon. "Spill your guts, honey."

Paige nodded and reluctantly turned back to the detective. "Senator Sutton called me to his office on Sunday afternoon. He made me delete the e-mails from the account, wipe it clean. He also made me delete my browser history."

Jackson and I exchanged glances again. This was big news, HUGE even. But the question was, would it be only Paige's word against his again? Or would we be able to prove Senator Sutton was directly involved in the evidence tampering?

"Walk me through what happened on Sunday," I said. "Step by step."

"Okay," Paige said. "The senator called me around two o'clock and said he'd heard I'd been arrested and that he'd like me to come to his office to talk about it. When I got there, he let me in—"

I interrupted her. "You don't have a key to the office?"

"No," she replied. "Interns don't get keys. Only the full-time staff."

"Okay," I said. "Go on."

"After he let me in he took me back to his office. He made me sign in to the system and show him my browser history. When he saw that I'd logged in to Gmail he went on a major rant about how the staff is not supposed to use our office computers for anything not directly related to our jobs."

"And then he asked you to delete the e-mails and your browser history?"

"Yeah." She frowned, her lips forming a pout. "He wasn't very nice about it, either."

"Of course not," the detective replied, giving the girl

a reality check. "You violated office policy and put his entire career at risk."

Paige looked at the detective and blinked, fresh moisture in her eyes. Her stomach began to lurch, as if she were fighting back a sob.

"You mentioned you were in his office," I said, trying to move the conversation forward before Paige could start crying outright. "Did you use his computer to delete the e-mails and browser history?"

She blinked again, three times in quick succession. "Yes."

"Is it a laptop or desktop?"

"Desktop."

"And I assume you each have your own user ID and password?" After all, that was standard office procedure.

"Yes," she said. "He had me log in as myself."

But he'd done it on *his* computer, in *his* private office.

The prosecutor, Detective Jackson, and I exchanged knowing glances.

There it is. The proverbial smoking gun.

If Paige had been at her own desk, the senator might have been able to pretend he wasn't aware what Paige was doing. But given the fact that he'd had to let her into the office with his key, as well as the fact that the removal of the information took place on his desktop computer, he'd have a hell of a hard time refuting the allegations. Of course he'd obviously never expected things to get this far, for anyone to be examining him with such scrutiny.

The prosecutor spoke now. "This might be circum-stantial evidence, but it's a crapload of it, more than enough for charges to be filed. Of course, we'd have to collect the evidence first."

Detective Jackson stood. "Officer Luz and I are on it." She turned to Paige. "If we have more questions we'll be back in touch."

"Done so soon?" Giacomo said, holding aloft the spoon he'd been using to eat Paige's blue Jell-O. "I was hoping I could convince the nurse to bring a second helping."

A couple of hours later, Jackson, Brigit, and I en-tered Senator Sutton's office armed with not only our department-issued weapons, but two other things, as well. The first was a search warrant we'd obtained in the interim. The second was a crime scene tech who spe-cialized in computer crimes. The detective and I would have no clue how to access cyberevidence, but this guy was a known whiz with all kinds of technology. Spald-ing had come along to continue watching our backs.

Jackson stepped up to the receptionist's desk, which was a built-in model situated behind a half wall and enclosed in what was likely bulletproof glass. Govern-ment officials couldn't be too careful these days. There were lots of crazies out there. Too bad my Smart Car's windows hadn't been bulletproof.

The woman looked up, quickly assessing us before sliding the glass open. Looked like we'd passed muster. "How may I help you?"

"I'm Detective Audrey Jackson with the Fort Worth Police Department." The detective angled her head my way. "Officer Luz and one of our tech specialists are assisting me in an investigation. We need to speak to Senator Sutton. *Immediately.*"

"May I tell him what this is regarding?" the woman asked, attempting to play her role as gatekeeper.

"It's a criminal matter involving an intern," Jackson said.

Her words were vague, but sufficient to let the woman know our business was serious. Paige had told us that she wasn't due back at work until the next day, and that she hadn't been in contact with anyone at Senator Sutton's office since the shooting. The news reports regarding the event had been cryptic, primarily because the information released by the Fort Worth PD's public relations office had been purposely so. The TV news and *Star-Telegram* newspaper had reported only that an "unidentified TCU student" had been shot three times in the back, the culprit and motive unknown, the victim's condition also unknown but presumed critical. Nobody here at Senator Sutton's office should yet be aware that Paige McQuaid was the unidentified student.

"You say this involves an intern?" The wide-eyed woman looked both bewildered and wary, her contorted expression belying the thoughts running through her mind. She was probably wondering whether there had been some type of sex scandal or bribe, but finding it hard to visualize the esteemed senator engaged in any such illicit activity. "One moment, please."

Rather than contacting the senator on her intercom where we might be able to overhear her conversation with her boss, she pushed back from her desk and scurried through an open doorway behind her. A minute or so later, a door that led from the foyer back to the offices swung open, the receptionist appearing in the doorway. She looked calmer, holding out a hand. "This way, please."

She led us to the end of the hall, where the senator's door remained open. On the way, we garnered concerned and curious glances from other seasoned staff members and young interns who sat at desks in the various offices and cubicles along the hallway. Clearly a visit from law enforcement wasn't a regular occurrence around here.

Sutton stood behind his desk, his American flag pin affixed to the lapel of his navy blue suit, a smile plastered on his face. Unlike his usual friendly, sincere smiles, this one appeared strained and forced. When his gaze moved from the detective and the tech to take in me and Brigit entering the office behind them, a look of utter surprise skittered across his face.

Hmm. Had he expected us to be dead? Or at the very least hospitalized?

As for me and Brigit, the news reports said only that an off-duty officer and her K-9 partner had been gunned down on a local highway. No clarification was provided, the listener or reader forced to draw their own conclusions.

My gaze quickly roamed the senator's office, taking in the colorful rug on the floor, the bookcases lined with tomes on politics and biographies of former presidents, as well as the Asian art hanging on his walls. *Classy digs.*

"Let me know if you need anything, sir." Sutton's receptionist stepped back out of the office, closing the door firmly behind her as if to hide his dirty secrets.

SIXTY
SIXTH SCENTS

Brigit

Brigit smelled a lot of things from the doorway. The acrid scent of the coffee in the mug on the senator's desk. The peppermint scent of arthritis cream. The smell of the man's shoe leather. Those loafers would make for some fun chewing.

But there was something else she sensed. She didn't scent it, not exactly. It was more like she smelled it with her brain.

Something here smelled rotten.

SIXTY-ONE
ABOVE THE LAW

Senator Sutton

The two cops, the dog, the detective, and the computer tech stood shoulder to shoulder on the other side of his desk as if playing an adult game of red rover, forming a human barrier.

He forced a smile. *How dare they?* These local yokels had no business confronting a United States senator, in his own office, no less. They'd been told in no uncertain terms that the federal government had taken over the drug case.

Why the hell were they here, wasting his time? Probably they wanted to ask about Paige, whether she'd been close to anyone on the staff who might know something that could lead them to her shooter. But that stupid girl and her problems were small potatoes. Didn't these people know he had more important things to do? Things of international significance?

Didn't they know he was above the law?

SIXTY-TWO
COMING CLEAN

Megan

Though his eyes were bright with alarm, Senator Sutton continued to smile and when he spoke it was with a practiced calm. Hours of media training and decades of speaking off the cuff under stressful circumstances had prepared him for this moment. "I'm surprised to see you folks."

I believed him. He seemed especially surprised to see me and Brigit, alive and well. Though his gaze roamed over the ugly cuts on my face, he didn't ask about them. It was as if he were afraid to acknowledge them, that by doing so he might draw a connection he was hoping to avoid. Instead, however, his failure to inquire about my obvious injuries seemed uncaring and unnatural. I suspected that he'd been responsible for what had happened last night. He might not have been the one to run us off the road or pull the trigger, but he knew something about it. I felt certain.

"I take it you haven't heard," he continued, looking

from one of us to the next, "the DEA is handling things now."

"They're handling the *drug* case," Jackson said, holding out the search warrant. "We've launched a separate investigation into evidence tampering."

His smile faltered. "Evidence tampering?"

"Yes."

He reached out to take the warrant, looking about as excited as one might be if handed a pair of someone else's dirty sweat socks. He unfolded the warrant and read it over before looking up again and continuing to feign innocence. "I'd be glad to be of service to you all, but I'm still a little unclear on what all of this has to do with me and my office."

Jackson took the warrant back, folded it, and returned it to her pocket. "We have reason to believe your intern hid evidence in the pending matter involving Officer Mackey."

"Mackey?" A red tint began to creep up the senator's neck. "The policeman who planted the drugs on Paige McQuaid?"

Jackson didn't miss a beat. "The policeman who is *alleged* to have planted drugs on Paige McQuaid. Our tech needs access to your system. We think your intern altered evidence that could have been valuable in the case."

The smile was entirely gone now, the red tint darkening Sutton's cheeks. "Altered what evidence, exactly?"

"E-mails," she replied. "We believe she deleted e-mails from a Gmail account and that she did so here in this office." Jackson was purposely keeping the focus on Paige rather than implicating the senator himself, probably to keep him off guard as much as possible.

"I don't follow," Sutton said, his brows drawing in to form lines between them. "How would e-mails sent from this office relate to the officer planting drugs?"

I chimed in now. "Because those e-mails would show that Paige herself was involved in selling Molly."

Panic flashed in Sutton's eyes. He seemed to finally realize he'd either underestimated the Fort Worth PD's investigative capabilities and dedication to justice, or overestimated his ability to sweep this matter under his colorful oriental rug.

"I'm sorry, folks," he said, pulling himself as tall as he could and crossing his arms over his chest in a defensive posture. "But there are matters of national security involved here. I'm sure you understand that I can't just give you unfettered access to my computer system."

Jackson eyed him pointedly. "Surely your classified files are password protected and interns have limited access to sensitive materials, correct? That's standard protocol for subordinates in any office. If your office failed to have such protections in place, you would look very foolish, Senator."

The tech chimed in now. "We'll only be logging in under Paige's credentials. We won't have access to anything confidential."

"Still," Sutton said, "I'm not entirely comfortable with this. It sounds risky."

The only risks were to the senator himself, that he'd find himself up shit creek not only without a paddle, but also without a boat or life jacket and with cement shoes on his feet.

He gestured to the phone on his desk. "I'm going to

need to call my attorney. Could you give me a moment of privacy?"

Jackson looked to the tech.

The tech angled his head to indicate Sutton's desktop computer. "We'll need to make sure the system isn't accessed."

In other words, we needed to make sure that Senator Sutton wasn't in here deleting more information from the computer system to cover his ass under the guise of speaking privately with his attorney.

Jackson reached over and unplugged the keyboard and mouse from the senator's computer, handing them to the tech. "You're free to call your attorney. We'll step into the hallway."

The senator had turned nearly purple now, clearly losing it. "You'll wait in the lobby!" he snapped.

No more Mr. Nice Guy, huh?

He personally escorted the five of us back to the foyer. Brigit glanced up at me, the expression in her eyes saying *Can't we go for a real walk rather than traipsing up and down this hall?* The receptionist appeared no more happy to be stuck with us than the senator had. She cut us furtive glances through the glass as she typed on her keyboard.

Once Sutton had stormed off down the hall, Jackson turned to the receptionist. "This office have a back door?"

"No, ma'am." The woman nodded to the entry door behind us. "That's the only way in or out."

Jackson lifted her chin in acknowledgment and stepped to the bank of windows on the exterior wall. Craning her neck, she looked down the side of the building as if she thought Senator Sutton might leap from his window in desperation or try shimmying down a drainpipe. As a seasoned cop and detective, she'd probably seen it all. I wondered what all I'd have seen once I had as many years of experience under my belt as she did.

We waited for twenty long minutes, Brigit leisurely sniffing her way around the room and the tech checking e-mails on his phone before the detective lost patience. She stepped up to the glass to address the receptionist. "Tell Senator Sutton we're coming back to get started. If he needs to finish his conversation, he can uproot one of his staff and use their office."

She didn't wait for the receptionist to respond before stepping to the door that led back to the offices and attempting to yank it open. It didn't budge. She turned back to the receptionist. "Buzz us in. *Now*."

The woman hesitated a moment, but seemed to realize disobeying armed police officers was not a smart idea. She pushed a button on her desk to release the door. *Bzzt.*

We went down the hall to the senator's office again. Jackson rapped loudly on the door. *Knock-knock.* "Let us in, Senator."

"I'm not done with my phone call!" he shouted from within. "I need to finish!"

"What you need," she replied loudly and firmly, "is to open this door and let us in right now or I will have Officer Luz arrest you for obstructing justice."

While there were gasps and murmurs of surprise from the staff members who'd left their posts and gathered in the hall behind us, there was no sound from inside the senator's office for several seconds. Finally, there was another *bzzt* as Sutton disengaged the lock on his door.

The door swung open to reveal the senator standing behind his desk, his hand placed over the mouthpiece on his phone. "My attorney says he's going to get a court order to stop this nonsense."

Enforcing the laws was nonsense? *Grr.* I was tempted to sic Brigit on the senator and take a bite out of him myself.

"More power to him," Jackson snapped. "In the meantime we're going to get to work. Step away from your desk, please."

Sutton sputtered, clearly not expecting the detective to act with such force. "I am a United States senator, ma'am!" he cried.

She raised her palms. "And? Do you think that makes you above the law?"

He sputtered some more, like a failing motor on a cheap johnboat. "What if I refuse?"

Jackson hiked at thumb at Brigit. "That dog will convince you otherwise."

Brigit wagged her tail on hearing the word "dog," knowing people were talking about her. But even with her tail happily going, it was clear Brigit was not a dog you wanted to mess with. With her size and fangs, she could take the senator down and hold him in place with her teeth for as long as necessary.

Sutton stood there a moment in defiance, his chest puffed out. But as we watched, he seemed to deflate in front of us, melting like a Popsicle dropped on a Texas summer sidewalk, realizing whatever power he had was dwindling.

He stepped aside. "You understand I'll need to remain here, to protect sensitive documents in my desk and file cabinet."

"Of course," the detective said. "We'd like you to stay."

It will make his arrest that much easier.

The senator pulled a chair over to the back corner by the window, where he could keep an eye on the tech but be out of the way. Jackson and I took seats in wing chairs. Spalding leaned back against the now-closed door, his hands hooked on his belt where his gun would be in quick reach.

The tech slid into Sutton's chair and logged on to the system.

Sutton's face contorted in concern as he eyed the screen. "You have Miss McQuaid's log-in credentials?"

"Yes," Jackson answered. "She gave them to us this morning."

Again, surprise skittered across his face. *Had he thought Paige was dead, too?*

As the tech continued to work the keyboard and mouse, Sutton became much more conciliatory. "I certainly hope that Miss McQuaid will not sully my office's reputation with criminal activity."

"It would be a bad time for s-something like that, wouldn't it?" I said. "What with you being in the middle of a campaign."

Sutton responded only with a scowl.

A mere ten minutes later, the tech waved Jackson over. I joined her.

He pointed to the screen. "The system backup shows Paige's browser history before it was deleted Sunday.

She accessed a Gmail account on several occasions in recent weeks."

I cut a glance at Sutton. He looked downright apoplectic now. Apparently he'd forgotten that the system had a backup drive.

The tech continued, clicking the mouse and pointing at another screen. "This shows that she logged in to her account Sunday afternoon and visited Gmail." With some more maneuvering, he was able to access the Gmail account. "The deleted e-mails are still in her trash."

Sutton bent forward now, putting his hands on his knees. I almost felt sorry for the guy. Having not grown up with or embraced computer technology, he'd been over his head when trying to hide the cyberevidence.

"And this," the tech said finally, "shows she was working on this very computer when she deleted the e-mails."

The three of us turned to look at Sutton, Spalding following suit.

Sutton's gaze darted around as if his eyes were seeking escape. Of course none was to be found. Not unless he wanted to end up splattered in the parking lot.

Jackson stepped over to Sutton. "You told Paige to delete those e-mails, didn't you, Senator?"

He looked up at her, his face mangled with emotion. "I absolutely did not!"

"Sorry, sir," she replied. "But I don't believe you. The only explanation for how an intern came to delete e-mails on your computer on a day when the office was closed and locked and she had no key was that you were involved. Now, will you come to the station with us voluntarily, or do we need to cuff you?"

He looked down at his shoes for a long moment before looking back up at the detective. "No need for cuffs," he hissed. "I'll behave myself."

Jackson led the senator from his office, while Brigit and I took up the rear, the tech trailing along behind us with the proof we needed to indict the senator for evidence tampering downloaded onto a flash drive.

"No need to worry, folks," the senator told the staff gaping along the hallways. "Everything's fine." As we entered the foyer and passed the desk of the bewildered receptionist, Sutton sent a forced smile her way and spoke in a calm voice that hid the emotion he'd just shown in his office. "I need to take care of something off-site. I'll touch base with you later."

We stepped out of his offices. He stopped in the hallway, standing stock-still and closing his eyes as if resigning himself to his fate. His term, it seemed, was coming to an end.

Over the course of the next few days, my face healed, Paige McQuaid was released from the hospital, and much more damning evidence against Senator Sutton came to light.

When Minister Wu attempted to board a flight to Beijing at the DFW airport Tuesday afternoon, an explosives-sniffing dog alerted on him. He was found to have gunshot residue on his clothing and was held for questioning.

A black Suburban Senator Sutton claimed to have

rented for use by his campaign in delivering yard signs was found parked behind his headquarters with damage to the front bumper. While he argued that someone must have backed into the vehicle, nobody was buying it. With the Suburban linking not only Sutton, but his campaign, to criminal activity, the FBI launched an investigation and discovered that a trade organization called the Texas Exporters League had made a half-million-dollar donation to Sutton's campaign, though they'd funneled the contribution through Sutton's personal accounts so that he could hide its source. Despite his campaign slogan that he was "The Best Representation Money Can't Buy," it was clear that Senator Sutton, like many other politicians, had been for sale. Looked like everyone had their price.

With Wu and Sutton directly linked not only to evidence tampering, but also to the attempted murder of two police officers and a college student, they were being held without bond. I bet the senator missed his American flag pin. It could have been used as a weapon in jail or traded for cigarettes.

The senator's approval rating plummeted, a diehard two percent unwilling to give up on the guy they were certain was being framed. Essie Espinoza's popularity soared even higher.

Derek was cleared of planting the drugs and returned to duty, though Captain Leone insisted he ride with another officer for the time being and that all evidence be handled by the partner. Straws were drawn, and poor Summer got the short stick. I made a mental note to buy her an air freshener for their cruiser. Derek was a big boy and could work up quite a sweat, not to mention those onion-loaded burgers he liked so much.

As for me, I was finally free to have that dinner with Seth and his mother, Lisa. Seth took us to a nice Italian place on a Sunday evening in late July.

While it was clear that things between Seth and his mother were still strained, my presence seemed to act as a buffer, and I could sense the two of them connecting through me. I still found it uncanny how much they resembled each other, from the blond hair to the chin dimple. It was as if Seth's absentee father had had absolutely nothing to do with his DNA.

I passed the basket of garlic bread to Lisa. "What do you think of Blast?"

"He's incredible!" she said, taking the basket from me and helping herself to a slice. "Such a sweetie, too. He helps me do the dishes."

Seth scoffed, but good-naturedly. "If by helping you mean he licks the plates clean with the same tongue he cleans himself with, then yeah."

"Brigit does the same thing at our house," I admitted. "She's better than a scouring pad at getting rid of sticky gunk on pans."

We kept the conversation light. All in all, it was a pleasant evening. I hoped it would be the first of many to come. Seth needed to get past his hurt, and it was clear Lisa needed to work through her guilt. I hoped I could help them do that.

In early August, Brigit and I were out on patrol, working the night shift, when a vandalism call came in.

"We've got a report of a broken window," the dispatcher said. "The victim reports she believes her ex-boyfriend tried to break into her home."

Ugh. Domestic violence is the worst.

I grabbed the mic from my dashboard. "Officers Luz and Brigit on their way."

. . . and don't miss the hilarious Tara Holloway novels!

Death, Taxes, and a French Manicure

Death, Taxes, and a Skinny No-Whip Latte

Death, Taxes, and Extra-Hold Hairspray

Death, Taxes, and a Sequined Clutch
(an e-original novella)

Death, Taxes, and Peach Sangria

Death, Taxes, and Hot Pink Leg Warmers

Death, Taxes, and Green Tea Ice Cream

Death, Taxes, and Mistletoe Mayhem
(an e-original novella)

Death, Taxes, and Silver Spurs

Death, Taxes, and Cheap Sunglasses

Death, Taxes, and a Chocolate Cannoli

Death, Taxes, and a Satin Garter

From St. Martin's Paperbacks